TWISTED

Also by Tracy Brown

Dime Piece

Black

Criminal Minded

White Lines

TWISTED

Tracy Brown

St. Martin's Griffin ❧ *New York*

TWISTED. Copyright © 2008 by Tracy Brown. All rights
reserved. Printed in the United States of America. No part of
this book may be used or reproduced in any manner whatsoever
without written permission except in the case of brief
quotations embodied in critical articles or reviews.
For information, address St. Martin's Press,
175 Fifth Avenue, New York, N.Y. 10010.

www.stmartins.com

Library of Congress Cataloging-in-Publication Data

Brown, Tracy, 1974–
    Twisted / Tracy Brown.—1st ed.
        p.   cm.
    ISBN-13: 978-0-312-33650-9
    ISBN-10: 0-312-33650-0
    1. African American women—Fiction.   2. Atlanta
(Ga.)—Fiction.   3. Adultery—Fiction.   4. Revenge—
Fiction.   I. Title.

PS3602.R723T86 2008
813'.6—dc22   2008003151

First Edition: May 2008

10   9   8   7   6   5   4   3   2   1

Though our roles as parent and child are clearly defined, we also share a friendship that has been forged out of disappointments, triumphs, heartbreak, and many lessons learned together.

We teach each other, encourage and inspire each other, and we pick each other up when we fall.

I want you to know that I love you, I admire you, and I am so very proud of the young lady I am watching you become. Sometimes, while we try to teach our children all about life, our children teach us what life is all about. Thank you. This novel is dedicated to you.

ACKNOWLEDGMENTS

Monique Patterson, I just can't say enough about you. Thanks for your support, your honest critiques, your patience and understanding. You are the absolute best there is and I am so honored to work with you. Thank you from the bottom of my heart for everything you do.

Kareem Moody, you always support me and you constantly include me in your latest ventures. You are always quick to offer your help, and you never let me down. You are a true friend and I thank you for all you've done.

Tanara Brown, Paulette Wilson, T'wana Denard, Jessica Forrest, Ayana Ellis, Angelique Poole, and Deidre Woodley: A friend is someone who knows the song in your heart and can sing it back to you when you have forgotten the words. A friend is one who believes in you when you have ceased to believe in yourself. A friend is someone who knows all about you and loves you anyway. A friend remembers what we were and sees what we can be. Friends are the angels who lift us to our feet when our wings have trouble remembering how to fly. Thank you for being my friends. I love you.

TWISTED

PROLOGUE

Once Upon a Time

Brooklyn, 2003

Celeste was distraught. The firefighters bravely battled the blaze as thick smoke hovered in the night air. Her beloved hair salon, Dime Piece, stood in smoldering ruins. Celeste wanted to cry in anguish and scream in triumph at the same time. She sweated from the intense heat at the scene and from the wide range of emotions stirring through her body. She now wondered if torching her shop had been the right thing to do after all.

Celeste was fed up with the life she was living. She was tired of being her man's mistress, sick of a life shrouded in secrecy and drama. For a long time she had been looking for a way out. And setting her beloved business on fire had seemed like a perfect way out. She could get the insurance money, pay her bills, and take the rest of the dough and get the hell out of Rah-lo's life for good.

Once she'd sent her salon up in smoke, Celeste had headed home for the night, preparing herself for the moment when someone would call her with the news that Dime Piece had burned down. She anticipated that it would take hours for anyone to notice the smoke and flames and report the fire. After all, she had only set a small fire in the back by the hair dryers. She estimated that it would take a while for it to spread across the entire salon. But she had gotten a call on her cell phone only minutes after she had closed up shop for the night and gone home. As she headed back home to Staten Island after putting her plan in motion, the ride had been smooth on her way to the Verrazano Bridge. She had put in the new Jay-Z CD, had the window cracked, and was feeling good about the decision she'd made. It was about time that she got some closure on what was a stressful chapter in her life. But just as she neared the entrance to the bridge, her cell phone had rung and she'd answered it. It was Sean from the barbershop across the street, calling to tell her that Dime Piece was in flames. He could see the fire from the front of his shop. Sean told her that he had already called 911 and they were on their way. Celeste had hung up and frantically turned back around, her heart thundering in her chest the whole time.

She went over it in her head. Had she left any clue about what she'd done? Did she leave anything incriminating behind? Had anyone seen her? She retraced her steps in her head and couldn't think of anything she'd done wrong. She had started a small fire in the back of the shop, careful not to use too much accelerant so that the fire wouldn't appear to be suspicious. Then she had shut off all the lights and locked up. How could the fire have spread so fast? When she arrived, the firemen were already on the scene. The neighboring stores had spilled out and the street was lined with spectators watching Celeste's dream go up in flames. She spoke with the fire chief and explained that it was her salon. After assuring him that she hadn't left any hot curling irons on and that there were no electrical problems with any of the wiring, Celeste began to frantically call her man, Rah-lo. Again and again she called him, each time her call going straight to voice mail. She sighed, disgusted that he was always so unavailable whenever she needed him. This was a typical situation with her in need and Rah-lo occupied elsewhere. Frustrated and in need of some comfort, she called Rah-lo's friend Ishmael, who had become a very dear friend of hers as well. Ishmael had answered immediately, unlike her man, and assured her that he was on his way. Now, as she stood in front of the salon, feeling weak from the second thoughts she now had about ruining her business, Ishmael stepped on the scene and took it all in.

"Damn, Celeste," he said, shaking his head as the fire ravaged the building before him. "How did *this* happen?"

She shook her head, both to signal that she had no idea how this had happened and to try to keep her tears at bay. "They said it looks suspicious. Somebody set my shit on fire, Ishmael." Her eyes were welling up so much that tears blurred her vision. Ishmael saw her and put his arms around her to console her. Celeste began to sob a little. She was scared to death that she would be found out. What if they figured out that she did it? Celeste told herself that she wouldn't be found out. The list of possible suspects grew longer the more she thought about it. Any one of her former stylists had a motive to destroy Dime Piece, as well as Rah-lo's wife. Celeste told herself to relax and tried to mentally convince herself that everything would be all right.

Ishmael held her tight. He was happy to be there for her but frustrated that she still wasn't fed up with her man. Rah-lo was never around when she needed him. At times like this, it was always Ishmael who held her together, and he was happy to do it. He wished he could be the one she depended on all the time. But her love and loyalty for Rah-lo stood in Ishmael's way. "You still willing to be second runner-up? Where's your man, Celeste?"

She was pissed. Here she was dealing with the realization that her hair salon was burning to the ground right before her eyes and her "friend" was rubbing salt in her wounds! "What the fuck, Ishmael?" she said in exasperation. "How do you sound right now? We both know that I should walk away. But I can't!"

Ishmael felt bad. Maybe this wasn't the right time to re-mind Celeste that she was only Rah-lo's mistress. Ishmael thought about why his friend wasn't here with the woman he claimed to love. Rah-lo was probably at home with his wife, not even realizing that Celeste needed him. In Ish-mael's opinion, Celeste deserved better than that. She de-served to be some lucky man's wife, not just a mistress. In fact, Ishmael wished that somehow she could be *his* wife. But Rah-lo had met her first. And Rah-lo was Ishmael's friend. He had to respect that.

As he stood there with Celeste in his arms, Ishmael tried to think of something reassuring that he could say to her, but the words didn't come. As he struggled to think of a way to make her feel better, Rah-lo appeared out of nowhere. Ish-mael had been so comfortable holding Celeste that he hadn't even seen her man approaching them. Rah-lo stared at Ish-mael with his jaw clenched, his eyes piercing right through his friend. Ishmael sensed Rah-lo's disapproval and stepped away from the embrace. Celeste also noticed Rah-lo's an-noyance. She stood back, feeling guilty, and quickly tried to fill the awkward silence.

"My shop is gone, Rah-lo. They said somebody burned my shit down." A tear fell from her eye and Rah-lo quickly wiped it away for her. Her heart raced nervously.

"Don't cry, mama. You got insurance on this place. You can rebuild it if you want to." Rah-lo hugged Celeste, eye-ing Ishmael the whole time. Rah-lo hoped his friend knew that he loved Celeste and would kill over her. But then he felt guilty for having doubts about his friend. Ishmael had been his friend since they were kids. He wouldn't do that to Rah-lo. He brushed off his suspicion, and Ishmael gave the two of them his condolences for the loss of the salon. He said good-bye, and Rah-lo watched Ishmael get into his truck and pull away.

Across the street from where Rah-lo and Celeste stood, Charly Hanson smiled a devilish grin. Things couldn't have worked out better! She had noticed the exchange between Ishmael and Celeste and thought they looked awfully cozy together. Charly had long suspected that there was more between Ishmael and Celeste than mere friendship. Now it seemed that Rah-lo was beginning to feel the same way. Charly noticed the look on Rah-lo's face—serious and suspicious of his so-called friend. She couldn't have been more pleased. It was about time that Celeste got what she deserved, and losing Rah-lo was *exactly* what she deserved.

Rah-lo stood looking down at Celeste. He told himself that she wouldn't betray him by fucking with his best friend. But Rah-lo still hated the closeness between her and Ishmael. He hated that, once again, Ishmael had beaten him to Celeste's side when she was in the midst of a crisis. Rah-lo had been focused on his paper chase, and on top of that his wife was giving him hell at home. But he still did his best to make it clear to Celeste that she was a priority to him every day, no matter how complex and hectic things were. He had been at home with his wife and his three daughters when he got Celeste's urgent message. He had raced to her side only to find her looking too comfortable in Ishmael's arms.

Rah-lo saw the tears in Celeste's eyes as she watched Dime Piece go up in smoke. That salon had been a gift from him to her, and she had turned it into a big success. The business was a venue for plenty of drama—from the stylists' constant bickering to a break-in and attempted rape. Celeste had had her share of difficulties trying to keep things afloat. But for her it was all a dream come true. She had a business all her own. Even though Rah-lo financed it, she was the one who'd had the vision and had made it a success. Now the shop was destroyed, and she looked heartbroken.

"Baby, don't worry," he said, his tone reassuring. "You can open up a new shop. Whatever you want to do, I'll make it happen." Celeste kept staring straight ahead as the flames ravaged her salon. Rah-lo pulled her close to him and held her tightly. "It's okay, baby girl. You know this shit is just a temporary setback." He stroked her back. "We'll find out who did this and I swear I'll make them pay for it. You'll see. We'll build you something bigger and better, ma. I promise."

She shook her head. "I don't want to rebuild it," she said.

Rah-lo stepped back, slightly surprised. "Why not?"

She shrugged. "Maybe this is some kind of sign that it wasn't meant to be." Unbeknownst to Rah-lo, Celeste wasn't just referring to the hair salon. She was also referring to her role in Rah-lo's life. She was beginning to want out, and this was the start of her dramatic exit from his life.

Rah-lo nodded. "I can see why you might feel that way," he said. He thought back on all the drama and pain that Celeste had dealt with since she opened Dime Piece. First one of Rah-lo's enemies had tried to rob and rape Celeste—an attack that Ishmael had saved her from and another instance when Rah-lo was unable to run to her rescue. Then there had been the constant arguments and fights between Celeste and her stylists. To add insult to injury, lately Rah-lo's wife, Asia, had been prank-calling the salon. As he looked at the smoldering ruins, he had to agree with Celeste. Maybe it wasn't meant to be. He reached out and touched her face gently. "You can have whatever you want, Celeste. A restaurant, a bookstore, a clothing store . . . you can even open up a funeral parlor if you want." That made her smile, which was the effect he had wanted. "There's that smile I love so much." He kissed her softly. "I mean it," he said. "Whatever you want. I'll make it happen. Just say the word and it's yours. You know that. I love you."

Celeste hugged him tightly. "I love you, too." She felt a surge of guilt. She knew that Rah-lo loved her. There was no question in her mind about that. She knew that he meant what he said. All she had to do was tell him what she wanted and Rah-lo would stop at nothing to get it for her. Regardless of his marriage and his children, she knew that Rah-lo loved her. And she loved him back. She was just sick and tired of being second in line. Celeste lived in a large home Rah-lo owned on Staten Island. The house was in a very upscale neighborhood amid beautiful views of what had been the classic New York City skyline before the World Trade Center was destroyed. His wife, Asia, knew nothing about this house. And until recently, she had not even known about Celeste.

For years he and Celeste had maintained a low-key relationship behind Asia's back. They didn't travel in the same circles and Celeste loved Rah-lo and had been content to play her position in his life as the other woman. But that lifestyle was getting tiresome for her. She was tired of having to share Rah-lo's time and having to share his heart. And when Rah-lo's secret house was raided and Rah-lo and Celeste were arrested together, their secret was out. Asia found out about the other woman in her husband's life, and she was livid.

The drama Rah-lo was enduring at home and Celeste's increasing unhappiness were enough to make him crazy. Both of the women in his life were giving him grief. But his main concern was Celeste. She was the one he was in love with. Asia was his wife and the mother of his three daughters. They had been together for years and they had learned to accept the mutual loss of interest in their marriage. Rah-lo was used to (but still hated) Asia's confrontational and ghetto-fabulous personality. He hadn't been in love with her for a long time. His daughters were what kept him in his marriage. He wanted for them what he hadn't had for himself—a two-parent household, structure, and stability. Asia was just part of that package.

But Rah-lo wasn't worried about Asia right now. He looked at Celeste and could tell that she was devastated. When the fire was completely extinguished, he helped her sift through the rubble to see if anything was salvageable. Unfortunately, everything had been destroyed. He drove Celeste home and spent the night by her side, holding her and comforting her the best way he could. He knew that Asia would be livid that he had spent the night out again. But he didn't give a fuck. Celeste needed him and he was determined to stay by her side that night no matter how much grief it caused him at home.

"Celeste," he said, lying beside her in bed with his arms wrapped securely around her thin frame. "What can I do to make this better?"

She sighed. "I just want to get away from all this shit, Rah-lo. I want to live without all the constant drama, all the bullshit. But you can't leave your wife—"

"Don't say that," he interrupted. "I *can* leave Asia. And I *will* leave Asia. I just have to make sure that my kids are old enough to understand that I'm not leaving them, too. It's not about Asia. As far as I'm concerned, *you* are my wife."

She shook her head. "But I'm not."

"Not yet." He kissed her, silencing her. His hands wandered to all of her hot spots, and Celeste acquiesced.

As she lay beside him, Celeste knew that there was no turning back now. She had started the process of withdrawing from Rah-lo. As they made love she reminded herself that no matter how perfect it felt, Rah-lo's sex wasn't hers alone. His sweet words and strong hands weren't hers alone. He was married to another woman, and Celeste was finally determined to walk away.

That night, as he lay beside her, Rah-lo watched Celeste sleep. He loved her so intensely that he wished he could protect her always. It killed him to think of her hurting in any way. As she snored ever so softly, he stroked her hair. Rah-lo wondered who had burned her shop down. In his heart of hearts he believed that Asia may have had something to do with it. Now that she knew about Celeste, Asia was borderline obsessed with getting revenge against her husband's mistress. He knew that Asia hadn't done it personally. After all, he had been at home with her and his daughters when he got Celeste's urgent messages. But he wondered if Asia had arranged to have Dime Piece destroyed. To Rah-lo it didn't matter. No matter what Asia did, nothing would come between him and Celeste. He wouldn't let it.

His thoughts drifted to Ishmael. Rah-lo wondered why he felt so jealous of Ishmael's friendship with Celeste. He believed that neither of them would ever cross that line and take their friendship further. Still, it killed him to think that any man—especially his best friend—had eyes for the woman he loved. Rah-lo was insanely jealous over her and would kill to keep her all to himself. As he drifted off to sleep he wondered if she had any idea just how much he loved her.

As the next several weeks passed, Celeste secretly began to pack her things. She got the insurance money and knew that this was her ticket to freedom. On a warm and sunny Sunday afternoon, Rah-lo walked into the house, hoping to surprise Celeste, and noticed immediately how quiet it was. "Baby girl!" he called out, his voice echoing off the walls. He headed up the stairs, calling her name. He got no response. "Celeste," he called out, wondering if she could still be asleep. She was typically an early riser. So if she were still asleep at this point in the afternoon it would be quite unusual. When he reached the bedroom, he stopped calling her. He knew immediately that she was gone. All of Celeste's clothes, shoes, and personal items were gone. The closet was empty except for the hangers. The pictures of the two of them, which had once adorned the nightstands, were also gone. All that remained was the king-sized bed in the center of the room. Celeste had left him.

Rah-lo's heart sank. Lately, Celeste had been talking about bowing out of his life. She was tired of being his mistress, and told him that she wasn't going to wait forever. Her patience had been wearing thin for a long time. The truth was Rah-lo never really thought she would find the courage to leave him. He thought she would wait for as long as he needed her to. He had afforded Celeste a very comfortable lifestyle—money, cars, clothes, trips, and expensive gifts. He had housed her in a lovely home with all the amenities any woman would wish for. He thought it was enough to keep her waiting contently. And now he realized how wrong he was.

CHAPTER ONE

The Truth Hurts

Four years later . . .

Rah-lo walked into his house, and wasn't surprised to find it empty. He assumed that Asia must be out somewhere with her good-for-nothing friends. Their daughters were older now—fourteen, eleven, and nine. The teenager—Rasheeda—was always out with her friends, and the two younger ones took a dance class three days a week. He went in the kitchen and looked around for something quick to eat. True to form, Asia hadn't gone shopping, so there was nothing in the fridge for him to snack on. He sighed and shut the refrigerator and wondered what type of mother Asia really thought she was. Did she think she was doing her best and that their daughters were learning good habits from her? This type of shit was the reason he sought shelter in the arms of other women. Although he loved his family and wanted to keep it intact, he wasn't getting what he needed from his wife. Rah-lo wondered for the thousandth time if he should walk away.

Instinctively, his mind drifted to thoughts of Celeste. Even after four years, his love for her had never waned. And try as he might, Rah-lo couldn't get over her. He walked over to the bookcase in the living room and pulled out the Bible on the second shelf. It was the only place in the house that he never worried about Asia searching. He pulled out the letter Celeste had left behind when she had walked out of his life four years ago. Rah-lo sat down on the couch and read the worn and folded page.

Raheem,

I love you so much. I always have and I always will. But I can't live like this anymore. Life is short and I don't want to look back on mine with any regrets. I don't wish I had done anything differently. Everything in life is a lesson. You taught me so much, and I want you to know that the love I have for you can never be replaced or duplicated. But it's time for me to move on and start treating myself the way I deserve to be treated.

I want to get my own mansion, my own diamonds and

furs, put myself through college. I want to start a new business
for myself. I wish you and Asia all the best and hope that you
forgive me for walking away. I had no choice. I was suffocating.
I will never stop loving you. Never.

Celeste

He folded the note once again and put it in his pocket, sighing. When he first discovered that Celeste had left town, Rah-lo had put his heart on the shelf and tried to tough it out. *Fuck it,* he had told himself. If she could leave him, she wasn't worth the heartache. He had even tried to put his all into his marriage at that point. One week after Celeste left town, Rah-lo had taken Asia and the girls on vacation to the Disney resort in Florida. His intention was to see if he could reconnect with his wife to salvage what remained of their marriage. Asia had been surprised by this spontaneous gesture and their daughters had been thrilled, surrounded by fun, sun, and their parents. Rah-lo had tried to make his time with his family fun enough to satisfy his longing for Celeste. But throughout their vacation, he and Asia had constantly argued. About the simplest things. They argued over what they would do each day, which rides they would get on, what the girls would wear, what they all would eat for dinner, how they would spend their evenings. It was ridiculous, and both Rah-lo and Asia were disgusted with each other by the end of their vacation.

But the girls had had a blast. Rasheeda, Raleigh, and Raven had been on cloud nine. The trip, to them, had been one big adventure. Granted, their parents were at each other's throats as usual. The kids were accustomed to the arguing and fighting that went on between Rah-lo and Asia. It was nothing new to them. But they were excited to have the luxury of a hotel suite and a rental car, room service, and the excitement of being someplace new and thrilling. They seemed oblivious to the tension surrounding them, and for that Rah-lo was grateful. At least the trip hadn't been a total waste. The girls had enjoyed themselves and Rah-lo was satisfied with that.

But it had only highlighted the fact that his relationship with Asia was unsalvageable. Even with the sun and beaches, the absence of Celeste or any other distractions, and the joy of giving their daughters a vacation they would never forget, Rah-lo and Asia failed to reconnect. Even though Asia still looked good, considering her age and the fact that she had had three children, Rah-lo wasn't attracted to her anymore. Seeing his wife in a revealing bathing suit and watching her ass jiggle as she walked around sweating sexily in the heat and humidity had done nothing to entice him. He had found himself counting the days to when he could get home and get back to the block. It was the first time he genuinely accepted that he no longer loved Asia. In fact, he no longer even liked the woman.

Every day after that had been difficult for him. Staying in his marriage for the sake of his kids was a noble gesture. But it caused him to neglect his own happiness. Each time he came home after a day of grinding in New York City's mean streets, Rah-lo wished that he could have the love of his daughters and the routine of tucking them in each night, without having to deal with their mother. It was wishful thinking, though. Asia wasn't going anywhere. He felt like he was stuck with her.

As he sat on the couch lost in thought, Asia came home. She was returning from a smoke session at her friend Kim's house. High off marijuana, eyes hanging low, Asia walked in the door and looked at Rah-lo. He looked back at his wife, trying to recall if he had ever been more disgusted by her. He was so sick of seeing her this way—coming home twisted with no dinner ready for her family and no intentions of doing anything productive.

"What?" she asked, looking confused.

Rah-lo just kept staring at her. "Where were you?"

She grinned. "You're jealous? I was just over at Kim's—"

"What are the kids supposed to eat when they get home?" he demanded. Rah-lo was seething.

Asia looked taken aback but still high. "Well, if you're so worried about it, why don't you go cook something for them?"

Rah-lo was amazed. "What's wrong with you? You think I should do it all—cooking, cleaning up, and the whole nine— and you don't do shit all day but go out and get high with your friends? What the fuck do I need *you* for then?"

"Who the fuck are you talking to like that?" Asia was outraged that her husband, whom she was used to having her way with, was challenging her this way as soon as she walked in the door. She looked around and saw no sign of her rambunctious children. "The kids ain't even home yet!"

"What about me, Asia? Don't I need to eat, too?"

She sucked her teeth. "You're a grown-ass man, Rah-lo. And the kids ain't babies no more. They can make themselves something to eat when they get home."

"But why should they have to?" Rah-lo was growing increasingly frustrated. "You're their mother. You don't work; you don't go to school; there's more than enough money for you to go shopping. But instead you sit around here all day and do nothing. I'm tired of that shit. I'm out there working my ass off and—"

"You *work,* Rah-lo? Is that what they call it now?" The expression on Asia's face was saying *Oh, please!*

He stopped talking and looked at her. Asia stared right back at him. She was frowning at him, seemingly amazed by his audacity. Rah-lo tried to reason with her. He figured he would lay it all on the line, stop beating around the bush, and really tell his wife what he was feeling. "I'm your husband, Asia. That's not just a title. There's supposed to be benefits that come with that shit. You know how being my wife affords you certain luxuries? Why can't you take care of me the same way I take care of you?"

"Please!" she shouted. "You always gotta bring up money.

So what, you give me money, Rah-lo! I'm tired of you reminding me that you pay for everything. So the fuck what?"

"I'm not just talking about the money. I'm talking about the things I do to make life easier in this house. Not just for you, for everybody. I'm around here cooking, doing laundry, picking the kids up, dropping them off. And where are you?"

"I do all of that shit, too, Rah-lo. And those are things you're *supposed* to do. You don't get a pat on the back or a damn medal of honor because you take care of your kids. That's what good fathers do. And I never told you I was gonna be a boring fucking housewife. Who wants to sit around all day cleaning and cooking and never having fun? I'm more than just the maid and the cook."

"What are you then?" he asked.

Asia looked hurt. "Fuck you!"

Rah-lo couldn't stand it anymore. He hated being in this mockery of a marriage. Neither of them was happy anymore. He and Asia never talked anymore, they rarely had sex, and they seldom even laughed in each other's presence anymore. Asia turned him off, and Rah-lo was sick of living in an unhappy home. Plus, something she had just said was echoing in his head. "You know what? You're right. The kids ain't babies no more. Why should we keep playing games like this is where we want to be?"

Asia put her hands on her hips. "What the fuck is that supposed to mean?"

Rah-lo watched her. Even her mannerisms at that moment

were typical. Asia looked ready for a confrontation. Her eyes glared right through him. She was impossible to talk to, she had a terrible attitude, and she was in denial about the state of their marriage. "I don't want to keep fighting with you, Asia. Word. This shit ain't working out. You got your own life and me and the kids have ours."

"So what are you, Father of the Year now? Rasheeda's failing two subjects and I don't see *you* going over her homework with her. But *I* gotta do it?"

Rah-lo shook his head. When he talked to Asia it felt like the two of them were speaking completely different languages. She wasn't hearing what he was saying, and he was tired of trying to make her hear it.

He walked away, and went to the living room. He sat down on the couch and grabbed the remote. Asia stood there for a few moments, replaying their conversation and becoming more and more pissed that he had ambushed her that way. As she stood there, Rasheeda came in and greeted her mother.

"Hi, Ma. Why are you just standing there like that?" Rasheeda asked.

Asia heard her daughter but ignored the question. Instead of answering, Asia stormed off to the living room and stood in front of the TV.

"What the hell is your problem?"

He looked up at Asia and wished he could make her disappear. "I'm fed up."

Asia laughed mockingly. "You're fed up, huh? Since when?"

Rah-lo shrugged his shoulders. "I've felt that way for years. I don't blame you, really, because you only did what I allowed you to do. The weed, the liquor, the partying, not taking care of the kids, the house being left a mess, I let you do that. I didn't complain because I didn't feel like fighting with you all the time."

"No, you didn't complain. You just replaced me with that bitch Celeste!" Asia yelled.

Rah-lo went back to ignoring her. This was part of the reason that he couldn't forget about Celeste. Asia brought her name up every time they had an argument.

"Now you ain't got nothing to say, huh? What, did I hit a nerve or something, Raheem?"

He shook his head at her. "You don't care about me and what makes me happy. You seem like you don't even care about your kids."

Asia had heard enough. Just as Rasheeda came into the living room to see what all the fuss was about, Asia let loose with a verbal tirade. "Let me tell you something, Rah-lo," she began. "I'm sick of some shit, too. You know what I'm sick of?" she asked rhetorically. "I'm fuckin' sick of you walking around here like King Tut, acting like everybody in here owes you something because you pay the bills. That's what any man is supposed to do. A man is *supposed* to pay the bills, and take care of his kids. And a real man is supposed to be faithful to his wife." Asia's words lingered in the air and Rasheeda soaked it all up. "Yeah, you ain't got nothing to say now, right? All these years I put up with you fucking somebody else. Then you went and got arrested with that *bitch*! Do you know how fuckin' embarrassing that shit was? All my friends finding out that my man is cheating on me. All that money you took out of this household so you could keep her living the good life, buying hair salons, cars, houses, and all that shit! How do you think that made me feel? But did I come in here accusing you of being a fucked-up father or husband?"

Rah-lo looked over and saw Rasheeda standing in the entranceway and he wished he could slap Asia for being so careless with her mouth. "Rasheeda, go upstairs," he said calmly.

"No! Why should she go upstairs? You don't want your daughter to know what kind of man you really are?" Asia's high was blown. Instead she was completely furious. "You wanted to call me out as a bad mother, but look in the mirror, Rah-lo!"

Rah-lo wanted to wring Asia's neck. "Why don't you have some class?" he asked her. "Why would you want to have this conversation in front of your daughter?"

"Why not?" Asia demanded, furious. "I ain't lying. You cheated on me for years with that bitch Celeste. And now you're mad because I'm not like her. What did she cook for you, Rah-lo? Did she clean your house and take care of you?"

He shook his head at Asia's ignorance and looked at Rasheeda seriously. She caught the hint and turned to leave.

Asia stopped her. "Rasheeda, am I a good mother?"

Rasheeda stopped in her tracks and looked at both of her parents. "You're both good parents," she answered diplomatically. She was conflicted by what she was hearing. She had no prior knowledge of her father dealing with any woman other than her mother. Rasheeda felt a kind of way about that. She wasn't sure what the feeling was exactly. But she knew that she felt something. Still, her father had always looked out for her and for her sisters. She wouldn't dare tell her mother what she really thought about *her* parenting skills. Not to her face anyway.

"Well, your father thinks I ain't shit."

"Asia, let her go upstairs. Don't put her in the middle of this." Rah-lo wished that he had never started this discussion.

Asia wasn't listening to reason. "She just said I'm a good mother. So what gives you the right to come questioning me about where I was or what I'm cooking for dinner?"

Rah-lo was exasperated. Motioning with his fingers as if counting off a list of charges, he yelled, "You're coming in here later every night, Asia! You're drinking more and more. You're lazy. You don't—"

Rah-lo was letting loose when Asia interrupted. *"Fuck you!"* She was in his face now. "You got a lot of nerve, you sorry son of a bitch!"

"Ma," Rasheeda called out, attempting to intervene. She felt like she should leave her parents alone, but she was afraid to leave them at the same time. Things were getting way out of hand. They were a volatile couple at times. But this was way beyond any argument she had ever seen them have.

But Asia was beyond reasoning now. "You backward-ass hustlin', hood-rich muthafucka! You walk around here like you're somebody important. Like I'm supposed to bow down to you like you're royalty. If I never lift another finger in this house, I'm entitled to that. I've paid my dues. I sat in court for you, went on trips upstate to visit you, and I had your muthafuckin' kids."

"Hey!"

"Hey, my ass, Rah-lo! I did all of that *and* I put up with you having a whole separate life outside of our marriage. I think I deserve to do what the fuck I want."

"Drop it," Rah-lo insisted. He turned to Rasheeda and pointed at the stairs. She took the hint and went up to her room, leaving her parents to battle it out. Rah-lo turned his attention back to Asia. "You got a real fuckin' psychological problem," he said. "What type of mother do you think you are? Really? Why would you say all of that in front of her?"

"The truth hurts, huh?" Asia asked, lighting a cigarette.

Rah-lo chuckled, frustrated. "You can't possibly think you're doing a good job or that you're setting a good example. Your daughters have seen you drunk; they've seen you high. You don't cook; you don't clean up most of the time. You have no job, no goals whatsoever. You have a mouth like a truck driver and you have no fucking class."

Asia sensed his fury, but she didn't back down. She

wanted to hurt him the way that his words had hurt her. "I may not be the classiest bitch in the world," she said. "But I deserve more than the bullshit I've put up with over the years from you . . . cheating, lying, going to jail. What kind of fucking role model have *you* been? What kind of lessons have you taught your daughters about following rules and being loyal and trustworthy? All of a sudden you're talking like you're a fucking Boy Scout or something. You're a *drug dealer*, Rah-lo. You're a criminal. A lying, cheating, half-assed hustler. I don't care if you don't want me. So the fuck what? *Go!* Leave! I can replace you in a fucking heartbeat."

Rah-lo sat there looking at her for a long time. He replayed in his mind the things she had said to him, how she belittled him. After all the years of putting his life on the line for his family, all the years of taking care of Asia's every want and need, here she was telling him that he was simply a criminal. Nothing more. None of his sacrifices or any of the risks he'd taken had mattered much to her after all. Rah-lo calmly walked away from Asia and out the door.

CHAPTER TWO

Beneath the Surface

Ishmael Wright set the flowers down on his sister's grave and stepped back. He looked at her tombstone and shook his head. *What a waste,* he thought. Tangela had been several years older than he but far less intelligent in her decision making. From the moment she became an adolescent, Ishmael had watched her throw herself at guys and do whatever it took to get and keep their attention. She had been promiscuous at an early age, sneaking out of the home she and Ishmael shared with their aunt. Their mother had committed suicide when Ishmael was seven years old. Ishmael's father had walked out on her and the pain of being abandoned by the man she loved was more than she could stand. On a sweltering August afternoon, while Ishmael and Tangela played in the park across the street from their building, their mother had shot herself in the mouth with the same gun their father had given her for protection. Tangela had been the one to discover their mother's body when she went upstairs to get a quarter-water. The scene Tangela witnessed was traumatic for her, to say the least, and it took countless sessions with child psychologists and trauma counselors to get her back to some semblance of normalcy.

After their mother's funeral, Tangela and Ishmael had moved in with their aunt Mary. Mary was a lovely dark chocolate–hued woman with no children of her own and a revolving bedroom door. Aunt Mary partied and drank herself into oblivion just about every night of the week, leaving little time for her to be concerned with her niece and nephew and the trouble they were getting into. Not that she didn't love them. Aunt Mary kept the house clean and the refrigerator stocked. But she depended on them to supervise themselves and to be independent as far as preparing their own meals and staying on track with school.

The trouble was that by the time the kids reached middle school, they figured out that no one was double-checking to ensure that they were doing the right thing. Tangela rebelled first, cutting school, hanging out with boys, and smoking cigarettes. Ishmael wasn't far behind. His problem, though, wasn't adolescent rebellion. He was eleven years old, trying desperately to keep his fifteen-year-old sister from fucking up her life. If he caught her smoking cigarettes he would threaten to tell Aunt Mary.

"Tell her, then." Tangela would shrug. "She ain't my mama."

Ishmael did tell on his sister in an attempt to curb her behavior. But Aunt Mary had merely laughed in her drunken haze and patted Ishmael patronizingly on the head.

"If cigarettes is all she's smoking, then that's not such a big deal, baby. Tangela is a teenager now. You just keep being good and do the right thing. You can be an example for your sister, believe it or not." Ishmael watched his aunt slip her feet into her heels and head out for another night on the town with another man. And he knew that he was going to have to be solely responsible for Tangela's well-being.

It was no easy task. Ishmael tried taking his aunt's advice to be a good role model for his older sister. The trouble was that Tangela had a mind of her own. It didn't matter to her that her brother was getting straight As in school and receiving perfect-attendance awards. All she cared about was guys. As he looked down at her grave, Ishmael wondered whether that dependency on male attention had come from their mother, their aunt Mary, or both. It didn't matter, he reasoned. The bottom line was that Tangela's thirst for male attention would prove to be her undoing.

The trouble with Tangela Wright was that she gave too much of herself to men. She would fuck, suck, and work magic in order to keep a man she'd set her sights on. It worked. She had her pick of all the guys in their neighborhood and she always managed to get them wrapped around her finger. Young Ishmael would watch as his sister plotted, planned, and schemed to get some unsuspecting sucker in her clutches before she sucked the life out of him skillfully. Tangela was hungry for money and power, and as she got older she sought out guys who had these things. Turned out that the dudes who had the money, power, and respect in the hood were the ones who were hustling on a very large scale. Tangela dated these guys and enjoyed the status that came along with being their wifey. She manipulated them with her explosive sex and she got everything she wanted.

One of the guys she dated was called KC. He had a reputation for ruthlessness and was more feared than respected in their Brooklyn neighborhood. When Tangela was with him, Ishmael was concerned because for the first time he genuinely feared his sister's man. Ishmael had just turned thirteen and he was feeling like a man. His voice had deepened, his shoulders were broader, and he had begun to sprout hair from his face to his private parts. He was almost taller than his sister but nowhere near as tall as KC, who stood a staggering six feet, four inches tall. Ishmael knew that he could never protect Tangela from her boyfriend if shit hit the fan. But Ishmael had no reason to worry. KC loved Tangela with all of his heart. He spent money on her, trusted her with his secrets, and slowly but surely gained the trust of her little brother.

KC spent a lot of time in Aunt Mary's household. He greased her palms with rent and grocery money and she never complained that he spent the night with her niece, locked in her bedroom with the radio blasting to drown out the sound of their lovemaking. When he wasn't digging Tangela's back out, KC talked to Ishmael about life, women, being a man, and getting involved in the drug game. Their discussions began innocently enough. KC would comment on some show that Ishmael was watching on TV or some song that was playing on the radio. Once he saw that KC wasn't the venomous monster in their house that he was in the streets, Ishmael began to relax around him more. Soon Ishmael found himself asking KC's advice on everything from what sneakers to wear with a particular outfit to what to say to a girl he liked in school. Slowly but surely, KC became a mentor to the young man.

The conversation about drug dealing began when Ishmael and KC were watching TV together. Tangela was asleep and Aunt Mary was out in the streets doing what she did best. Ishmael sat on the tan sofa with his legs stretched out on the coffee table in front of him. As he often did when he was getting comfortable in their house, KC took his gun off his waist and laid it on the end table beside him. He then laid a stack of dollar bills as wide as his fist next to it. Ishmael wasn't immediately impressed, since he could see that the cash was mostly one-dollar bills wrapped in a large rubber band. Still, he surmised that it must be at least a hundred dollars, since the stack was thick. He also figured that while one hundred dollars wasn't necessarily a lot of money, KC was lavishing Tangela with gold jewelry and expensive clothes and sneakers. He was paying Aunt Mary's rent and driving an Acura when not many dudes in the hood were living that large. Ishmael was curious and decided to ask some questions.

"What's it like to sell drugs?" he asked.

KC sat forward in his seat and looked at the young teen before him. He smiled. "It's crazy," he explained. "These muthafuckas will do anything for these drugs, Ish. I mean anything. Word." KC shook his head as if he was still amazed at the lows people would sink to in order to get high. "It's easy money. The shit sells itself. Any fool could stand out there and make enough money to dress nice and eat right." He lit a Newport and exhaled. "But that's all fools want. They hustle to eat Chinese food when they want and cop the new sneakers when they come out. But the true hustlers are the ones who drive hot cars and live in hot cribs. We're the ones with enough money to support our family so that nobody has to want for nothing. Trust me. If you ever want to get in the game, make sure you do it big. You should never risk your freedom for crumbs off someone else's plate. For the amount of time you'll get if you get caught, you better be out there making major figures. Seriously."

Ishmael liked the way that KC talked to him. KC didn't lecture him or talk down to him like he was a little kid. When KC spoke to Ishmael he gave it to him straight. KC cursed, he spoke freely, and this endeared him to Ishmael. It made him feel like a man who could think for himself and decide which direction his life would go. Ishmael grew to have tremendous respect for the guy.

Tangela, meanwhile, had her eyes on the prize. She knew that KC was a good man, and she did care for him. But she cared for herself more than she ever cared for anyone else. Tangela was selfish and could be cold at times. She played her position with KC well, though, mindful of the fact that he was one of the top players in his class. She didn't want to fuck up the good thing she had going on. So she did whatever it took to keep him. She even professed her love for him when, in fact, all she loved was his money and his status.

About a year after she began dating him, KC was locked up on federal charges and was sentenced to eight to ten years in prison. Tangela was devastated, and she wasn't the only one. Aunt Mary had grown accustomed to having the rent and phone bill paid and to having spending money every week to go out and do as she pleased. Faced with the prospect of having to make ends meet on her own, she had no idea where to begin. She couldn't go back to the welfare agency for assistance as she'd done years ago when she first took custody of her sister's children. Now—because of KC's money and influence in their neighborhood—Aunt Mary could never swallow her pride enough to ask for a handout. What would her girlfriends think? The same girlfriends she had bragged to and flossed in front of would now surely laugh at her.

Tangela, too, was in a panic. She had depended on KC to

keep her living the lifestyle she had become accustomed to. She visited him in jail and he sensed her fear and her concern for her and her family's well-being. KC loved Tangela. So he told her where his money was, told her who to talk to in order to get what she needed to keep her and her family afloat. And Tangela thanked him, assured him that she loved him and would be there waiting for him when he came home, and when the visit was over she walked out of the jailhouse and never looked back.

Ishmael began to dislike his sister. He couldn't understand how she could be cold enough to not write, visit, or accept the collect calls of a man who had single-handedly lifted her and her family out of poverty. He couldn't fathom how a man could love a woman and give her the world, only to have that woman turn around and give that man her ass to kiss. Aunt Mary, too, had seemingly forgotten about KC. Once, when Tangela wasn't home, Ishmael had accepted a collect call from KC. Ishmael tried to rationalize his sister's behavior by making empty excuses for her—maybe she was feeling a lot of pressure or perhaps she didn't visit because she didn't want to see her man encaged like that. He tried to say something that sounded like a suitable reason to turn your back on the person who helped you most. But as he was talking to KC, Aunt Mary came in.

"Boy, who are you talking to on my phone?" she'd asked.

"KC," Ishmael answered her.

The look on Aunt Mary's face had vacillated from surprise

to anger and then outrage. "Hang that phone up!" she demanded. "Tangela don't want to talk to him."

Aunt Mary marched over to the phone and hit the button to end the phone call. KC called back, but Ishmael didn't dare answer. From that day on, he didn't look at women the same. He had learned that you could give them the world and they would seldom appreciate it.

After that day, it wasn't long before KC's stash money ran out. Within months, they were struggling to make ends meet and keep a roof over their head. Neither Ishmael's aunt nor his sister was willing to get a job, so Ishmael did what came naturally. He started to hustle. Taking the advice that KC had imparted to him about the drug game, he and his friend Raheem "Rah-lo" Henderson started a crew and together they hit the block, eager for a slice of the pie. When Raheem moved to Staten Island with his mom, Ishmael feared that he would be left on his own to get money. But instead of their operation shutting down, it simply expanded. On Staten Island, Rah-lo scouted out some young men who were anxious to get involved in the game as well. Soon, Ishmael and Rah-lo were joined by Harry, Pappy, and J-Shawn, and together they got money in Brooklyn and in Staten Island.

Aunt Mary happily accepted Ishmael's illegal money and allowed him to take over all the bills. But his success on the streets wasn't enough to keep Tangela from seeking out her next sponsor. She was done with KC and his money was spent. Tangela wanted status as well as riches. And even though Ishmael tried to give her enough money to keep her from fucking for it, she moved on to the next big-time hustler in Brooklyn. His name was Biz, and he would be the next sucker for love that Tangela sank her claws into.

Tangela and Biz had gotten involved with each other almost a year after KC was incarcerated. Knowing that it would be at least another several years before KC saw the light of day, Tangela had sought out the next baller. At the time, Biz was the man in their hood and Tangela was eager for a new sponsor. Biz became her man, and she was once again living the lifestyle she had become accustomed to. When she turned eighteen, Tangela moved in with Biz and he took care of her. She was one of the first in the hood to drive a Lexus and most of the chicks around the way hated her. But that hate only fueled Tangela's ego. She reasoned that as long as she had haters, she was doing something right. Biz wanted children, and Tangela refused, claiming that she had no desire to be a mother—yet. She assured him that eventually she would have his child, and Biz believed her. The truth was, Tangela never wanted children. She was too selfish to be a parent, and she knew that. And she really wasn't in love with Biz. She cared for him because of the things that he did for her. But there was no love on her part. Still, she strung him along and enjoyed her status in the hood as Biz's wifey and Ishmael's sister. Both were ballers and she was the recipient of the fruits of their labor. Years passed this way, and everyone forgot all about KC.

When KC was released from jail and came back to the hood, he was a man on a mission. All of his money had been spent, and throughout years of incarceration Tangela had abandoned him. No letters, no visits, and she had changed her phone number so that he couldn't call. To make matters worse, the word on the street was that she had moved on to another hustler and was living lavishly, flaunting her wealth and status while KC had to start over from scratch. It was more than he could bear. He waited for her outside of Aunt Mary's apartment building one day and sat perched on top of her car eager to confront her. Tangela had emerged from the building, spotted KC, and scowled at him in disgust.

She strolled over to her car and looked at him. "Excuse me," she said. "Can you get off my car?"

KC smirked. "That nigga bought this for you?" he asked.

Tangela frowned and waved her hand, dismissing him. "Don't worry about all that. You didn't buy it."

KC felt his blood boiling. "I must have bought you *something* with all that money you took from me."

She laughed. "You gave me that money. Don't twist the shit around now to make yourself sound like a fucking victim."

KC nodded. "Okay, okay," he said. "So why couldn't you visit a nigga? Send a letter or a food package—something? Why'd you leave me out there by myself like that after everything I did for you?"

Tangela shrugged coldly. "Nobody told you to go to jail.

I'm not putting my life on hold for nobody." She hit the alarm button on her key chain and unlocked her car. "Can you excuse me? I got shit to do."

KC sat there and stared at her for a long while. He didn't budge. He was hurt and he couldn't believe that she was being so cold toward him after all that he had done for her.

Tangela was losing patience. "Okay, now you're acting like a fucking deaf mute! *Move off of my car, muthafucka!* It's over! You're broke, you lost your spot in the hood, and you're nobody now. Don't be mad at me!"

KC stood and towered over her. "I should kill your trifling ass right here," he threatened.

She smirked at him. "And you *still* wouldn't be shit!" she hissed. She reasoned that with Biz and Ishmael having her back, KC would never have the balls to harm a hair on her head. She was wrong.

He pulled a Taurus nine-millimeter from his jacket and shot her in the face twice. Then he took her car keys, jumped into her Lexus, and sped away. Tangela died immediately and KC fled town, knowing that he was a wanted man. Ishmael was devastated. And so was Biz, since the autopsy uncovered the fact that Tangela had finally gotten pregnant with his child.

Ishmael had always taken it as his responsibility to look after his sister. In his heart he felt that he had failed miserably. He and his boys hunted for KC, eager to settle the score. But the authorities caught up with him first and arrested him in

Baltimore. They brought him back to New York to face murder charges as Ishmael buried his sister.

As he looked down at her grave now, he couldn't help feeling guilty. Not just because he had failed to protect Tangela from an untimely death, but also because a part of him didn't blame KC. Part of Ishmael understood why the man had done what he did. In Ishmael's heart, he was happy that the cops had caught up with KC before he did. KC was serving a life sentence without the possibility of parole. Ishmael was satisfied with that. Tangela had played KC and she had been remorseless. Ishmael did miss his sister, and it broke his heart that she had died such a horrible death. Still, the way that Tangela had treated KC, the way Aunt Mary used men to get what she wanted, these things changed Ishmael's perception of women. In his mind, most of them were manipulative and self-serving. He didn't trust most of them and got real joy out of toying with their emotions before they had the chance to toy with his.

He looked down at his sister's tombstone and smirked. Tangela had taught him valuable lessons about females. Today would have been her thirty-fifth birthday. Instead, she lay six feet beneath the surface. Again, he shook his head.

"Happy birthday, Sis." He laid the flowers on her grave and coldly turned and walked away. Once he climbed behind the steering wheel of his SUV, Ishmael let out a deep sigh. He put his key in the ignition and prepared to head home but was interrupted by his ringing cell phone. "Hello?" he answered.

"Where are you, Ish?" Nina asked.

Ishmael frowned, confused. "Why? Wassup?" He didn't feel like explaining his whereabouts to Nina. He hadn't shared *all* the details of his relationship with his sister, so Nina had no clue as to how profoundly Tangela's life—and her death—had affected Ishmael. He hadn't even bothered to tell Nina that today was his sister's birthday, let alone the fact that he was visiting her grave.

"What do you mean, 'Wassup?' " Nina asked. *"Where . . . are . . . you?"* Nina pronounced each word slowly and loudly for emphasis.

Ishmael pulled his cell phone away from his ear and looked at it as if it were foreign. He was sick of Nina's desire to know his every move. It was becoming more apparent to him that even though they had been together for years, Nina didn't completely trust him. Ishmael remained a very private person. He had always been that way, a man of many secrets. Very few people knew the details of his past. So whenever Nina got pushy like this he resisted. "I'm out handling business. What's the deal?"

Nina sucked her teeth. "What's with all the secrecy, Ishmael? I'm only asking where you are because I wanted you to come and pick me up. But if you're far away, I can get home on my own."

Ishmael could hear the irritation in Nina's voice and he

wasn't in the mood for it. Not today. "I'm not in Brooklyn," he lied. "So I guess you can get home on your own."

"Fine, then," Nina reluctantly agreed. She wanted to protest, but Ishmael hurriedly hung up the phone. He decided that he would head to downtown Brooklyn. Might as well do some retail therapy to get his mind off of his dead sister and his nagging girlfriend. He was feeling restless. For years Ishmael had been faithful to Nina. Well . . . as faithful as he was willing to be. He had not been seen with or spoken of another female besides Nina since they moved in together. He had others, of course. In other boroughs and with discretion, Ishmael kept company with several sexy ladies of various shades and shapes and sizes. Today, instead of going straight home, Ishmael was going to prowl. Plus, a shopping spree would give him an alibi for his whereabouts when Nina inevitably interrogated him later on.

Ishmael drove to downtown Brooklyn and parked his truck. He stopped in Dr Jays and picked up some jeans and a few T-shirts. Then he strolled past Lawrence Street and glanced over at where Celeste's salon had once been. Ish had had a lot of fun at Dime Piece. Each of the stylists had kept him entertained at some point in time. But Celeste was special. From the moment Rah-lo introduced them, Ishmael had felt more for her than he should have. She was Rah-lo's shorty. Ishmael wasn't supposed to be watching her ass whenever she walked past. But he was, from the very beginning. As he grew to know her, he only felt more affection for her. Ishmael liked the way she thought. She wanted more than the average chick and she wasn't scared to put in work to get it. In Ishmael's eyes, Rah-lo didn't deserve her. Ishmael thought about her a lot and he really couldn't believe that she hadn't bothered to call him over time. Looking at where Celeste's shop had been, now the site of a Dominican hair salon, Ishmael headed up the block to pick up a pair of kicks.

As he walked inside Foot Locker, he was surprised to see Nina's old coworker Robin Hunter emerging with her son in tow. Ishmael hadn't seen Robin in a very long time and he smiled at her, pleased with what he saw. Robin had gained a little weight in all the right places. He observed her wide hips and thick thighs, her small waist and perky breasts. He was mesmerized by the transformation. The last time he had seen her, she had looked pretty and simple, nothing to write home about. But now she looked like she could go on that VH1 show *Flavor of Love* and outshine all those bitches.

"Hi," he said, sizing her up. "Long time no see."

Robin smiled, noticing him taking in her newly voluptuous physique. "Hey, Ish. How you been?"

He nodded. "I'm doing all right." He looked down at Robin's son. "Hey, little man."

"Hi," Hezekiah said simply, wondering who this man was who was talking to his mom.

Robin couldn't help noticing how good Ishmael still looked. He looked like he had been working out and his muscles bulged through his button-up. He looked sexier than ever. "How's Nina?" Robin asked, hoping that he'd tell her that their relationship was over.

Ishmael unconsciously rolled his eyes slightly, much to Robin's amusement. "Nina's doing good," he said dryly.

"I knew you couldn't stand being locked down with one woman for too long," Robin said with a chuckle. "Nina got you bored already?"

Ishmael hated that he had been so obvious about his frustration with Nina. He did love her. But lately she had been nagging him about settling down, getting married, having kids, and the whole thing. He didn't want that—not yet—and Nina was losing patience. She was a wonderful woman—pretty, intelligent, a talented artist, devoted girlfriend. But she was not enough to get a player like Ish to commit to marriage or kids. The last thing he wanted was to feel like a woman was trying to force his hand. He didn't want to feel bullied or manipulated into commitment—the way he had watched Tangela bully and manipulate men for most of her life. He wanted a woman who was the opposite of his aunt and his sister. Lately, Nina had begun to remind him of them more and more. "I'm not bored," he lied.

"You're bored," Robin insisted, with a giggle. "I can tell." She thought about how good their sex had been the one time they had been together. She would give almost anything for another episode with Ishmael. "Come and find me when you need some excitement." Robin smiled and walked away, leaving Ishmael to watch her ass as she strolled out of the store.

Ishmael browsed the sneaker store briefly and didn't see much that he liked. He drove home with visions of Robin on his mind. Nina was in her usual withdrawn and slightly irritated mood. She wasn't saying much. Ishmael welcomed the silence, but he was still annoyed that Nina seemed to be wallowing in negativity these days. He wondered what she had to be stressed about. She had her own shop. Nappy Nina's did good business and she had no major problems on the surface. But something seemed to be tormenting Nina. In the beginning, Ishmael had wondered what it was. But over time he began not to care. Here she was, beautiful and talented, and all she could do was sulk around, wondering if her man was ever gonna give his love to another woman. It drove her crazy, and it drove him away. Ishmael watched her mope around the kitchen for about an hour before he went to bed. He was physically tired and emotionally drained. It was his sister's birthday, and thinking about her made his heart heavy. He went to bed, making every effort to block Nina's foul mood and Tangela's mistakes out of his mind.

CHAPTER THREE

Time for a Change

The next day, Rah-lo sat in his car in the parking lot of the United Artists movie theater on Staten Island. He watched as Ishmael's truck pulled up close by and he climbed out. Ishmael got into the passenger side of Rah-lo's Benz.

"What up?" Ishmael and Rah-lo greeted each other with a handshake.

Rah-lo puffed on the blunt he held in his hand and passed it to Ishmael. "Shit," he said. Rah-lo leaned his head back against the headrest and gazed off into space.

Ishmael waited for Rah-lo to say what was on his mind, but Rah-lo seemed lost in thought. Ishmael puffed on the blunt, wondering how long he'd have to wait for his friend to tell him what had him so entranced. He had known Rah-lo for many years. The two of them had grown up together in Brooklyn, and when Rah-lo's mother had moved her family to Staten Island, Ishmael had kept in touch with his friend. They had been through a lot of things together, and made a ton of money together also. Ishmael knew Rah-lo well enough to tell that something was troubling him now.

Rah-lo took the blunt back from Ishmael and shot him a sidelong glance. "I got some shit on my mind," he said, and he sighed. "I been thinking a lot about the old days. Thinking about J-Shawn and how they killed him, how Pappy got killed, and how Harry's doing twenty-five years." Rah-lo took another puff.

"What you thinking about all that for?" Ishmael was surprised at Rah-lo. He was usually so stoic, so fearless and at times ruthless. Rah-lo had always been the stone-faced one who led them into battle. But their crew had suffered severe blows in the past few years. Rah-lo's friend J-Shawn had been slain after being kidnapped by a rival crew. Pappy, the dust head of the crew, was killed with a gunshot wound to the head. His body had been found on the roof of a building in a Brooklyn housing project. Pappy had gotten dusted and shot his stepfather. The man had survived, and some suspected that Pappy was murdered in retaliation. With all the enemies that he had, it was tough to pinpoint who might have actually killed him. For both the police and Rah-lo's crew, Pappy's murder remained unsolved. Harry, the hothead of their crew, was serving a twenty-five-year sentence for having an arsenal in his home that rivaled that of an army platoon. He had been the stickup kid, the troublemaker, and the one with all the connections. While he was away, Rah-lo had managed to hold the crew together, with Ishmael's help of course. But it would be a lie to say that things were easy with just the two of them getting money.

The game wasn't the same for Rah-lo anymore. The money was slower, the risks were greater, and the allure was fading. Back in the day, he and his crew had been a force to reckon with. They had all gotten money together, came up together. Then it all went wrong so suddenly. Five childhood friends had dwindled down to two. Rah-lo was tired of worrying about who was out to get him or whether or not the police were on to him. He wanted out so badly, yet he didn't want to come out looking like a quitter to Ishmael. That's what Rah-lo really wanted to say to his friend.

Instead he said, "I been thinking about a lot of things." He shrugged his shoulders. "You ever get tired of this shit?"

Ishmael pondered Rah-lo's question, thinking about his own recent developments. Ishmael had been laid off from his legitimate job in a local law firm. His job in the mailroom at the firm had never been his primary source of income. He had kept the job for the benefits and for the illusion of being a workingman. It kept him off the police's radar and made him appear to be harmless to his neighbors. The hustle had always been his main career, and he loved it more than any nine-to-five. When he was laid off from his day job, Ishmael hadn't seen it coming. They'd explained that they were downsizing and had given him a benefits package to soften the blow. Since then, he had turned up the heat. He was going harder than ever. Getting money was his number one priority, and he was ready to really grind. To his surprise, Rah-lo was talking about being tired of the life they led. Ishmael was far from tired. He was intoxicated by the game—in love with the grind. Nina had been encouraging Ishmael to get another job, to give her a ring and a baby. That wasn't the life that Ishmael wanted. He was already married to his hustle.

"Sometimes I get tired," he said. "But I think about how I like to live, the way I like to eat, the clothes I like to wear. And I get refocused." Ishmael looked at Rah-lo. "Why? *You* getting tired of it?"

Rah-lo thought he detected a hint of condescension in Ishmael's tone. He wasn't sure, though. "Nah," he said, shaking his head. "I think I'm just getting tired of my wife." They laughed, but both of them knew that he was serious. "She just don't make me happy anymore."

Ishmael nodded. "So, what? You got all them other broads you fuck with to keep your mind off shit like that."

Rah-lo shrugged. "Yeah, I do. Still," he said. He did have several women he dealt with outside of his marriage to keep his mind off of Asia's shortcomings. But none of them compared to the love affair he had once had—with Celeste.

"So why don't you just leave her? People get divorced every day."

"I would have divorced her years ago if it was that simple. I just worry about my baby girls. I don't want them to have to deal with Asia's bullshit without me being there to keep her under control."

Ishmael shook his head. "That's why I don't want no kids. I don't want to get stuck with a girl just because we have a child together."

Rah-lo lit a Newport. "Nina's not the one?"

Ishmael, a true player for real, didn't answer the question. Instead, he sucked his teeth and looked away.

Rah-lo laughed. "All right. Let's get down to business." Rah-lo sat up in the driver's seat. "This is yours." He handed Ishmael his part of the profits from the work they had on the streets. The two of them were responsible for dealing with their connect, getting the work to their street soldiers—young dudes eager for sneaker and clothes money—and picking up the proceeds. They split these duties, rotating so that neither of them was doing the same thing constantly. This time it was Rah-lo's turn to divvy up the proceeds. The envelope felt a little light to Ishmael and he frowned.

"Bad week?" he asked, holding the envelope aloft to demonstrate its lightness.

Rah-lo nodded but didn't look at his friend. "Yeah," was all he said.

Ishmael sat there and looked at Rah-lo for several silent moments before realizing that he had no intention of elaborating. Ishmael's sixth sense bugged him. He had a nagging feeling that Rah-lo was holding out on him. He hated to think that way about his friend. Ishmael cleared his throat.

Rah-lo turned to face Ishmael and shook his head. "You know how it is. Some weeks are better than others. It'll be better." He lit another cigarette, exhaled the smoke.

Ishmael looked out the window. "What are you doing tomorrow?" he asked, changing the subject.

The two friends made small talk for a few minutes longer before they parted ways. Once out of the parking lot, the two went in opposite directions.

Ishmael headed for Harlem. As much as he loved Rah-lo, this was no time for money to slow up. Ishmael had bills to pay, moves to make, and he wasn't going to sit idly by and let the game get the best of him. For years he had been in Rah-lo's shadow as his foot soldier, even his errand boy. He was tired of that role and now he wanted more.

The cash that Rah-lo had given to Ishmael seemed significantly less than what he was used to. Rah-lo's refusal to explain the "bad week" they'd had only bolstered Ishmael's determination to succeed on his own merit. He had to do his own thing. There were no friends when it came to business. So he went uptown and cut a side deal with Cito— their connect—to get some product for himself without including Rah-lo in the deal. Ishmael had to take care of himself and make sure that the success he deserved would be his. He was tired of playing second fiddle, and Rah-lo was going soft on him.

CHAPTER FOUR

Starting Over

It was one of those days when winter's crisp wind gives way to a soft spring breeze, and Celeste Styles and her friend Keisha Russell were on their way to a social event. Keisha was so glad Celeste was finally coming to one of the events she'd been inviting her to for months. Celeste was accompanying her friend to a dinner party being thrown by a women's group that Keisha belonged to. The group of female entrepreneurs met each month to mingle, listen to guest speakers, and support one another's business. Among them were publishers, agents, real estate brokers, teachers, lawyers, bankers, and assorted other professionals. Keisha had been trying to get Celeste to join for the longest time, but Celeste was reluctant. To her it sounded like the "Uppity

Bitches Club," and Celeste knew she wouldn't fit in. After all, she had once lived a lifestyle in which she was surrounded by hustlers and the women who loved them. The last thing she wanted was to sit around a bunch of Ivy League or holier-than-thou women who had nothing in common with someone like her.

Upon moving to Atlanta, Celeste had gotten back into college, continuing her pursuit of the business degree she had abandoned upon meeting Rah-lo. She had worked at a hair salon in Buckhead and tried to grow accustomed to her new life. But in the beginning she couldn't help feeling like she had taken a huge step backward. After all, she had once owned and operated a successful salon of her own. Suddenly, she was merely working in one. She found that she had *far* less money than she was used to having, and frankly, she missed the lifestyle she had enjoyed courtesy of Rah-lo. But she told herself that she was ready for a new day. She wanted a love of her own, when her heart was ready. One that she would never have to share, or hide, or be ashamed of. She wanted her own success. Success that she wouldn't have to relinquish if a relationship turned sour. What Celeste had pursued—and gained—was a new life, with her own success and triumph to make it sweeter.

She worked for a marketing firm in downtown Atlanta and she was slowly moving up the corporate ladder. She owned a condo and a nice car, she went to church with her mama and nana on Sundays, and she had a dear friend and coworker in Keisha. Celeste had lost about ten pounds as part of the clean slate she had given herself. She was looking and feeling better than she had in years. The only thing missing was a man to share it with. Keisha was also single and having a great time dating man after man in her search for Mr. Right. But Celeste seemed far more hesitant to get out there and find someone to settle down with. She was testing the waters, but she was in less of a rush to find her Prince Charming. And Keisha couldn't understand why.

Tonight, Keisha's group was opening their doors to men. It was a cocktail party/fund-raiser to support AIDS research, and many male professionals would be there to offer information and services related to the charity. Celeste had broken up with her boo Damon only weeks prior. She had dated him for close to a year, and she enjoyed his company. But after being with him for so long, to Celeste it seemed to be going nowhere. The relationship had lost its thrill and Celeste was wasting no time on a relationship that no longer excited her. She was feeling brand-new, after cutting her hair into a cute and sassy style and updating her wardrobe. Ending her relationship with Damon made her feel alive again. Not that he was a bad guy—in fact, quite the opposite. He was a gentleman and a success story. She just couldn't help being bored. Tonight, Celeste looked forward to having fun.

Keisha was driving her Escalade and Celeste hung on for dear life. Keisha had a lead foot and riding with her was an adventure, to say the least. When they arrived, they parked and checked their makeup in the car mirrors one more time before going inside. Celeste wore a breezy white Nicole Miller dress and very sexy Stuart Weitzmans. Keisha was sharp in a tailored red Escada pantsuit with a ruffled neckline. She wore no bra or blouse, and the jacket was cut as low as possible for full effect. She was sexy and she knew it. They both looked amazing. Celeste's short hairdo was styled to perfection, and Keisha wore her hair long and wavy, with one side dramatically shielding one eye. They stepped out and headed inside, eager to mix and mingle.

They were not disappointed. All the ladies from Keisha's group were dressed to impress. Designer labels and pricey baubles were everywhere. They made the rounds with Keisha introducing Celeste to many of her entrepreneurial sisters along the way. With champagne flutes in hand, they worked the crowd, flashing dazzling smiles, cracking jokes, and having stimulating conversations. Dinner was served and several speakers followed as dessert was presented. They all talked about the importance of wealthy, successful black people donating to finding a cure for the number one killer of black people in almost every demographic. The biggest donors received special recognition, and Celeste surveyed the room.

There were a number of handsome men there that evening, although several of them looked as if they may have been homosexual. Still, there were quite a few men with potential. Keisha set her sights on one handsome middle-aged man seated elsewhere in the dining room. She knew she would meet him before the night was over. The formal part of the evening was capped off by a solo performance by a gospel singer doing a soulful rendition of the Lord's Prayer. After a big round of applause, a deejay took the reins and the party went into full swing. Drinks and hors d'oeuvres flowed and Celeste was having a great time. She couldn't help noticing a tall brother who stuck pretty close by one of Keisha's fellow members. Celeste surmised that they must be a couple, but she couldn't help glancing in his direction from time to time. He was tall and he was well proportioned. His haircut was fresh, his goatee was perfect, and his lips were inviting. She watched him gesture with his big hands while he talked to the sister at his side. He had great teeth, too, which Celeste noticed whenever he flashed his megawatt smile. She was captivated.

Keisha was holed up in the corner with a man she'd had her sights set on all evening. He was a new district court judge, and she sat beside him with her legs crossed invitingly and her eyes fluttering flirtatiously. He never stood a chance. Celeste chuckled at her friend's aggression and went to the bar to order another drink. "Hennessy this time, please," she told the bartender.

"That's a big drink for such a delicate lady," a voice behind her remarked. Celeste turned around to find the beautiful stranger she had been watching standing behind her. She immediately looked for his girlfriend. Celeste had already gotten out of one relationship where she had been the other woman. She didn't want to find herself in that position again. Instead of responding, she smiled and looked away.

"My name is Bryson. Are you one of my sister's group members?" he asked, extending his hand to Celeste in greeting.

She took it and smiled broadly. "Is that your sister?" she asked, nodding in the direction of the woman she had assumed was his wife. Celeste was relieved.

Bryson nodded. "She didn't want to come by herself to another charity event. So I got suckered into coming with her."

Celeste's smile broadened. "My name is Celeste," she offered, shaking his strong hand. "I'm not part of the group. I came with my friend Keisha."

Bryson nodded as the bartender brought Celeste her drink. She reached to pay for it and Bryson held his hand up to stop her. "This one's on me," he said. He ordered a glass of Patrón and leaned against the bar. "You don't want to join their group?" he asked. "It seems like you're somebody important, so you'd fit right in."

Celeste laughed. "Well, thank you. I think." She wasn't sure if he had given her a compliment or not. "I guess I do all right for myself and I could probably benefit from making the good connections in their group. But I've never really been tight with a bunch of women like that. Most of the women I've encountered are backstabbers or haters."

"So you have a lot of male friends?" Bryson asked, with one eyebrow raised.

Celeste sipped her drink. She wasn't sure what Bryson meant by the question. "Keisha is my best friend since I moved to Atlanta. I like her. We get along real well. But I don't think I could stand meeting with fifty women once a month talking about women's issues."

Bryson smiled. "You're from New York, right?"

Celeste nodded.

"I can tell by your accent," he explained.

Celeste wanted to tell him that he was the one with the accent. But she didn't want to hurt his country pride. "Everybody says New Yorkers have an accent. I guess it's true."

"How long have you lived in ATL?"

"A few years. I like it. I needed a change of pace."

"You got a man?"

"You get straight to the point, don't you?"

"Well, I thought New Yorkers don't like to beat around the bush." Bryson downed his shot of tequila.

Celeste smiled flirtatiously. "Nope. I don't have a man. Why? You wanna take me out?"

Bryson smiled back. "Yeah."

Celeste nodded. "Okay. I'd like that," she said. He was confident, straightforward, and he seemed to be pretty intelligent. So far, Celeste was feeling optimistic about this man.

The bartender brought Bryson another drink and Celeste watched, impressed, as he handed the bartender an American

Express Centurion card. The black card spoke volumes about his wealth, and Celeste's curiosity was piqued. "So what do you do?"

"I'm an entertainment attorney with a prominent Atlanta firm. Reed, Maxwell, and—"

"Forrester," Celeste completed his sentence. "I'm a junior executive with a marketing firm downtown. Your firm represented us in a case against a rival company."

Bryson smiled. "It's a small world. I've been practicing for twelve years and been a partner at the firm for two of those years."

"Wow," she said. "Sounds interesting. Who is your most famous client?"

He shrugged. "I have a few famous clients. After a while they don't impress you with their fame and wealth as much. They're human just like the rest of us. The famous clients are no different for me than the average Joe."

"All of their money is green, right?" Celeste asked, sipping her drink.

"That's right. It's all the same," Bryson said. "So how do you like working in marketing?"

She sat on a bar stool and crossed her legs, perching her clutch bag on her lap. "The work is exciting, I get to travel often, and the pay is competitive. I like it."

"That's great. When you get paid to do what you love to do, it's a wonderful thing." Bryson sized her up and liked what he saw. Celeste was a beautiful woman, stylish and sophisticated. She was successful and intelligent. And she had a fat ass, just the way he liked. "So," he said. Why are you single?"

She sighed. "Actually, I just got out of a yearlong relationship."

"So is it too soon for me to ask you out? I don't want to be your rebound romance." Bryson smiled as he said it.

Celeste laughed. "It's not too soon. It wasn't a bad split. In fact, we're still friends. The whole relationship just lost its thrill for me, and I got tired of going through the motions."

Bryson looked at her, wondering what man would be foolish enough to allow a woman this beautiful to get bored. "So, you're a thrill seeker, huh?" he asked facetiously.

She smiled. "Yeah," she said. "I guess you could say that."

Keisha came over, looking exasperated. The man she was trying to snag had turned out to be gay and she was dismayed. "This party is wack!" she spat. "I'm ready to go."

Celeste looked at Keisha, confused. "What happened? I thought you were having fun!"

Keisha looked at Celeste sidelong. "Don't ask."

Celeste turned back to Bryson. "She's ready to go," she said, nodding in Keisha's direction. Celeste handed him her business card. "Call me."

Bryson nodded. "I definitely will."

Celeste grabbed Keisha's arm gently and they headed for the exit. She felt bad that Keisha's night hadn't gone as well as hers had. But she was thrilled that she had connected with

Bryson. He had a sexy swagger about him and a law degree to match. It seemed like he may have potential. Celeste wasn't that interested in the white-collar suit and tie—wearing men she came into contact with most often. But Bryson might be an exception. She still wanted a bad boy, only without all the bullshit that went along with it. She was finished with guys who went to jail, had crazy baby mamas and multiple kids.

Since Celeste had left New York, the closest she had come to finding a roughneck who fit the bill was her ex, Damon. She had met him at the gym where she worked out regularly. In the beginning, their relationship had been purely physical, with no strings attached, and Celeste liked it that way. The two of them shared occasional movie nights at her place or his, which were always capped off by great sex. Then they'd talk and have a few drinks before round two of their passion began. Celeste was content with them being friends with benefits. But eventually, for Damon, the relationship grew more serious. He began to want to see Celeste more often, he called numerous times each day, and Celeste got scared. When he started dropping hints about wedding bells, Celeste made herself scarce. Marriage and families were the furthest things from her mind.

On the other hand, Keisha, the southern belle, *craved* marriage to a wealthy man and socialite status. To her, marriage was the golden carrot that every woman should be in pursuit of until she got it. Keisha couldn't understand her friend's desire to remain single and date without commitment.

Anyone who knew Celeste could attest to the fact that she was staunchly independent. Despite the fact that a man had financed her lifestyle for several years, it had been Celeste who had made the dream of owning her own salon a reality. She had been responsible for the decor, the ambiance, and it was she who had chosen the best stylists in Brooklyn to keep the clientele consistent. Celeste was a visionary. Always had been, always would be. In her youth, Celeste had been a straight-A student, a popular girl among her peers. She was well behaved and seldom rocked the boat for her single mother, Zara Styles.

Celeste had been raised by her mother and her grandmother, and their maternal wisdom had served her well. While many of her peers were getting high, getting in trouble, or getting pregnant, Celeste had had her head in the books and her future clearly mapped out for herself. She had envisioned herself as a successful businesswoman from an early age. She pictured herself in pricey shoes, strutting into a boardroom and setting her expensive briefcase down on the table, wowing the crowd of stiff suited businessmen with her knowledge and her expertise. Celeste had been ready for the world in those days. And then she'd been sidetracked by her love for a thug. When she fell in love with Rah-lo, college had fallen by the wayside, much to her mother's chagrin. Celeste had given up her collegiate dreams in search of the American dream—or at least a ghetto-fabulous version of it.

Now, years later, she was back on track. But she was still

having the sweetest dreams about one man in particular. In her dreams, they made love with a passion that blew her mind. He would hold her and she would feel so safe and loved. Then she'd wake up and find herself living a beautiful life in a beautiful city, and still feeling empty despite it all.

Celeste thought often about the man in her dreams. Rah-lo had been her everything. She remembered the night she met him so many years ago. He was so thugged-out, so sexy. Out for a night on the town in New York with her girlfriends, Celeste had found herself in Staten Island's notorious Park Hill section. As she sauntered across busy Targee Street in search of a pay phone, several men had called out to her, hoping for a chance to talk to the pretty young stranger in their midst. They called out to her from across the street.

"Let me holla at you."

"Damn, baby! You *wearin'* them jeans!"

"Can I talk to you?"

She was flattered, but she didn't respond to men who called her out that way. She felt that she was too classy a bitch to answer these types of greetings. Approaching the pay phone, she prepared to place her call but noticed a tall and rather handsome guy crossing the street in her direction. She thought his walk was sexy as hell.

"Excuse me. Can I talk to you for a minute?" he asked. The smirk on his face was a mixture of flirtation and mischief. "Don't listen to them. It ain't every day that they see somebody as fly as you are stepping out on the block. My name is Rah-lo." He extended his hand and Celeste hesitated before she shook it. She looked him over, feeling strangely attracted to this rugged stranger with a mischievous grin on his face. "You ain't gonna tell me your name?" he asked.

She smiled and told him her name. She took in his attire—a black hoodie, jeans, and Timbs. A typical block hugger, she surmised. But his smile was disarming, and she was impressed that he'd had the guts to cross the street and risk rejection in front of all of his friends. All of his boys stood on the opposite sidewalk, watching to see what would happen. She liked a confident man, and the one standing before her exuded not only confidence but cockiness as well. His arrogance coupled with his charm was irresistible. She liked his style. So she engaged him in conversation, and when he walked away he had her number. And Celeste had been with him from that day forward.

But not now. Still, Celeste thought about him all the time. She might see a designer handbag she couldn't fit into her budget and she would recall how Rah-lo had spoiled her, lavished her with all the material things a woman would want. She had never had to concern herself with such trivial things as budgets or financial limitations when they were together. She had lived in his large home on Staten Island, New York, and she had been Rah-lo's well-kept secret. He took care of her, buying her cars and jewelry, supplying her every need. He had bankrolled her hair salon—Dime Piece—as a gift to her, and he made sure that she had any and every material thing she wanted. But what she hadn't had was his time. She hadn't had his love exclusively. And she hadn't had the title. Asia was his wife. Celeste had been little more than his chick on the side.

Secretly, the one thing she had yearned for most of her life was a father. She had never known her dad and had often envied the few of her friends who had fathers active in their lives. More than anything, Celeste had always wanted the luxury of being Daddy's little girl, being spoiled and taken care of. She had never had many friendships with females. They had always proven themselves to be jealous or untrustworthy. Friendship, popularity, belonging to a clique—those things had never been of importance to Celeste. That was one of the reasons she had managed to keep her head in her hair salon amid the stylists' constant bickering and cattiness. Celeste was always able to tune them out. She didn't need or long for girlfriends. But she did long for her father. Although her mother and grandmother had done an outstanding job of raising Celeste to be a strong and respectable woman, she still had a void where her dad should have been.

Celeste had always shared an open and honest relationship with her mother. So when Celeste had fallen in love with Rah-lo she had never hidden his marital status from her mom. She told her the truth of what she was dealing with. Her mother, of course, disapproved. Not only because Rah-lo was a married man. But also because he made his living in the streets—something that Ms. Styles had always wanted her daughter to steer clear of. Celeste was an intelligent young lady with a bright future ahead of her when she met Rah-lo. Her mother saw her daughter's potential and couldn't help being disappointed in her choice of whom she'd given her heart to. But Ms. Styles didn't protest too loudly. After all, Celeste was an adult. She had made her decision. And Ms. Styles knew all too well that when a woman gave her heart to a man, wild horses wouldn't be able to tear her away.

In the months before Celeste decided to leave New York City, Zara had noticed that Celeste's lifestyle was wearing her down. Without being told, Zara could sense that her daughter was fed up. She could tell by the forlorn look on her daughter's face every time she saw her. It hadn't always been that way. In the beginning of their relationship, Rah-lo had Celeste floating on a cloud. The pure happiness that she felt from being loved by him was evident in her smile. Celeste had always smiled back then. She had always been optimistic that the situation was only temporary. Rah-lo would leave Asia eventually. Celeste had believed that Rah-lo couldn't love her like he did and not want to be with her exclusively. Naively, she had held out hope. But that hope had begun to fade. And Celeste's mother knew long before Celeste ever told her. When Dime Piece had burned down, Celeste had been sad but also oddly relieved. For the first time, Celeste began to talk about needing a change. Zara saw it as the perfect opportunity for her daughter to start over. Zara and her aging mother were moving to Atlanta. Celeste's mother invited Celeste to come along and prayed hard that she would accept her invitation. When Celeste had finally called to say that she was coming to Atlanta and leaving Rah-lo behind, Zara had danced and shouted around her house like a church lady filled with the Holy Ghost. She couldn't have been happier.

Unfortunately, the same couldn't be said for Celeste. When she had first left Rah-lo, she had felt so many different emotions. Happiness was not among them. She felt hurt that Rah-lo hadn't loved her enough to leave his wife. Celeste had believed that he loved her. But obviously not as much as she had loved him, because if he had, he never could have continued in an "empty" marriage with another woman. Celeste was also angry with herself for the choices she'd made, angry about all the times she had allowed herself to be taken for granted.

Part of her hoped that he would come after her, that he would somehow find her and rush in, declaring his love for her. But part of her was relieved to be free of him. She felt like she had sold herself short in some ways. True, she was living an enviable lifestyle. She had all the material things any woman could ever yearn for. But how she'd gotten those things weighed heavily on her conscience. In the beginning, she hadn't let herself think about it. She told herself that Rah-lo was the one selling drugs, not her. She convinced herself that dropping out of college hadn't been a mistake, reasoning that Rah-lo had been a fast track to the life she would have inevitably led eventually. But when she really thought about it, she was merely a mistress with a bunch of meaningless perks.

The salon was hers, but she hadn't earned it. The clothes and jewelry were beautiful, but she would have given them all back to have Rah-lo as her man exclusively. Celeste had been feeling so trapped with Rah-lo, so stuck and stagnant. And life was too short to continue feeling that way.

Rah-lo had protected her and cared for her and she admitted to herself that in some twisted way Rah-lo had been the daddy she had longed for for so long. In so many ways Rah-lo had raised her. He had taught her the ways of the streets and the ins and outs of being a hustler. And Celeste still carried that hustler's spirit with her to this day. For that, she would be forever grateful to Rah-lo.

Celeste loved him with all of her heart. But she had begun to ask herself if love was enough. Atlanta offered her a clean slate. It was time for her to stand on her own two feet for once. This time she would be a success without the security of a relationship. She was a single woman surrounded by wealthy and accomplished single men. Celeste dove right in.

Now, four years had passed since she'd left the man and the city she loved behind. And no matter how she tried to get him off her mind, Rah-lo was still there. He would invade her thoughts at odd moments, and she quickly brushed those thoughts aside. But he was there in her dreams, kissing her just the way she needed to be kissed and spanking her when she needed to be spanked. He had never needed instructions or guidance. He just knew. That excited Celeste, and that excitement was something that no other man had been able to duplicate for her. She dated different men and moved on with her life. But none of them were *him*. Damon was sexy, tough, well-groomed, and a very successful businessman. But to Celeste, sex with him lacked much excitement—because she was comparing him to Rah-lo. On the surface, she had moved on. But on the inside, she hated herself for still holding on to the long-ago love that she had hoped would fade with time.

But as she and Keisha climbed into Keisha's truck and buckled up for the ride home, Celeste gazed out the window and smiled. She hoped that Bryson would be the perfect candidate to fill the void in her life. Thinking about his smile—and his black card—Celeste hoped he'd be the one to sweep her off her feet.

CHAPTER FIVE

Just Like Old Times

Brooklyn, New York

H*ow can I love somebody else . . ."*
"Mary J. Blige is the truth! She said a bitch gotta love herself before she try to love anybody else." Charly Hanson snapped her fingers to the beat of the song "Be Happy" playing on the hair salon's radio. Her hair salon, Charly's, was packed with saints and sinners alike, but all Charly saw was dollar signs. She didn't notice some of her patrons wincing as she referred to women as "bitches" within the earshot of a few church ladies and several children. Charly didn't care. It was *her* shop. And she did as she damn well pleased.

People knew this about her and they still kept coming each week. That was because the stylists in her shop were some of Brooklyn's finest. Dimitri and Lauren had the cuts and weaves on lock. Tina's clientele was composed of mostly kids and old church ladies. And Charly's friend Robin handled braids, dreads, and natural styles. Charly had an interesting relationship with Robin. While they had bonded during the time they worked together at Dime Piece, things between them had changed.

There was a sense of friendly competition between the two of them. Charly was single and loving it. She was successful with her salon and she looked better than ever. She had no children, no steady man, nothing tying her down. Charly partied hard and traveled often. She shopped constantly and ate dinner out at restaurants far more than she ever cooked at home. And because of her looks, she had men lavishing her with these things. Charly was good at what she did. She liked to say that she had a hustler's spirit.

Robin, on the other hand, was more humble. She was the single parent of her son, Hezekiah. She loved him tremendously and her life felt fuller with him in it. Robin worked hard to keep him dressed well, eating right, and looking good. He went to private school, played in a football league, and scored excellent grades. She had never expected to be a single parent. But his father had died while Hezekiah was just an infant, and she was forced to do it all on her own. She had the odds stacked against her, but she managed to keep her head above water. And Robin was focused. She had gone back to school, paying her younger sister a tidy sum to babysit Hezekiah while she did so. Robin worked hard and made good money. And instead of spending it on frivolous fashions and costly baubles the way that Charly did, Robin invested in her education. Now it was paying off. She was about to graduate from John Jay College and she knew that Charly was hating that. Robin was doing more as a single mother than Charly could ever accomplish with no one to worry about besides herself. Robin wore her education as a badge of honor, which only grated on Charly's nerves.

"Robin, you need to sweep all this hair up off the floor between clients." Charly's face was twisted into a disgusted grimace. "This shit looks horrible." Her tone was condescending and everyone noticed.

Robin kept right on braiding extensions into her client's hair, ignoring Charly's comments. This only further pissed Charly off.

"Hellooooooo," Charly said.

"I heard you," Robin replied, locking eyes with Charly. "When I'm done, I'll sweep it all up. Okay?"

Charly wanted to curse her out, but Robin hadn't given her a good enough reason to. Instead, she rolled her eyes and walked away. Just then, fine-ass Ishmael Wright walked through the door of the salon, bringing almost all chatter to a complete halt. Charly felt a shiver go down her spine as she looked him over from head to toe. Charly and Ishmael had shared an intense sexual relationship years ago. For Charly, it had been so much more than just that. For her, it had been love, for the first time in her life. Unfortunately, Ishmael didn't share the sentiment, and he had broken her heart. At least that was Charly's version of events.

During her time as a stylist at Celeste's shop, Dime Piece, Charly and all the other stylists had come to know Ishmael as a friend of Celeste's man, Rah-lo. When Rah-lo went to jail, Ishmael came by the shop often to escort Celeste upstate or to drop off messages or gifts from Rah-lo. In that capacity, Ishmael spent a lot of time with Celeste. In turn, Ishmael spent a lot of time at the salon. And one by one he had sampled the stylists. Charly had been first, and that distinction meant something to Charly. She and Ishmael had shared subtle flirting that blossomed into a sexual relationship. They had gone out a couple of times—dinner and a movie for the most part. Ishmael had bought her pricey gifts and even given her a car to drive when hers was giving her trouble. But Charly had bragged about his generosity in the shop, and when Ishmael became aware of that he was turned off. Then she began to exhibit jealous and possessive behavior, which was the final straw for Ishmael. What had started as something fun and passionate had turned into something ugly, and he was finished. Ishmael dumped Charly.

Next he slept with Robin, although that had only been a one-night stand. And after their physical encounter, Ishmael moved on to Nina. Nina Lords was a lovely girl with a troubled past who had somehow gotten the notorious play-boy to settle down. She had also been one of the best stylists at Dime Piece, working with and sparring with both Robin and Charly. It was Ishmael who had come between the women at that time, and he and Nina were still together after all these years. Which was why Charly couldn't understand seeing him walk through the doors of her salon now.

She strutted over to him and smiled sexily. "You must be lost, sir," she joked, pointing at the sign above the door. "This is Charly's beauty salon, not Nappy Nina's."

Ishmael smiled. Nina's hair salon (which he had financed for her, just as Rah-lo had done for Celeste) was located just a block away from Charly's. He was taking a chance by coming in there today, since Nina would surely have a fit if she knew that he was seen anywhere near her rival. "Hello, Charly. Good to see you again." Ishmael gave her a friendly kiss on her cheek. "I actually came to see Robin."

Charly's jaw immediately clenched. She glanced over her shoulder at Robin, who was smiling at Ishmael from her station in the back of the shop as she continued braiding her client's hair. Robin winked at the both of them and chewed her gum giddily. She knew that Charly wanted to gag.

Ishmael walked past Charly and over to Robin. Charly was tempted to cause a scene, but she managed to hold her composure. She had never gotten over Ishmael. No matter how many ballers tricked their dough on her, no matter how many thugs she had in her life with that unmistakable Brooklyn swagger, no matter whom she spent her nights with, she still had a weakness for Ishmael Wright. She hated that she had been silly enough to mess up what they'd had once.

Robin, meanwhile, wondered why he was taking such a chance by visiting her at her job in broad daylight. She didn't care, truthfully. *Fuck Nina!* she thought. *And Charly, too, for that matter.*

Ishmael was sexy as hell. He smiled at Robin as he approached, and she smiled back. They were having a private joke, and no one else got it but them. "Hi," Robin said. "This is an unexpected visit."

Ishmael sat on her stool as she stood and continued to braid her client's hair. "Surprise," he said. "I was in the neighborhood, so I just stopped by to say hello."

Robin glanced at him, smiling slyly. She surmised that their conversation the night before had piqued his curiosity, which had been precisely what she had wanted. It had obviously worked, because here he was.

Ishmael had replayed their conversation in his head over and over that night. And the next day, once he was sure that Nina was busy in her own salon with a customer's relaxer, he had slipped away to come and see what Robin had in mind to excite him. He had to admit that he was intrigued.

Robin finished her customer's braids and handed her the mirror so that she could see the end result. Robin got paid, thanked her client for the generous tip, and turned to Ishmael. "So, hi," she said, smiling. Robin noticed Charly stealing glances in their direction. She knew that this was not the time or place for the two of them to speak freely.

Ishmael also noticed Charly looking. He stuck his hands in his pockets and looked around. "You wanna go get something to eat?" Ishmael asked. He looked around. "You got any more clients waiting?"

Robin shook her head. "Nope. My next appointment is at four thirty."

"Come on." Ishmael led the way, with Robin following closely behind.

As they passed Charly, Robin smirked. "I'll be back in a few. I'm going to get some lunch."

Charly said nothing. Instead, she watched, seething as Robin followed Ishmael to his truck. Charly saw him open the passenger door for Robin, and she climbed inside. Charly wondered what was going on. She knew about Robin's dalliance with Ishmael years prior and wondered if history was repeating itself. She was tempted to make a scene, but she wasn't sure what the two of them were doing and she didn't want to come across as the jealous ex. She decided instead to wait for Robin to return, and swoop down on her like a hawk attacking its prey.

Robin watched Ishmael bite into his burger as she picked at her salad. She couldn't help wondering what was so wrong with Nina that Ishmael was being so reckless as to have lunch with her in broad daylight just blocks from her salon. "So, tell me why you're bored with Nina," she said. She shoveled a forkful of salad into her mouth as she waited for his response.

Ishmael finished chewing his food and looked at Robin. "I don't want to talk about Nina right now," he said simply.

Robin took a gulp of her Snapple and Ishmael watched her swallow, intrigued. "Okay," she said. "So what do you want to talk about?" she asked.

"I wanna know what kind of excitement you have to offer me. Last night it seemed like you had something in mind." Ishmael sat back, waiting for her response.

Robin looked at him with a sexy expression. "I'll level with you, Ishmael. I know what kind of man you are. . . ."

"What kind of man am I?"

"A man who plays the field. A man who's used to getting what he wants from women and has a hard time being faithful to one woman."

Ishmael smirked and took another bite of his burger. She continued to eat her salad and she looked back at him. "Am I wrong?" she asked.

Ishmael took a swig of his soda. "Well, you left out one thing," he said.

"What's that?"

Ishmael wiped his mouth with his napkin. "I'm a man who knows how to please a woman."

Robin smiled. "Yes, I know that," she said. Robin had a

flashback to when she had sex with Ishmael in the backseat of his SUV. Even though it had been quick and unemotional, she had never experienced anything like it. "So what kind of excitement are you looking for, Ish?"

He shrugged. He wasn't about to spell it out for her. "You got a man yet?" he asked.

Robin stopped chewing. She was slightly annoyed by the question. She was tired of everyone acting as if having a man were a sign of success—as if her life were somehow incomplete because she wasn't tied down to one person. "Yeah," she answered. "Hezekiah's my man."

Ishmael chuckled. "I like that. Little man is big now, too. When I saw you and him in the store yesterday I was shocked. Last time I saw him he was a shorty." Ishmael took a gulp of his soda. "You've changed a lot since the last time I saw you."

"For the better, I hope." Robin smiled.

Ishmael nodded. "Definitely. You look . . . good!"

She sat back in her seat. "I feel good," she said. "I've changed a lot in more ways than one. Like take Charly, for instance. I know how to tune her out now. She's miserable and that's why she behaves the way that she does. She meets men, parties all the time, picks fights with bitches, starts trouble, all for attention. I figured that out and I ignore her."

"How come you don't need all that? All the drama and all the bullshit to keep life interesting?"

Robin scrunched her lips up in disgust. "I have an interesting life as it is. I don't need drama or constant parties—or a *man*." She met his gaze for emphasis. "I have my son, school, my job, and that's all I need. When the right man comes along, he'll recognize me as the catch that I am." Robin smiled and shoveled more salad into her mouth.

Ishmael stared at her, watched her chew her food. He liked what he was hearing. More than anything, Ishmael liked a woman who was a go-getter. It was what had attracted him to Celeste—and to Nina in the beginning. A woman who went out and chased her own wealth and her own power, as opposed to waiting around for some man to hand it to her, was a turn-on to Ishmael. Nina had been like that once. She had worked at Dime Piece, promoted parties in her spare time. Nina had an amazing talent for sketching and painting. Those things had made him fall in love with her. Lately it seemed that all of that had changed. Nina nagged him to spend time with her, nagged him to commit to her, nagged him about what she needed for the shop. She seldom sketched anymore, and Ishmael missed that. He used to love watching her sit at her easel with nothing but boy shorts on, sketching away at a new masterpiece. He loved watching her create, seeing her motivated to finish a project. But her watercolors and chalks had been replaced by bridal magazines and books of baby names. Suddenly she was everything he never wanted—needy, unmotivated, and pushy. Hearing Robin speak of contentment without a relationship was refreshing.

"So you almost finished with school?" he asked.

She smiled broader now. "Yup. A few more weeks and I'll have my bachelor's degree. It feels good because I did it on my own. Financial aid helped, but I did all the hard work on my own. All those late nights sitting up writing papers and early mornings in the library paid off." She finished her salad and sat back. "I remember when I never thought I'd make it to this point," she confided. "When Hezzy was little and his father passed away, I thought my whole life had ended. I thought I could never raise a child all by myself. Everything was so fucked up. I didn't even want to live anymore, because I thought that was the end for me." She shook her head at the thought of what she would have missed out on had she given up back then. "But it was just the beginning," she said. "You ever felt like giving up?"

Before he could answer, his cell phone rang and the caller ID revealed Rah-lo's phone number. Ishmael held his hand up, excusing himself, as he answered the phone. "Yeah."

Robin listened to Ishmael's part of the conversation. True to form, he revealed little as he spoke. Most of his end of the discussion consisted of a series of "yeahs" and "uh-huhs." He hung up and summoned the waitress for the check. "I gotta go," he explained to Robin as he fumbled in his pockets for some cash. "Gotta go handle some business for Rah-lo."

Robin nodded and reached for her purse. Ishmael stopped her, insisting that she let him handle it. He paid the waitress and left a nice tip. As Robin rose to leave, he held her hand, stopping her.

"I want to see you, but I can't keep coming to the shop. If Nina sees me there, it's gonna be some bullshit. Plus Charly is about to have a fit seeing me with you."

Robin laughed, knowing that he was right. At least about Charly.

Ishmael continued, "Let me get your number and maybe I can stop by. You know, when your son is asleep." The last time they'd been together physically, Robin had gotten caught up. It seemed to Ishmael that she had wanted more than the sex, and that was all that he had been willing to give. All he had wanted was some sexual gratification. He didn't want to get to know her son or to lead her to believe that his attraction to her was on any level other than a physical one.

Robin smirked. She knew he wanted another taste. And so did she. "All right," she said. "It'll be our little secret." She gave Ishmael her number and they headed out to the parking lot. Once he dropped her back off at Charly's, Ishmael peeled out and headed for Staten Island.

CHAPTER SIX

All or Nothing

R ah-lo couldn't believe his eyes. He sat in his car outside
of his house and watched as Asia snuck Neo out of the
house's side entrance. Rah-lo had been away from home for
three days. He had been staying at the house he had once
shared with Celeste. That house held a lot of memories for
Rah-lo, and it helped him come to a difficult decision. Celeste was long gone and he hadn't been truly happy since she
left. He decided that he would try to talk to his wife one last
time, try to honestly explain to her what was making him
unhappy. Rah-lo felt that he owed it to his daughters—and
to himself—to try to get Asia to change.

But now it was close to two thirty in the afternoon, and
his daughters would be returning home from school at any

moment. Rah-lo had hoped to surprise his daughters by being home to greet them when they got back. Instead, he was the one surprised. He was shocked to see Asia and his arch-rival slipping out of the side door of Rah-lo's house. His instinct was to rush across the street and kill both of them for having the balls to rendezvous in the house he owned. But rather than go ballistic Rah-lo calmly walked across the street. Outwardly, he was cool, but inside, Rah-lo was enraged.

He walked toward Asia and Neo, now standing in the side yard. Asia spotted Rah-lo as he approached them, and she panicked. "Oh, shit!" She turned to run back inside the house as Neo looked on. Rah-lo caught her by the collar of her shirt and snatched her backward, yanking her back into the yard. Asia stumbled and Rah-lo jerked her upright again, pulling her face to within inches of his.

"You got this muthafucka in my house, Asia? *In my muthafuckin' house?*" Rah-lo's voice boomed, and Neo instinctively stepped back. Rah-lo kept a tight grip on Asia's collar and turned his glare toward Neo. "I should kill your punk ass for being bold enough to set foot in my house!"

Neo shook his head. "She said it was over between y'all, so I don't know what's going on here."

"You're fucking my wife in my house; that's what the fuck is going on." The bad blood between Rah-lo and Neo dated back years prior, when Rah-lo, Ishmael, and their crew had slain one of Neo's workers—Jack—in a bloodbath on

Staten Island. Ever since then, the beef between them had simmered. So Neo knew that Rah-lo was even more pissed off to find him of all people digging Asia's back out.

"She said y'all were finished. I thought you moved out and shit was all good, you know what I'm saying?" Neo figured fucking Asia was payback for all the times he and Rah-lo had bumped heads in the streets. He had flirted with Asia for years on the low. Every time he got a wink from Rah-lo's wife or a seductive smile, Neo had felt victorious. The previous day he ran into Asia and she invited him over. And now here was her man flipping out in the middle of the afternoon. Neo knew that he should have known better than to come to another man's house to fuck his wife. But the temptation to disrespect Rah-lo on that level had been too sweet to resist.

Rah-lo wanted to crack this bastard's skull open. "So why sneak out the side entrance then? That's what you do when shit is all good?"

"She said her kids were coming home from school. I was just trying to be respectful."

Rah-lo looked at Asia and then back at Neo. He really wanted to hurt both of them for disrespecting his house so boldly. Rah-lo felt like a fool.

He punched Neo hard in the face, knocking him backward. Neo regained his footing and ran toward Rah-lo. But Rah-lo was too quick. He caught Neo again, this time with an uppercut. As Neo crouched defensively, Rah-lo pulled out his gun. Neo saw it and took off running toward his car parked on the corner. Rah-lo started to chase him and then changed his mind. Instead he shoved Asia aside and walked into the house. Asia followed him inside.

Rah-lo looked into Asia's eyes and smiled. "You know what, Asia?" he said. "I feel like fucking you up right now."

"Why? 'Cuz I cheated on you? Well, that's how the fuck I felt when you were out with Celeste all them years. Now you see how it feels. Get over it."

Rah-lo stared at his wife. He knew that he now had a bigger beef with Neo. Rah-lo shook his head. "Your stupid ass ain't worth me getting mad." As pissed as he was that some clown was fucking his wife in his house—and most likely in his bed—Rah-lo reasoned that this was the final straw. Asia had finally given him the last reason he needed to walk away from her for good.

"So this is how it is, Asia?" Rah-lo looked at his wife, disgusted. "You fucking niggas in our house now?"

Asia shook her head and laughed softly. "This is *our* house now, Rah-lo? You walked out of here, remember?"

Rah-lo turned to her, wanting to wring her neck. "Nah, it's *my muthafuckin' house!*" he yelled in her face. "Nothing is yours!"

"Please, Rah-lo!" Asia walked away from him. "Save that shit! Don't be mad 'cuz I called your bluff. You thought you was gonna hurt me by walking out of here the other day. But I don't give a fuck!"

"Good. Remember you said that." Rah-lo took out his cell phone and called Ishmael. "Ish, I need a favor. Come to my house and help me get my shit out of here before I hurt this girl." Rah-lo briefly explained about finding Neo exiting his house. Rah-lo needed Ishmael to hold him down and keep watch for an ambush while he moved his stuff.

Asia sucked her teeth and walked away, leaving him standing in the middle of the living room. She wasn't buying it. In her mind, Rah-lo would never leave her. She stormed off toward the kitchen, muttering under her breath while Rah-lo headed upstairs. He took his luggage out of the closet and started to pack his things. Piece by piece he filled up his luggage, listening to Asia downstairs on the phone talking shit about him to her friends. As he zipped up his last piece of luggage, he noticed his daughter Rasheeda standing in the doorway of his bedroom. He hadn't even heard her come in from school.

Rasheeda watched her father preparing to leave, and was surprised by the sense of relief she felt. Finally, her father was standing up to her mother. For years Rasheeda had heard her mother talk shit and put Rah-lo down. Rasheeda had watched her father swallow his pride and bite his tongue while Asia ranted and raved. Rasheeda looked into her daddy's eyes and smiled a sad little grin. "Daddy, I just wanted to tell you that I'm not mad at you for leaving," she said. "I don't blame you for wanting to get away from her. You deserve to be happy."

Rah-lo was stunned to hear his daughter speaking this way. She sounded so mature for her age. She had a poor relationship with her mother; that much he knew. Rasheeda was going through her teenage rebellion and she had chosen Asia as the target of it. But what Rah-lo didn't know was that it wasn't just teenage angst that made Rasheeda so mean toward her mother. It was Asia's ways that Rasheeda despised. She hated that her mother did so little and her dad did so much. Rasheeda had noticed long ago that her mother had no interest in the things that were important to her. If Rasheeda came home eager to talk about something that had happened at school, Asia often snapped at her, telling her that she didn't care about that silly shit. All Asia cared about was herself. At times, Rasheeda felt that her dad was the mother *and* the father in their household. Other times, Rasheeda felt like she herself was a single parent, always having to pick up her sisters, cook for her sisters, babysit them, and help with their homework when her dad was out making money. It was always her or Rah-lo doing their part, never Asia doing hers. So Rasheeda understood her father's decision to leave. She couldn't wait until the day when she could leave, too.

Rah-lo sighed. He hated that Rasheeda had witnessed their fight the other day. He especially hated that she had heard about his infidelity. He had been his daughters' untainted hero for all of their lives. All they knew was that he took care of them, he seldom raised his voice, he paid attention to them, and he loved them more than anything in the world.

"Come here," he said. He sat down on his king-sized bed and Rasheeda came and sat beside him. "I never claimed to be perfect. I don't want your mother to ever tell you anything about me that will make you see me differently. Don't let her change the way you see me. I need you to always see 'Daddy' when you look at me, no matter what she says to try and change your mind about me. Know that I always got you and I won't let nothing hurt you. But I'm not perfect."

"You didn't have to tell me that," Rasheeda said. "I know how she is."

Rah-lo hated that his daughter felt this way about her mother. But he was glad that Rasheeda understood that he was unhappy. "Your mother has some foul ways, Rasheeda. But she does love you. So do I. But we just don't make each other happy anymore. That happens sometimes. You start out loving each other and understanding each other's faults. And then sometimes it gets to the point where you don't love each other the same way you used to. And then all the things you used to be able to tolerate start to get on your nerves. Neither one of us is happy being together anymore. Maybe if I go, your mother can be happy on her own. Maybe I can, too. We'll both be better parents, maybe even better friends, when we're apart. But it has nothing to do with you or your sisters. I will always be here for y'all. I swear. Nothing will ever change that."

Rasheeda nodded. "Can I come with you?" she asked.

Rah-lo felt his heart break. He wanted to tell her that

she could, but he knew that Asia would fight him tooth and nail, if only to make his life miserable. "Not tonight. You should stay here with your mother and explain to your sisters that I'll be by to see them soon. I need to go get my place set up and all that, and then if you want to, you can come and stay with me for as long as you want. I promise."

Rasheeda threw her arms around her father's neck and hugged him tight. He held her in his arms, thinking how it seemed like only yesterday that she was a little girl in love with her daddy. Now she was a teenager approaching adulthood. But he was happy to see that in her heart she was still that same little girl who adored her father. He kissed her forehead and held her face in his hand. "Call me if you need me," he said. "Anytime, day or night. You let me know what's going on around here. Let me know if you and your sisters are okay. Nothing is changing, except that I won't be sleeping here anymore. I'm always just a phone call away."

Rasheeda nodded and took a deep breath. Rah-lo reached in his pocket and dug out a few twenties. "Go pick your sisters up from dance class and take 'em to Papa John's and get pizza on your way home." He kissed her, hugged her, and waited until she left the house and he heard the door close behind her. He grabbed his belongings. He could hear Asia downstairs on the phone with one of her ghetto girlfriends.

"That muthafucka ain't going nowhere!" Asia was saying.

Rah-lo came out of the room with his bags packed, and his facial expression warned that he was not to be fucked with. Asia immediately hung up the phone and blocked his exit. He stared her down and said, "Move."

Asia stood her ground and held her husband's gaze. "So this is how you leave me?" Deep inside she wanted to cry. But her pride and stubbornness stood in the way of her heart. She wouldn't give him the benefit of seeing tears rolling down her face. "You gonna act like you were always innocent and none of this shit is your fault?"

"Nothing is ever *just* your fault, right?" Rah-lo asked rhetorically. "It doesn't matter what you say. You told me to leave, right? So that's what I'm doing."

"So what, you gonna run off and find Celeste now?" Asia stepped closer to him.

"Maybe." He was antagonizing her on purpose.

Asia looked at him without flinching. "You thought that was gonna hurt me?"

Rah-lo shook his head. "I'm not trying to hurt you. I just wanna walk away. This shit was over years ago."

"So then why did you keep getting me pregnant?" Asia's pain was apparent as she stood, hearing Rah-lo verbalize what they had both known long ago. True, she had known that the thrill was gone years before this moment. But even when she had acted like she didn't care, truthfully Asia would've never left Rah-lo. And here he was leaving her.

Her heart was broken, but her foolish pride said, *FUCK YOU!*

"No, why did you keep *getting* pregnant? We don't even have sex that often and yet you kept getting knocked up."

"So what are you accusing me of, planning the shit that way?" Asia yelled. In her mind, none of the children had been planned. Well, except their first daughter, Rasheeda. Asia *had* set out to have Rah-lo's baby then. But that didn't count.

"Nah. But you never tried to prevent it, either. All that complaining about being a mother wasn't getting any better with you not using protection."

Asia laughed. "So why didn't *you* use some damn protection then? Stupid, it takes two to make a baby!" Asia got in Rah-lo's face and mushed him hard. "I'm the one that needs the fucking protection! All those years you were fucking that nasty bitch!"

"You know who's a nasty bitch?" Rah-lo was tired of hearing the woman he sincerely loved being referred to as a bitch. He smirked snidely and threw Asia's own words back at her. "Go look in the mirror."

Asia lunged at her husband, swinging. She wanted to kill him, more for the fact that he was defending his mistress than because he had called Asia a bitch. Rah-lo caught a left hook to the side of his head, and he stumbled a little. She followed that with a barrage of slaps and punches. She scratched him on the side of his neck as he shoved her off of him. Her back hit the wall hard, and ironically, their family

TRACY BROWN

pictures came crashing to the floor. The frames lay shattered, glass covering the snapshots of their smiling daughters. Rah-lo was furious. He wanted to hit Asia back but caught himself just as he swung at her.

"I think you forgot who the fuck I am," he said, his chest heaving as he glared into her eyes. He stood over her and watched her shrink away from him defensively. Suddenly she wasn't so tough anymore. He almost wanted to laugh. "I let you raise hell around here and get drunk with your girlfriends instead of being a real fucking wife and mother. Let you talk your bullshit, put me down, and neglect your kids. But don't get it twisted. Just because I learned to tune you out over the years doesn't mean that I don't still run this fucking house. Don't ever raise your hand to me, Asia. And keep that nigga Neo away from this house."

Asia knew he meant business. But she didn't back down, either. "Well, you can't run this house from outside of this house. So how you gonna leave me for another bitch?"

Rah-lo grabbed her face roughly. "I'm not leaving you for another 'bitch.' I'm leaving because *you're* a bitch."

"What about the kids?" Asia could hardly speak due to the tight grip he had on her jaw.

It hurt Rah-lo to think of having to live apart from his baby girls. That was the hardest part of this whole thing. He let go of Asia. "Let me take them with me. I *will* take them. And you know I'll take good care of them."

"Hell no!" Asia yelled.

Rah-lo didn't argue. He had expected her to say that. "Then as long as we gotta deal with each other, you *will* respect me. I don't want them living like this anymore." Rah-lo shook his head, full of regret. "They can't be happy if we're not happy. You don't make me happy anymore, Asia. Obviously, I don't make you happy anymore, either." He stepped away from her slightly. He looked around at the mess they'd made. "This whole shit was a mistake."

"*Mistake?* Is that what you think your daughters are? Mistakes?" Asia looked incredibly hurt. Rah-lo could see it even though she tried to hide it.

"Not at all. And you should know that by now. But we're a mistake. You and me being together is a mistake."

"You shoulda told me that a long time ago and let me move on with my life." Asia couldn't help the tears now. But she quickly wiped them away.

"What life, ma? What life you wanna move on to? Hanging outside in the hood with bitches in the summertime, smoking weed and drinking beer? Playing cards and gossiping with your moms all day? What did I stop you from doing?"

"Hold the fuck up! You do all that shit, too, Rah-lo."

"But you're a fucking female!" He couldn't believe that she saw no difference between them. "You got daughters, Asia! And they watch *you* as an example of what it is to be a lady. And you're in the street day in and day out conducting yourself like a fucking hoodrat! That's what you want to teach your daughters?"

The doorbell rang and interrupted them. Rah-lo answered it and ushered Ishmael inside. Ishmael greeted Asia and assessed the scene around him—shattered glass, Asia's tearstained face, and Rah-lo's luggage. He felt like he had just walked in on some very personal marital drama.

"Thanks for coming over here," Rah-lo said. "Can you help me take my shit out of here? There's a bunch of bags upstairs plus this shit here." Rah-lo gestured toward several stuffed duffel bags by the front door.

Ishmael nodded and avoided making eye contact with Asia as he grabbed some of Rah-lo's stuff and took it out to the car. When Ishmael was gone, Asia turned to her husband with tears in her eyes.

"You know what? Fuck you *and* your little fuckin' *bitch*! I can't believe you're standing here putting me down 'cuz I ain't the goody two-shoes that she is."

"I'm not even talking about Celeste. You're the one who keeps bringing her name up."

"'Cuz you act like I'm not as good as her. Because I drink and I get high? She don't drink? She don't get high, Rah-lo? So what, I'm not good enough for you anymore? You forgot where the fuck you came from, Rah-lo. You forgot who was with you from day one. But it's all good." Asia shook her head in defiance.

Ishmael came back in and noticed the thick tension in the air. He pretended not to hear them arguing as he headed upstairs to retrieve the rest of Rah-lo's belongings. Ishmael climbed the stairs, grabbed some bags, and headed back out to the car. Asia waited until he left before she turned and glared at Rah-lo once again. She hated him at that moment and her facial expression showed it. "I don't need you to make me happy, muthafucka." She moved out of his way. "I'll be better off without you!" she hissed.

That had to be the hundredth time he had heard her say those words. "Show me, then." Ra-lo reached for his jacket and headed for the door. He was out of there. Asia hurled obscenities at him and ranted and raved. But all of her noise was like a current that carried him straight out of their house, into his car, and on the road headed for the house he had once shared with Celeste. He vowed that he would never go back to Asia. Their marriage was over.

Ishmael couldn't believe Rah-lo and Asia had called it quits. Within an hour of Rah-lo putting his car in drive, Asia started blowing up her husband's phone, calling again and again. Rah-lo ignored her calls, shutting his phone off altogether after she speed-dialed him repeatedly. Asia eventually started calling Ishmael, knowing that he knew where Rah-lo had gone. The two were such good friends that she was sure Ishmael knew Rah-lo's plans. But Ishmael hadn't heard from Rah-lo since he moved into his second house. And Ishmael had tried to call his boy numerous times with no luck. Rah-lo's phone kept going straight to voice mail, and when Ishmael went by the house to see him his car wasn't there and no one came to the door. Ishmael figured that Rah-lo was laying low to let his beef with Neo die down.

Unfortunately, Asia didn't believe Ishmael when he told her that he knew nothing. So she kept calling him to vent and to demand to know her husband's whereabouts. Now, after more than four days, Ishmael was checking his caller ID and ignoring Asia's phone calls, too. He marveled at how he always managed to be caught in the middle of Rah-lo's bullshit.

During one of Asia's rare breaks in speed-dialing him, Ishmael checked his full voice mailbox. All of them were from Rah-lo's wife. He deleted most of them, but one caught his attention. He heard a name he hadn't heard in a while, and he had to replay the message twice to be sure that he had heard correctly.

"Yo, Ish, this is Asia. I know you see me calling you all these times. And I just spoke to you, so you can't act like you don't know why I'm calling. This muthafucka left me here with these kids to go off and find Celeste and I'm supposed to just sit here and . . . what? Sit here and do *what*? I ain't got no fucking money. I ain't got no fucking job. And I'm stuck with the kids while he runs off to that *bitch*! Ishmael, you know more than what you're telling me. I don't want to kill Celeste. So please don't make me go find him. Tell me where my husband is so I can talk to him before he gets to her."

Ishmael had never heard Asia sound so vulnerable and so desperate. After replaying the message, he frowned. *Celeste.*

When did Rah-lo make that decision? Ishmael couldn't believe Rah-lo had left to look for Celeste. He hadn't mentioned Celeste during their conversation the other day. Ishmael hadn't even heard her name mentioned in his conversations with his friend in recent years. He wondered if Rah-lo had been in touch with her. Strangely, Ishmael felt an odd twinge of jealousy. The only thing that had made Celeste's move to Atlanta easier to deal with was the fact that neither of them had her. If he didn't have her, he certainly didn't want Rah-lo to have her. That would have been too much to bear.

But it sounded like that was exactly what Rah-lo had told his wife, and now he wasn't answering his phone. What had made Rah-lo go after Celeste now? It all seemed strange to Ishmael, and he found himself deep in thought. He was so distracted that he didn't notice Nina standing beside him as he stared out the kitchen window. When he realized that she was standing there (and had apparently said something to him that she was waiting for an answer to), Ishmael was at a loss for words. He had no idea what she had just said to him and was wondering how long she'd been standing there. He silently chided himself for giving so much thought to Rah-lo and his relationships. Now he had to act like he had been paying attention to Wifey.

Nina threw her hands up impatiently. "Do you like it or not?"

Ishmael looked her up and down, trying to see what was

new so that he could guess what he was supposed to judge for her. Her bangs looked a little different. As a hairstylist, she was often asking his opinion about different hairstyles. "I like your hair. It don't matter how you change it, you're still pretty."

Nina frowned. "I asked you about the new pillows I bought for the couch." She shook her head and walked away. "It's nice to know that you still listen to me."

Ishmael could see that she was gearing up for some bull-shit. She was going into her zone of feeling "unappreciated and unexciting." He didn't feel like hearing that shit all night. He waited until Nina went in the bedroom and turned on *The Quiet Storm* and then he grabbed his jacket and made his way out the front door.

He went to his quiet place. Ishmael kept a small two-bedroom apartment on Hall Street in Fort Greene. Nina knew nothing about this spot. Few people did. He came here whenever he needed to escape his surroundings and be left alone. This was one of those times. He thought about what Asia had said on his voice mail. Celeste. Had Rah-lo really gone after her? On a whim, Ishmael turned on his computer and logged onto the Internet. He figured he'd check out MySpace and see if he had any messages. He'd had a page on the Web site for about a month, and he was amazed at all the broads who had never met him and still sent him explicit pic-tures and comments. His and Rah-lo's connect—Cito—had put Ishmael on to the site. Papicito was a ladies' man with a handful of kids with different baby mamas. Once Ishmael had asked Cito where he found some of the bad bitches he fucked with state to state. He told Ishmael to set up a Web page and the rest was history.

Tonight he checked his usual friend requests, messages, and comments. Then he decided to search for Celeste's name. He was new to the Internet and the wonders of cyberspace. And for that reason, he had never thought of searching for Celeste this way. But ever since he'd heard Asia mention Celeste's name in her message earlier, he couldn't get her off his mind. The computer scanned the records for a few brief moments before Ishmael found what he was looking for. He clicked the link and sat back and smiled. Celeste Styles's smiling face stared back at him. Clad in a tiny bikini in some tropical setting, she looked as lovely as the last time he'd seen her. He checked her stats—single, no children, hometown: Atlanta, Georgia. He looked through her pictures and found several shots of her out with friends, traveling to different exotic locations, and looking better than ever. She had lost weight and cut her hair. But she was the same as he remembered her—better even.

Celeste had been special to Ishmael for a very long time. When Celeste was with Rah-lo, Ishmael's relationship with her had been strictly platonic. They were friends who shared private jokes and great conversations. In fact, they bonded not just because Ishmael had saved Celeste from an attempted rape but because the two of them were often taken for granted by Rah-lo. As his mistress, Celeste was relegated to playing second fiddle. Rah-lo didn't intend for her to feel that way, but with Asia being his wife Celeste had little choice but to play runner-up. Ishmael was also often overlooked. He had been Rah-lo's sidekick for so long that Rah-lo grew to depend on Ish without fail, especially when the rest of their crew fell apart. It got to the point where Ishmael was the one Rah-lo called for business reasons and personal ones. When Rah-lo was locked up, it was Ishmael's job to take care of both Asia and Celeste. It was then that he really got to know his friend's mistress. And it was then that Ishmael began to feel that she deserved so much more.

On their way upstate to visit Rah-lo, Celeste and Ishmael had shared many heart-to-heart conversations. He had always liked her as a person. He thought she was very pretty, witty, and seemed to have a good head on her shoulders. But during their trips up north, he discovered something even more endearing about Celeste. She was a go-getter. She didn't want a handout. Instead, she was willing to work hard for what she wanted out of life. She insisted on paying Rah-lo back for what he had invested in Dime Piece, and that impressed Ishmael. Unlike his sister, Tangela, or his aunt Mary, Celeste wanted success and she wanted it on her own terms. She didn't nag Rah-lo or beg to have more of his time the way that Nina did to Ishmael. Instead, Celeste waited patiently, allowing Rah-lo space to breathe, and she was available to him when he wanted her. While most women would have been content to be a baller's bitch—running their own business and enjoying all the fruits of Rah-lo's labor—Celeste wanted nothing more than to have Rah-lo's time. She was unlike any other woman Ishmael had ever known—beautiful, intelligent, patient, faithful to Rah-lo, and hopeful that he would be hers alone someday. Ishmael never meant to fall for her. But he did, and he fell hard. Soon, he was not only impressed by her character and her determination to succeed. He also wanted to help her succeed, wanted to give her the key to his heart. But Rah-lo had met her first. And for that reason she was off-limits. But Ishmael still pined for her. Even after all this time.

He clicked the message button and typed away: "Hello, stranger. This is how I have to find you? You can't keep in touch no more? I miss you. Shit ain't the same since you left. Get at me."

Ishmael clicked "send" and sat back. He hoped she didn't take long to answer him, and he also hoped that Rah-lo hadn't gotten to her first this time.

CHAPTER SEVEN

If It Don't Fit, Don't Force It

Rah-lo watched Sherry stroll naked over to the bathroom. She turned on the shower and stepped inside. Once she was out of sight, he lay back against the pillows and exhaled. Sherry was one of his favorite pastimes, and now that he was no longer with Asia, he was enjoying even more time with her. It had been four days since he walked out on his wife, and in that time he had been holed up at Sherry's crib. He didn't know what Neo would do in retaliation for Rah-lo pulling his gun on him. And Rah-lo wanted a break from Asia. He had turned his cell phone off and only checked his voice messages periodically in order to make sure that nothing was wrong with his children. They were all he cared about. He was finished with Asia, and he didn't care about how business was going. He needed some time to himself, away from the drama in his marriage and his responsibilities in the street. He knew that Ishmael would handle business. Right now, all Rah-lo was concerned about handling was Sherry. She had a perfect body and a gorgeous face. His only complaint was that she talked too fucking much. She was a real chatterbox and Rah-lo now found himself feeling anxious for her to disappear.

He reached over to the nightstand and picked up his pack of cigarettes. Lighting one, he sat up in bed and took a long drag. He had started to second-guess himself. Although he had no regrets about leaving his wife, he missed his daughters terribly. He had been ignoring Asia's phone calls and each time she left a voice message more profanity laden than the last. He knew that if he went over there or even called he would have to deal with Asia's bullshit. And he was in no mood for that.

As Sherry exited the shower, Rah-lo realized that he was in no mood for her, either. She had good pussy, but that was about it. True to form, she started talking almost as soon as her foot hit the bath mat.

"Don't you think we should go out and get something to eat? You're not with Asia anymore, so there's no point in us sitting cooped up in this house all day. I was thinking we should go to the new—"

"Nah," Rah-lo cut her off. "*You* should go to get some food while I go get my head together. I'm gonna go home," he said, sitting up in bed and reaching for his clothes. "I need some time to myself. I'll call you tomorrow." His tone was very clipped and matter-of-fact and Sherry looked momentarily stunned. She regained her composure, not wanting to turn him off by whining or appearing overly sensitive.

"Oh," she managed. "Okay then. I'll call you tomorrow."

Rah-lo exhaled some more of his Newport. "No," he said. "I'll call *you* when I get ready." He didn't mean to be rude to Sherry. She wasn't a bad person. She just wasn't the one for him. All she was to him was a way to pass his idle time, and he didn't want her to think differently now that he was separated from Asia. "I'm not trying to play you or nothing, sweetheart," he explained. "But I just left my wife, and I got a lot of shit on my mind. I appreciate you keeping my mind off it for a little while, but now I gotta face reality and there's a bunch of shit I need to handle. Don't take it personal."

Sherry shrugged as she put on her clothes. "I'm not taking it personal. It's all good," she lied. She felt as if she'd been dismissed, and she didn't like it one bit. "Call me when you handle all your shit." Rah-lo got dressed and left her house, and Sherry was pissed that he hadn't even bothered to kiss her good-bye.

Rah-lo didn't give a damn whether she was upset or not. He was finished with her for now, and she just had to get over it. He shook his head, wondering why women had to be so complicated all the time. Every one of them seemed to be overly emotional and incredibly needy and demanding. Well, almost every one of them.

Celeste had been the only woman he'd ever encountered who didn't stress him for anything. Celeste hadn't made demands; she'd made suggestions. She hadn't craved his attention constantly, which only made him more eager to give her his undivided attention whenever he could. She had seemed to understand him both as a man and as an individual, and she had fallen into step with him perfectly. He loved that—and so much more—about her. He had thought about her constantly over the four years since she'd left him. And after his argument with Asia he had thought about Celeste even more. In some ways, Asia had been right. He did often silently compare Asia to Celeste. He just couldn't help noticing that she had been as good for him and to him as any woman could ever possibly be. He wished that Celeste had been more patient. She would have been pleased to find out that he had finally left his wife. But Celeste was long gone, and his heart still ached for her despite him telling it not to. He drove to his new bachelor pad, figuring it was time for him to move on with his life. Celeste had left him and now he had left Asia. Both relationships were over, he reminded himself. No more living in the past.

Robin walked into the shop and right into the midst of a heated debate.

"Good! Robin's here!" Lauren yelled, happy to have their resident intellect present to weigh in on their latest topic of discussion. "Do you think they should have fired that guy? What's his name?" Lauren waved her hand as if willing the man's name to pop back into her head.

"Don Imus," Dimitri offered.

"Yeah, that's him! Do you think they should've fired him for calling those basketball players nappy-headed hos?"

Robin slipped out of her jacket and hung it on the coat-rack. She smiled. "Okay, first of all, good morning, every-body."

Everyone greeted her (except for Charly, who was stand-ing in the back of the salon shampooing a client and pre-tending not to have heard Robin's greeting).

"Yeah, yeah, yeah," Lauren said impatiently. "Answer the question."

Robin walked to her station and began to tie on her cape. "I think he was wrong."

"Thank you!" Lauren yelled. "I told you they were right to fire his ass!"

Robin shook her head. "You didn't let me finish."

"Exactly," Dimitri said sarcastically. "So *desperate* for a cosigner!"

Lauren waved her hand at Dimitri and waited for Robin to finish her thought.

"I think he was wrong. He always says foul things on the air about pretty much every ethnic group. But what makes him different from Howard Stern? What about all the rap-pers who use the same language in their songs and make millions? Where are all the outraged black activists when a rapper shows up to an awards show with black women on leashes, or when one of them swipes a credit card down the crack of a black woman's ass in a video? It's a double standard. We think it's okay that we use the 'n' word, or that we call each other bitches and hos. But if a white person does it, we're ready to kill somebody. If we don't want to be referred to that way, we shouldn't refer to *ourselves* that way."

"Amen!" Miss Pat called out. She had her head in the sink, but she was still engrossed in the conversation. As a woman of a certain age, she was tired of hearing the foul language young black people were using in music and in their everyday conversations. "You're a very smart young lady, Robin. *Ow!!*" she yelled. Charly was washing Miss Pat's hair, and just as she cosigned on what Robin had said, the water mysteriously turned scalding hot.

"Sorry," Charly said halfheartedly. But she wasn't. Charly had changed the water temperature in order to shut Miss Pat the fuck up. Charly hated that everyone made Robin feel like she was a genius. True, Robin was doing well in college and had learned a lot in the course of her education. But the bitch wasn't a prodigy or anything.

Lauren wasn't satisfied with Robin's answer. "Okay," she said. "But you still didn't say whether or not you thought he should be fired."

Robin called her client over to her chair and sighed. "No," she said, knowing that her answer was going to spark another debate. "I don't think they should have fired him."

"Thank you!" Dimitri said triumphantly. "That's what I've been trying to tell these ignorant heifers in here all morning. Why would you fire him for that when you got people on the air who say worse shit than that every day?" He shook his head in disgust.

Lauren frowned and stood with her hands on her hips. "You're crazy! That man is a racist. What did them girls do to make him classify them as hos? They weren't out there dropping it like it's hot. They acted like athletes, not hos."

Robin nodded in agreement. "You're right. He was dead wrong. But 'ho' is a term that black people use. White people say 'whore.' So he obviously heard the term 'ho' from somebody black, and then he used it to describe a pre-dominantly black group of women. But my point is that the term wouldn't be commonly associated with black people if we would stop using it to describe one another."

Charly was going to be sick. "Robin, how can you blame black people for what he said? He said it because he felt like that's all black women are—nappy-headed hos."

Robin started to defend her position, but Charly cut her off.

"His ass should have been fired. Period." Charly led Miss Pat to the dryer and adjusted the settings. "I'm going to the store. I'll be back in a few minutes."

On her way out, Charly eyed Robin. Robin smiled at Charly, knowing that she wasn't really upset about Robin's stance on the Don Imus situation. Charly was heated about

Robin's visit from Ishmael. Ever since he had come into the salon to see Robin, she had been dying to know what was going on. But she had too much pride to ask. Instead, she had sulked around the shop for days and made evil eyes at Robin. It made her happy just knowing that Charly was so clearly jealous. Robin knew that Charly would be even more upset if she knew that Robin had spent an evening with Ishmael at his secret apartment. Their lovemaking had been intense and almost violently passionate. And she couldn't get it off her mind.

As the salon conversation turned to whether or not Jay-Z would ever marry Beyoncé, Charly left and headed for the store. She zipped her jacket up a little higher, amazed by the cold fifty-degree weather New York City was having in April. It was supposed to be warm, she thought. But a chill was in the air and she shivered a little. She thought about something Robin had talked about called global warming. Charly thought that maybe that was one of Robin's rants that may have made some sense. Charly walked to the bodega on the corner and was at the counter purchasing a VitaWater and a pack of Altoids when in walked Nina Lords.

Charly smirked as Nina rolled her eyes at her and walked on by. The two of them had gotten into their share of battles as coworkers at Dime Piece back in the day. And for some reason Nina still harbored resentment toward Charly. True, Charly had been intimate with Ishmael years ago. But that had been long ago, and Charly felt that Nina needed to get over it. After all, Nina was the one who had walked away with the prize—Ishmael.

Charly paid for her items and lingered at the counter, pretending to put her change into her wallet. Nina approached, prepared to pay for her snacks, and saw Charly standing there. She rolled her eyes again and placed her items up on the counter as if Charly weren't even there.

Charly stood within inches of her, smiling provokingly. "Hi, Nina."

Charly waited for a response but got none. Nina handed the store clerk a twenty-dollar bill and waited for her change, wishing Charly would disappear. No such luck.

"Damn," Charly said. "You can't even speak?" Charly shook her head as Nina turned to leave. She stood in Nina's way, blocking her exit with a wicked smile plastered across her face. "I saw Ishmael the other day."

Nina's jaw clenched visibly. She looked Charly dead in the eye, warning her silently to go away. Still, that last statement had piqued Nina's interest. "And?"

Charly was still grinning. "And nothing. He came to my shop, actually. I was surprised to see him there because—"

"He came to *your* shop?" Nina was frowning now. Ishmael knew better than to step foot in that shop. He had slept with both Charly and Robin back in the day. He had to know that Nina wouldn't approve of that shit.

Charly couldn't be happier. "Yeah. Like I said, I was surprised, too. I even told him, 'This is Charly's beauty salon, not Nappy Nina's.' He laughed when I said that. But he wasn't there to see me. He came in to see Robin." Charly grinned ever so slightly, pleased with herself for baiting Nina this way.

Nina was vexed. "Robin?"

Charly nodded. "He waited until she was done with her client and then they left together. She came back about two hours later." Charly was exaggerating. But she was so enjoying the changing expressions on Nina's face that she couldn't resist fucking with her. "Is everything okay with you two?" she asked. "You two didn't break up or anything, did you?"

Nina glared at Charly, knowing that she was antagonizing her. Charly knew damn well that Nina and Ishmael were still together. This was one of the things she hated most about Charly. "No. We didn't break up. And I'm sure Ishmael and Robin didn't do anything wrong."

Charly shook her head. "I wouldn't be too sure, Nina. What about—"

"It was good seeing you, Charly."

Nina breezed past Charly and walked out of the store. With a sinister grin plastered across her face Charly watched Nina walk away. Sometimes it felt so good to be so bad.

Nina called her salon and told her employee Jackie to hold everything down while she handled some business. Jackie agreed and Nina headed straight for the home she shared with Ishmael. As she drove there, she began to think about what Charly had said to her. The more she thought about it, the angrier she became.

She was also thinking about the state of her relationship with Ishmael. Things between the two of them had been strained lately. She wanted so much more than he seemed willing to give her. Whenever the subject of marriage, children, or any kind of next step in their relationship was brought up, he clammed up. Nina was fed up, and as she approached her house, she saw Ishmael's car parked out front. She knew there was about to be a showdown and she was more than ready for it. It was about time.

She parked her car and then she walked into her house. She saw Ishmael lying on the couch watching TV, cell phone in hand. She wondered who he was talking to and decided to listen.

Ishmael smiled, surprised to find her home so early. "Hey, ma."

Nina flashed him a fake grin and then went in the kitchen.

"Yo, Rah-lo, lemme call you back." Ishmael hung up the phone and got off the couch. He hadn't really been talking to Rah-lo. In fact, he hadn't heard from Rah-lo since he left Asia. Ishmael had been talking to Robin. He stretched his tall frame and smoothed his goatee. Then he followed Nina into the kitchen.

Nina stood at the counter, pouring herself some juice. She heard Ishmael come in but didn't acknowledge his presence.

Instead, she opened the refrigerator, replaced the juice carton, and stood with her back to him as she drank her juice. Ishmael immediately sensed that something was wrong.

"You left work early," he said.

Nina swallowed and then turned to face him. She hated herself for loving him so much. He was such a terrible choice of a man to give your heart to. She was disappointed in herself. After all, he was a playboy, a smooth-talking hustler with a warm cocoa complexion and flawless style. She should have known that he was going to be that way even after things got serious between them. Still, she loved him. She wanted him to be content with their relationship and to give all his love to her. His sex was amazing, especially his oral skills, which were out of this world. Nina (and many other women besides her) would do just about anything to keep him all to herself. He always had money, he looked good, and he made a woman feel golden. Nina was steamed at the thought of him creeping with Robin—or anyone else, for that matter.

"Yeah," Nina said. She looked at him standing there in a wifebeater and jeans and she watched his eyes for signs of deceit. "I saw Charly today."

Ishmael didn't react at all. He stood waiting for her to finish, but Nina stood silent. "Okay," he said in response.

"She said you came in her shop recently. Looking for Robin."

This time Ishmael was the one who stood silent. That

fucking Charly. He almost wanted to laugh at how persistent she was, but he knew Nina wouldn't find it funny. Ever since Ishmael stopped dealing with Charly more than three years ago, she had tried to get with him every chance she got. The more he shot her down, the more havoc she'd wreak in an attempt to ruin his relationships with other women. She'd caused drama with Celeste and Nina because of her jealousy. She was impossible. But he would deal with her later. Right now, he needed to deal with Nina.

"Yeah. I went to talk to her about Celeste," he lied. He was always quick to find the escape route in a confrontation. He showed no emotion on his face, but the truth was his dealings with Robin had absolutely nothing to do with Celeste.

Nina was caught off guard. "Celeste?" There was a name Nina hadn't heard in a while. "Why would you need to talk to Robin about her?" Nina was now doubly pissed, because Ishmael had long ago admitted to her that he had feelings for Celeste. Nina believed that Ishmael loved Celeste, even though he couldn't have her because she was in a relationship with his best friend. So hearing that Ishmael had gone to talk to Robin about Celeste did nothing to make the situation better for Nina.

Ishmael leaned against the counter. "Rah-lo left Asia."

"What? Why?" Nina asked, frowning.

Ishmael was happy to have her following his lead. "He said he wasn't happy with her anymore. He still loves Celeste.

So now he wants to find her. He went down to Atlanta to look for her, but he doesn't know where to start. He wanted me to talk to Robin to see if she ever kept in touch with Celeste." He folded his arms across his chest.

Nina felt like she was going to be sick. *Celeste.* Nina had thought that she was finally rid of Celeste when she had left town. Now here she was again, giving Ishmael an excuse to talk to Robin and Charly. "I don't think Robin talks to Celeste," Nina said. "They stopped being friends when Robin brought Charly around the shop to start trouble after Celeste fired her." Robin and Nina had in fact come to blows in a fight Charly had instigated. Then, after the fire that destroyed Dime Piece, Charly had hired Robin to work in her shop. That would give Celeste even more reason to steer clear of both of them.

"That's exactly what Robin said. I only talked to her away from the shop so that Charly wouldn't hear our conversation and start some bullshit. Just like she's trying to do now." He inched closer to Nina. "Don't let that jealous girl cause trouble in our house." He smiled at Nina in the way she liked and inside she melted.

"That better be all you were talking to Robin about," Nina warned him.

Ishmael smiled. He scooped her up and began to undress her. Nina didn't resist. Piece by piece her wardrobe hit the floor until her naked ass rested in the palms of his hands. They kissed fervently and Nina moaned in anticipation. Ishmael took her right there in the middle of their kitchen. It was a spontaneous midafternoon quickie. Afterward, they lay on the kitchen floor, breathless.

Ishmael looked happy, and he was. He was happy that Nina had stopped beefing. Nina looked at her man and was unsure whether he was telling her the whole truth. But it didn't matter. His story made sense. She decided to have faith in him. Looking at him sitting there with the afternoon sunshine shrouding him, Nina pondered how much she really loved him. All she wanted was to take the next step. "Ishmael, when are we gonna get married?" she asked.

Inwardly Ishmael groaned. *Not this shit again.* He sighed and tried a witty comeback. "Method Man said, 'You don't need a ring to be my wife.' I'm going with that." He laughed at his own joke.

But Nina wasn't smiling. "Seriously, Ishmael. Do you want that? I mean babies, marriage, and all that. Is that what you want?" Her voice was sultry as she spoke. She was trying to entice him with the thought of sealing the deal.

Ishmael looked at her and then he shook his head. "No. I don't really see that for me in the near future. I told you that and—"

"I know what you told me, but how long do you think I'm going to keep waiting, Ish? It's going on five years." She couldn't even hide her impatience.

"Why we gotta have this conversation now?"

"Because I haven't heard you say what I need to hear."

Ishmael got up and headed for the shower. Nina was hot on his trail. "Why do you always walk away? That's always your response."

He turned and looked at her. "Ma, please. Not now with all that."

"Then when, Ishmael?" She stood with her hands on her hips and her expression was dead serious.

Ishmael looked at her standing there like that—making demands, wanting commitment. This was the part of relationships with women that he hated the most. The part where the woman couldn't see the line between where her man ended and she began. Ishmael didn't want a needy, clingy, nagging woman in his bed each night, didn't want to wake up to that every morning. What he did want was for Nina to listen to him once and for all.

"Ma, I don't know what to tell you. I'm not ready for all that. Kids and marriage and all that. I want it someday. Maybe one kid or even two, when I find the right woman." The minute he said the words, he wished he could eat them.

"So, I'm not the right woman?" Nina asked. "Is that what you're saying?"

"No, that's *not* what I'm saying." Ishmael shook his head, wondering what he was actually saying. "I'm not looking for a wife right now, Nina. Kids are not part of my plan. Maybe one day I'll change my mind. But I don't see that happening any time soon. I don't want to lead you on, or sell you dreams. I know you want all of that. But I really don't. Not right now."

Nina shook her head. "So, in other words, I'm not the woman you want to have babies with and get married to?"

Ishmael felt like he was standing in a pool full of quicksand. "I didn't say that. If I wanted to get married right now, I would ask you. You would be the woman I would want for my wife. But I'm *not* interested in getting married right now. That has nothing to do with you not being the woman for me. It doesn't mean that you're not good enough for me. It just means that I'm not looking for any of that *right now.* All I want is to enjoy my younger years as a single man. When I'm forty years old, I'll probably be ready for marriage and kids and a white picket fence and all that. But I'm still a young man. I want to be a little selfish for a little while longer."

Nina stood there silently for several moments. "Forty? You're not going to be ready to settle down until you're forty?"

Ishmael was growing increasingly frustrated. "I'm estimating!" he yelled, worn out. "What's the problem, Nina? It's like all of a sudden this shit is all you talk about, babies and getting married and—"

"We have been together for four years, Ishmael. Four long years and I still don't have a ring. You don't want to talk about marriage or kids, so where does that leave me? I don't want to wait until I'm old to start having kids. And I don't think marriage means that you have to stop having fun. We could still have fun."

He heard what she was saying, but he didn't care. Ishmael wasn't going to be pressured into marriage or parenthood just because Nina was operating on some type of schedule. He sighed. "I don't want to fight with you, ma. But we might as well drop this now. I'm not getting married until I'm ready to be with one woman for the rest of my life. Right now, I think that woman is you. But I'm not gonna lie to you and say that I know that for a fact. I *don't* know. Things change. I don't see why we just can't go with the flow and see where it leads us."

"I'm wasting my time with you," Nina said, exasperated.

That was it. Ishmael was fresh out of patience. "Well, fuck it then," he said. "Don't waste your time with me anymore. I swear I'm tired of arguing about this shit. I'm not gonna let you pressure me into doing something if that's not what I want. I'm not trying to get married and cheat on you the way Rah-lo did with Asia all those years. Celeste was the one he should've married, but he missed out on that by marrying someone he didn't really want to spend his life with in the first place."

That was the last straw for Nina. "You talk about Celeste like she's fucking Mother Teresa or something, Ish. How do you know he should've married her?"

"Because he still loves her, that's why."

"So do you." Nina spat the words at him venomously, and they lingered in the space between Ishmael and Nina.

He shook his head. "You're still on that shit, huh?" he asked. "I haven't even seen the girl in years."

Nina laughed, although she didn't find a damn thing funny. "But you still love her. I can tell. Whenever you say her name you sound like you're talking about a priceless diamond rather than Rah-lo's mistress."

"Today was the first time we talked about her in how long, Nina?" Ishmael felt that she was looking for things to fight about now.

"All of a sudden, Rah-lo needs *you* to find her for him? Why couldn't he ask Robin himself whether or not she's spoken to Celeste? Why couldn't he, Ishmael? Is it Rah-lo who's trying to find her or is it really you?"

Ishmael's eyebrows were raised in shock. "You can't be serious."

"I'm not stupid, Ishmael. Can you honestly deny that you still love her?"

He shook his head in dismay. "I love *you,* Nina."

"Not enough to marry me, though."

Ishmael turned on the shower and adjusted the temperature. He ignored Nina's last remark and stepped into the shower as if she weren't even there. The subject was closed as far as he was concerned. Nina stood there staring at the shower curtain, watching Ishmael's silhouette through the vinyl. He lifted his arms and scrubbed his armpits, then lathered up the rest of his body. She watched his outline step into the stream of running water and rinse off. The bathroom began to fog up around her and she felt like it was swallowing her. This relationship was beginning to fall apart.

She walked out of the bathroom and shut the door. She threw her clothes back on, fuming the whole time. Strolling into the kitchen, she retrieved her car keys and her purse and walked out of the house. Once inside her car, she turned her key in the ignition and drove straight to Charly's.

CHAPTER EIGHT

Sticks and Stones

Charly was doing a roller set in the front of the salon when she saw Nina's car come to a screeching halt out front. She looked up in time to see Nina step from her ride and charge toward the salon. Charly smirked, figuring this had something to do with their exchange earlier that day. Robin was in the back, preparing to cornrow a little boy's hair and unaware of what was headed her way.

Nina burst through the shop door and grumbled an incoherent "Hello." She spotted Robin in the back and made a beeline for her. Robin looked up and saw Nina and she could not hide the shock she felt. She wondered what the hell had gone wrong in order to prompt this visit. Nina didn't give her much time to wonder. "Hi, Robin. Can I talk to you outside for a minute?" Nina asked.

The little boy in Robin's chair looked up at her to gauge her response. He could tell that the pretty lady talking to his hairstylist was very angry. Nina was clearly steamed. Robin wondered what she should do. "Sure," she said. She excused herself from her young client and followed Nina to the door. Charly, by chance, happened to be standing outside smoking a cigarette.

Nina and Robin stood face-to-face. Nina got right to the point. "What did Ishmael come to see you for the other day?"

Robin wondered how Nina had found out about that. Instinctively, Robin looked at Charly. She smiled knowingly, and Robin knew instantly that Charly had been the one to orchestrate this somehow. Robin shook her head and looked back at Nina. She had packed on a few pounds over the years, but she was still a pretty girl. Still, Robin understood why Ishmael was creeping with her. The expression on Nina's face was that of a woman obsessed. Robin sighed. "I don't remember," she lied.

"You don't remember?" Nina rolled up her sleeves, wanting to beat Robin's ass for telling such a bald-faced lie.

Charly stepped discreetly closer. Robin didn't want to tell Nina the truth. She wasn't out to break up Nina and Ishmael's relationship. Robin and Ishmael shared an explosive sexual connection. She recalled their recent rendezvous and had to suppress a smile. She and Ishmael had wonderful sex and she knew that she would do it again when the opportunity presented itself. He wasn't married to Nina. So, to Robin, he was still fair game. But by no means did Robin want to break up their relationship. She wanted to cover Ishmael's back, but she didn't know what explanation he had given Nina.

"Nina, what's the matter with you? He came to talk to me in broad daylight, just a few feet from your own hair salon. Would he be that dumb if he was up to no good?"

"Just tell me what he came to talk to you about. What's the big secret?" Nina asked. Several of Charly's customers were standing in the window, watching the events unfold.

Charly walked over near the two women and leaned against the wall, watching their exchange. They both ignored her. Nina waited for Robin's response. Not knowing what she should say, Robin attempted to walk around Nina and go back inside the shop. But Nina grabbed Robin by the arm and pulled her back.

Robin yanked her arm away defensively. "Don't grab me. I'm not gonna stand here and be interrogated just because you're insecure."

Nina was growing increasingly aggravated. "Stop using all your vocabulary words, Robin."

Charly laughed at that one. It was about time somebody else called Robin's bourgeois ass out. Robin was too smart for her own good sometimes, Charly thought.

Nina continued ranting and raving. "Would you be

insecure, *bitch,* if your man was going to see some chick he once fucked in the backseat of his truck?"

Robin wanted to slap Nina but didn't want to give Charly the satisfaction of seeing her plan succeed. She knew that Charly wanted nothing more than to see a fight. Robin felt like telling Nina how many times Ishmael had called her in the past three days and how she came in his mouth the other night, but she held her tongue. She didn't want to make a big ghetto scene in front of the beauty salon. That was years ago when she had stooped to that level. She wasn't going there this time. She told herself that she was bigger than that. She was a mother, a student, a hardworking woman with class. She wouldn't stoop to Nina's level. Robin shook her head out of frustration and smirked at Nina. "Okay. You got that," she said. "You feel better now?"

"No, I don't," Nina said. "I'll feel better when you tell me what the fuck you were talking to my man about."

Charly heard a car pull up close by and turned to see Ishmael frantically parking his ride. He wasn't paying attention to how he parked, and his car was left at an angle near the curb as he jumped out and quickly crossed the street in their direction. He looked pissed, and he was. He had gotten out of the shower only to find that Nina had left the house. He felt bad about the argument they'd had and how he had shot down her desire for commitment. He had decided to go and see her at her hair salon. Maybe what they both needed was a nice night out on the town. They hadn't done that in a while. He figured it would improve things between the two of them. But on his way, he noticed Charly standing next to two women who seemed to be in the midst of a heated discussion. When he looked closer, he saw that it was Nina and Robin. He only hoped that he had arrived in time to prevent Nina from finding out the truth.

He walked up to where they stood and asked, "What's going on?"

Nina turned to face him, but Robin answered first, pointing at Ishmael's jealous girlfriend. "*This one* came here to approach me about why you came to see me. I was just telling her that she shouldn't be so insecure—"

"Fuck that!" Nina said. "It has nothing to do with being insecure. I just want to know what's up with you two. Why can't you just answer the fucking question?"

"Calm down!" Ishmael yelled. He was growing more and more disgusted by Nina. "I told you that I came to see her to ask about Celeste."

"*Celeste?*" Charly asked. "What did you wanna know about Celeste for?"

"Mind your business!" both Ishmael and Robin barked at her.

"This *is* my business!" Charly reminded them, pointing to her name on the sign over the door for emphasis.

Ishmael sucked his teeth and turned his attention back to Nina. "I told you. I only wanted to talk to Robin to see if she heard from Celeste because Rah-lo was looking for her."

Charly digested this information, as did Robin. Since that wasn't really what Ishmael had talked to her about, Robin wondered if Rah-lo was indeed looking for Celeste, if he had really left his wife.

"So, Rah-lo and Asia broke up?" Charly asked.

"Yeah." Ishmael scowled at Charly as he said it. He blamed her for this whole mess. If she hadn't been running her mouth to Nina about him visiting Robin, none of this would even be happening. "Why you always gotta start shit, Charly?" he asked.

Charly feigned innocence. "What did I do?"

"You put all this shit in Nina's head about me coming to the shop to see Robin! You always gotta be the one to start some shit."

Charly had the most innocent expression on her face. "All I said was that I had seen you and I asked if everything was okay between the two of you. That's it. How is this all my fault?"

"Listen, I'm going back to work," Robin said, walking toward the salon.

Nina blocked Robin's path once more. Her instincts were telling Nina that she wasn't hearing the whole truth. "I'm asking you woman-to-woman to tell me if you're fucking with Ishmael."

Robin sighed. *"No!"* She turned and stormed off and went back to her patiently waiting client.

Charly stood right there with Ishmael and Nina. Ishmael was irate. "Yo, I can't believe you came down here and made a scene like this," he said. "You're acting just like her." He pointed to Charly.

Charly shrugged it off and continued to stand there. Nina had tears in her eyes. This was getting good.

"It's a wrap, ma. I'm serious. I'm not fucking with you no more." Ishmael was motioning with his hands for emphasis. He was enraged. "Word." He looked at Charly. "And you need to mind your business."

She exhaled her cigarette smoke. "I told you—"

"Yeah, this *is* your business," Ishmael finished her sentence for her. He stuck his middle finger up at her as well.

As he crossed the street, Nina followed him. "Ish, hold up."

"Nah." He stormed off toward his poorly parked SUV.

"Wait a minute!"

Ishmael ignored her. He climbed behind the wheel and peeled out, leaving Nina standing by the curb. She figured she'd follow him in her car to make him talk to her. But as she turned to walk back to her car, she looked across the street and locked eyes with Charly.

Nina stopped dead in her tracks. She looked at her nemesis standing there with so many tricks up her sleeve. Nina hated Charly. She also hated Robin, and any other bitch, for that matter, who got too close to Ishmael. Now Nina had to go and try to mend what was left of their relationship because of the seed that Charly had planted. Nina was angry at herself also for ever feeding into Charly's bull-shit and questioning Ishmael. She shouldn't have taken it as far as she had. And she never would have, had it not been for this bitch standing across the street. Charly blew the smoke from her Newport out through her nostrils and flicked her cigarette butt into the street. Then she turned and walked back inside her salon.

When she got inside she went right over to Robin, who was clearly still angry. As Robin's fingers maneuvered ex-pertly through the little boy's hair, her brow was furrowed. She was clearly agitated after her run-in with Nina. Charly seized the opportunity to make nice.

"She's really bugging out," Charly said. "Why did she have to come here and make a scene like that?"

Robin shot Charly a treacherous look and then directed her attention back at the client in her chair. Charly wasn't giving up that easily.

"You were right when you said that she's insecure. She is. Ishmael looked pissed, too. He told her it's over. Do you think he meant it?" Charly was excited by the thought that Ishmael could be a free agent again. She looked at Robin, wondering how she could have ever thought that Ishmael would have entertained the likes of her for anything besides information. Charly felt silly for ever suspecting that some-thing was going on between Robin and Ishmael. What would he want with her?

Robin had heard enough. "Charly, please! You started

that whole shit. Why did you say anything to Nina about Ishmael coming in here in the first place?"

Charly shrugged her shoulders. "It just came up in conversation. I was telling her that I had just seen him, and I asked her if they were still together. It was an innocent question. I didn't expect for her to go run off and make a big deal out of it. How was I supposed to know that she's so sprung?"

Robin kept working and Charly kept pushing. "Did Ishmael really come to ask you about Celeste?"

"Yup," Robin lied.

"Wow. So, Rah-lo left Asia." Charly shook her head in disbelief. It had been years since she had seen or heard from Celeste, and to Charly's knowledge the woman had left town and never looked back. But suddenly Rah-lo had left his wife to be with Celeste. And Ishmael had conveniently broken up with his wifey. Suddenly, the whole game had changed. Not only was Ishmael a free agent now, but so was Rah-lo. Charly felt like she was a contestant on a game show called *Who Wants to Snag a Baller?*

Robin said nothing as Charly got lost in thought. Charly thought about the possibilities. After she and Ishmael had ended their brief romance, Charly had trouble getting over him. Truth be told, she never had. And when he got serious with Nina, Charly made an attempt to move on—albeit a spiteful one. She had started dating Neo, the well-known rival of both Ishmael and Rah-lo. The relationship hadn't lasted long and it failed to get Ishmael's attention as Charly had hoped it would. She wondered now if her relationship with his enemy would prevent Ishmael from giving her another chance.

As she stood there contemplating these things, Robin watched Charly closely. She was so predictable, Robin thought. She could almost see the wheels in Charly's head turning as she processed the information. Ishmael was single, and Robin knew that Charly wanted nothing more than to be next in line with him. Robin told herself that she didn't give a damn. She wasn't about to get into another competition for Ishmael's affection. Charly, Nina, or even Celeste, for that matter, could have him. Robin was done with it. No man was worth this much trouble. At least that's what she kept telling herself.

CHAPTER NINE

Misery Loves Company

Asia charged into Nappy Nina's and looked around for the owner. She spotted Nina in the back talking to a client and sipping a cup of hot tea. Asia wasn't here for pleasantries today. She didn't need her hair done and there was no time for small talk. She was on a mission to save her marriage.

She walked over to where Nina sat and stood there. Nina looked up and saw Asia and sensed trouble immediately. "Hello," Nina said.

"Yeah. Hi," Asia said rather snottily. "I need to talk to you for a minute."

Nina excused herself from her conversation and stepped over to a secluded part of the salon with Asia. She couldn't imagine what Asia wanted with her and she was eager to find out. "What's up?"

Asia got right to the point. "I need to know where my husband is," she said. "Ishmael is not answering my phone calls and I'm about to really hurt somebody." Asia was desperate to find Rah-lo, and that was clear, judging by the look on her face.

"Well," Nina said, looking at the floor, embarrassed, "Ishmael isn't really talking to me right now, either. He came home last night, took a shower, changed his clothes, and went back out. He hasn't been back since."

Asia wondered if Nina was lying. Ishmael had been ducking Asia, so maybe he had told Nina to lie for him. But the dejected look on Nina's face signaled that she was telling the truth. "So you two are breaking up?" Asia asked.

Nina shrugged. "He's mad at me. Hopefully, he'll get over it." She didn't tell Asia that Ishmael was ignoring her phone calls, too. "What happened with Rah-lo?"

Asia shot a treacherous look at Nina, and for a moment Nina was sorry she'd asked. Asia said, "Don't act like you didn't hear it already. I know how people talk." She realized that she was taking her frustration with Rah-lo out on Nina and softened her tone. After all, Nina was going through a similar situation with Ishmael from the sounds of it. "He walked out and he won't answer my calls. If the kids call him from their cell phones, he answers. But the minute I get on the phone he hangs up. And I know that Ishmael knows where Rah-lo is. But he won't answer my calls, either. I need to know where my husband is because I know he don't think he can just walk out on me and leave me with three kids. He must be crazy."

Nina sympathized with Asia. She knew how bad it felt to have your phone calls ignored by the man you loved. She shook her head sympathetically. "I don't know much," Nina began. "But one of the reasons me and Ishmael had a fight was because of how Rah-lo walked out on you."

Asia was confused. She frowned and asked, "What do you mean?"

"The other day I ran into Charly. She asked me if everything was okay with me and Ishmael because he had come into her hair salon a few days ago to see Robin."

"Robin?" Asia asked suspiciously. She didn't know the former Dime Piece stylists too well. She knew only what she had been told. Since the salon had been owned by Rah-lo's mistress, Asia had never been there personally. She only knew Nina because she was Ishmael's wifey and, therefore, traveled in the same circles as Rah-lo and Asia. Over the years, Nina had filled Asia in on the other stylists—Charly and Robin—and how they had both slept with Ishmael. Nina had told Asia about Celeste's close relationship with Ishmael and how uncomfortable that had made her. And Asia knew more details of Rah-lo's affair with Celeste, thanks to all the things Nina filled her in on. "Why did he go to see her?"

Nina nodded. "That's what I wanted to know. So I asked him, and he told me that Rah-lo wanted him to find out if Robin had heard from Celeste. He said Rah-lo's in Atlanta trying to find her and he wants to know if any of us have an address or a phone number for her there. I didn't believe him, so I went and asked Robin myself. She backed up his story, but now Ish is mad at me for questioning her."

Asia processed the information she had just been given. Rah-lo had actually gone all the way to Atlanta to find Celeste. Asia kept her poker face on, but she was inwardly seething. "Did Robin tell him anything?" she asked.

Nina shrugged her shoulders. "I don't think so."

Asia stared off into space. She felt even more desperate than ever to find her husband so that she could patch things up between them. With Celeste back in the picture, Asia feared that her husband might be gone for good. "Thank you, Nina." Asia took a deep breath and then exhaled, trying to calm herself down. "Call me if you hear anything else, please. Or if you need to talk." Asia really didn't want to hear about what was going on in Nina's relationship with Ishmael. But if she could get any more information about Rah-lo's whereabouts it would be most helpful. Asia walked out of the salon. Now she had to figure out her next step.

Celeste couldn't believe her eyes. She sat in her office at work, checking out her MySpace page, and was floored to find a message from Ishmael Wright. It had been years since she'd seen his face and he still looked incredibly fine! She scrolled through all the pictures he had posted on his page and all but drooled. There was one of him behind the wheel of his truck, one of him leaning against a graffiti-covered wall, and then she saw another one. Celeste gasped audibly when she saw it. The picture of Ishmael and Rah-lo dressed to impress at some party almost stopped her heart.

When Celeste had left New York four years ago, she had brought with her a bunch of pictures of Rah-lo alone, pictures of them together, pictures of Ishmael, Pappy, Harry, J-Shawn—of days gone by and all the fun they'd had. But she hadn't allowed herself to look at those pictures in years. They brought back too many memories for her, and she had tucked them away in the back of her storage closet. Now, seeing pictures of Rah-lo and Ishmael sent her right back in time and she found herself on a journey down memory lane. Rah-lo's beautiful lips were spread into a smile, and Ishmael's sexy physique filled out his button-up perfectly. For a moment, as she stared at the photograph, Celeste couldn't decide which one of them she missed more—the man she'd loved for years or his best friend, who made her panties wet.

"Hey, girl, what time are you leaving today?"

Celeste was startled by Keisha's voice as she entered her office, and she nearly jumped out of her skin. Celeste had been so entranced by the image on her computer screen that she hadn't heard her friend come in.

Keisha frowned. "What the hell is wrong with you?" she asked. Keisha came around to the other side of Celeste's desk to see what had her so engrossed that she hadn't heard her approaching. When Keisha saw the picture of Ishmael and Rah-lo she fanned herself with her hand as if she had suddenly encountered a heat wave. "*Whew!* Girl! Who are they and where do I sign up?"

Celeste laughed. Pointing at the screen, she explained, "This one is my ex. And this one is his best friend."

Keisha's jaws opened in shock. "Damn!" she said. "They're both fine as hell!" She peered closer. "But the friend is sexier, in my opinion. Is that the one you told me you were starting to develop feelings for?"

"Mm-hmm." Celeste sat back in her chair and gazed at the picture, nodding.

"Well, I can see why," Keisha said. "He looks like a cross between LL and Reggie Bush! Damn!"

Celeste laughed at Keisha's assessment. "Well, Ishmael somehow found me on MySpace and sent me a message."

Keisha pulled up a chair. "What did it say?" she asked, anxious for some juicy details.

Celeste guided her mouse across the computer to take them back to the previous screen. Ishmael's message popped up in front of them. Keisha read it out loud and looked at Celeste suggestively. "He still loves you, girl!"

Celeste waved Keisha off. "What are you talking about? He didn't say anything like that."

Keisha sucked her teeth. " 'I miss you. Shit ain't the same since you left. . . .' Would you read between the lines? The man is crazy about you!"

Celeste rolled her eyes at Keisha but thought about what she was saying nonetheless.

"Did you write him back?" Keisha asked.

Celeste shook her head. "No, not yet. I don't really know what to say."

Keisha had heard enough. She was sick and tired of Celeste being so nonchalant about her love life. Before Celeste could protest, Keisha leaned over her friend and typed a response to Ishmael's message:

I miss you, too. Call me. (404) 555-0217.

Before Celeste could stop her, Keisha clicked "send."

"What are you, crazy?" Celeste protested. "I don't want him to call me!"

Keisha was unfazed. "Why not? It's not like you're with Rah-lo anymore. It can't hurt. Plus he wants to call you. He went through all that trouble of searching cyberspace to find you . . . and the man is *fine*! He don't have to waste time on shit like that if he don't want to. I bet women throw themselves at him all the time."

"That's the problem," Celeste mumbled.

"So, if you don't want him, when he calls you can give him *my* number."

Celeste couldn't help laughing. Keisha was crazy. "I would like to hear from him," Celeste finally admitted. "Just to find out how everybody's doing and—"

"Save that bullshit for someone who don't know you, girl! You want to find out if he's single and if he can still lay the pipe good enough to make bitches claw each other's eyes out!"

The two women laughed and slapped each other a high five before Celeste logged off and the two of them headed home for the night. In the back of her mind, Celeste knew that Keisha was absolutely right. As Celeste climbed behind the wheel of her Benz, she sighed. She knew exactly what she needed. Seeing pictures of sexy Rah-lo and Ishmael had only reminded her that what she needed more than anything was some good sex. It had been weeks since the last time she'd been with Damon, and she was long overdue for some good loving. Trouble was, there were no viable candidates to replace Damon in her bed. Except, perhaps, for Bryson. She called him and he answered after the third ring.

"Hello?"

"Hi, Bryson. It's Celeste."

"Heyyyy," he crooned. She could hear the smile spread across his face. It made her smile as well.

"I was just leaving work and I thought I would call you. What are you doing tonight? Feel like having a drink?"

Bryson took off his watch and set it on the bed, removed

his cuff links. "See?" he said. "That's what I like about New York women. You take the initiative."

"I guess that's a yes?"

"Definitely. I just got home a little while ago, so why don't you come by here? I have a full bar." Bryson had much more than that. His home was simple, understated, and expensive. He owned a home on ten acres of land in Decatur, which had been passed down to him by his grandmother. He gave Celeste his address and brief directions and they hung up.

On the way to Bryson's place, Celeste thought about what she wanted from Bryson—from any man, for that matter. She had money of her own. She didn't need or want a man to take care of her ever again. It gave them too much power. It felt too much like charity. Even if they were kind enough to give you the illusion of control, they always held the reins. She wanted her own shit—her own money, name, success, and power. But she also wanted the security, the comfort, of a man. A man who didn't come with baggage and issues. She wanted to be held, touched, and talked to—listened to. But tonight she would settle for being fucked.

She felt like a seductress as she drove over to Bryson's place. This was how she should be living, she told herself. Foot on the gas, headed up the highway for a cozy night of drinks and intimacy, Celeste felt sexy as hell. She let the spring breeze blow through her open car window as she listened to Jay-Z's new CD. Ishmael's face flashed in her mind, then Rah-lo's. Where the hell had they come from and why now? She glanced at her reflection in the rearview mirror and licked her lips. It didn't matter. Tonight was all about Bryson.

She arrived at his house in no time and was impressed by what she saw. His home was a beautiful colonial-style house on such well-manicured grounds. As she stepped out of her car, Bryson came outside to greet her. He wore an unbuttoned dress shirt, a wifebeater, and a pair of tailored slacks. Celeste checked his shoes out and approved. This was gonna be a good night.

He greeted her with a kiss on the cheek. "It's good to see you again."

She smiled. He smelled good. "I'm glad to see you, too. Your house is gorgeous."

"Thank you," he said, smiling at her New York accent once again. As he ushered her inside and showed her around, he told her about his family. His grandparents had married young and given birth to two daughters before Bryson's grandfather was killed in an accident. His grandmother had single-handedly raised her daughters and put them through college. Bryson's mother, Alice, and his aunt Clara held degrees in education and psychology, respectively. And they had raised their children to achieve greatness. College was not an option, it was a requirement, in his family. The question was not *if* he would go to college but *where* he would go. And when his grandmother passed away at the ripe old age of ninety-seven, she left each of her four grandchildren property.

As they reached the huge master bedroom on Bryson's guided tour, Celeste gasped. The room was triple the size of her own and the only things inside were a king-sized bed, sitting atop plush cream-colored carpet, and a huge wooden armoire. One plant stood in the corner, as tall as a ballplayer. This was a lovely place for a single man to live alone. She realized that she was in the big leagues for real now. This was a fine brother with legitimate money, old money. He was as charming as ever as he led her back downstairs and poured her a glass of her favorite drink. He poured himself a shot of Patrón and sat beside her. Kanye's "Graduation" played at the perfect volume, and Bryson's cologne caught her attention again.

"You smell good," she admitted. "What are you wearing?"

He smiled. Perfect teeth. "Thank you. Unforgivable."

She smiled back. "It's nice."

She thought she caught him blushing. She loved this southern boy's charm. "You always look this nice when you go to work?" he asked.

Celeste glanced at her black pencil skirt, Stuart Weitzman heels, and cleavage-baring ruffled blouse and smirked. "If you call this sexy," she purred.

Bryson nodded. "That's definitely what I call sexy. But I thought you were sexy from the minute I saw you at the party." He sipped his drink.

Celeste crossed her legs. "Thank you." She looked around at his home once again. It was sparsely decorated but so lovely regardless. "How long have you lived in this big house all by yourself?" she couldn't help asking.

"Since about a year ago. At first my sister lived here with her husband and their kids. But they all moved when her husband got a job in Columbus. I moved into this house about two years ago."

"No woman to share it with?" Celeste wasn't necessarily auditioning for the part. But Bryson seemed almost too good to be true.

He shrugged. "I thought I had that. But it didn't work out, you know what I mean?" He sipped his drink again. "Her name was Desiree. She had a daughter named Tiffany. I really thought I was gonna get married and have the whole perfect family."

Celeste was intrigued. "And? What happened?"

He smiled at her impatience. "She cheated on me. Not like one-night-out-on-the-town-with-your-girls kinda cheating, either."

Celeste laughed. "Is that what you think girls do when we have our nights out?"

He chuckled and watched her swallow her Hennessy. "Well, you know what I'm trying to say. It wasn't just like a onetime thing that maybe I could forgive over time. She was still fuckin'—pardon my language."

"No, it's fine," Celeste assured him. "Shit!"

He laughed, and so did she. Bryson continued, "She was still fuckin' her daughter's father behind my back. I'm playing daddy to his kid and she's still letting him hit it. It was crazy."

"It sounds crazy." Celeste wondered why his ex would be so stupid. Here was a man who seemed to have it all. What was he lacking that would cause her to slip back to her deadbeat baby daddy? Celeste sighed, wondering if Bryson had a little dick. That would explain Desiree's problem.

"What about you?" Bryson asked, snapping Celeste out of her thoughts. "Where's your man?"

She threw her hands up. "I can't find him!"

The two of them laughed and Bryson refreshed their drinks. He slid back into position, a little closer to her this time. "He'll come when you're not looking."

She liked having Bryson this close. "Well, I didn't see you coming up behind me at the bar when we met. Does that count?"

He smiled, his lips so close to hers that she breathed his air. "Yup." He saw a sexy look of passion in her eyes. He liked it. She was in a naughty mood and he could tell. He kissed her.

Celeste tongued him expertly and he was drawn in. Her aggression was a turn-on! He pulled her closer to him and Celeste took the initiative once again and straddled him. He smiled. She kissed his face, feeling the Hennessy. Bryson was open. He liked Celeste's whole style.

She pulled back as if suddenly aware of what was happening. "Damn," she said, smiling and touching her lips softly as if she could still feel the kiss there.

Bryson looked into her eyes. "Don't pull back now. I won't bite."

She wanted him to bite her. She wanted him to fuck her, ravage her, devour her completely. But she knew that she shouldn't let him. Bryson was a good catch. He had a broken heart and she wanted to play her cards right. "I shouldn't be this aggressive," she said coyly. "You're used to southern belles."

He wouldn't let her climb off of him. Instead, he grabbed her ass and held her there. She liked it; he could tell by the slow smile that crept across her face. "I can get used to this," he assured her.

She stopped trying to fight it. She kissed him and he held on to her ass like it was a life raft. She had no idea what she was in for. He was gonna tear her little ass up. Her lips tasted so sweet. Celeste was feeling the effects of the cognac, and she aggressively unfastened Bryson's belt and unzipped his slacks.

His lips spread into a sexy grin. "That's what you want, huh?"

Celeste simply nodded and unleashed his thick, juicy dick, which was already hard and ready for action. *Size couldn't have been Desiree's problem,* Celeste thought. *Stupid bitch!* She rubbed it, kissed it, stroked him, until he was panting her name. "Look at you," he whispered. He was loving it. She stopped and sat back breathlessly, and Bryson unbuttoned the blouse she wore, unleashing her breasts. She kicked off her shoes and he tugged off her skirt. She led him to his own bedroom and he anxiously followed. Celeste climbed into the bed and Bryson climbed on top of her.

Celeste was in paradise. Bryson buried his face deep inside her pussy and ate her like lunch. She was gone. By the time he came up for air, strapped on a condom, and entered her, she was eager to feel him inside of her. He stroked her like an expert, careful not to hurt her with his ten inches but forceful enough to ensure that she felt him.

"Ohhhhhhhh . . . ohhhh . . . *shit*!" Celeste moaned with pleasure and he watched her facial expressions vacillate involuntarily. "Yeah!"

He switched up his rhythm and she followed his lead. Stroke for stroke she matched his intensity, and he was feeling that. She made him want to really fuck her. When Celeste turned over and stuck her ass far in the air as if she needed him to get it, he panted. "Shit! You want to get fucked tonight?"

"Yes!" Celeste grabbed the sheets as Bryson plunged his dick deep inside of her, stroking her so well that she moaned from deep in the pit of her soul. He was taking her there! Celeste shrieked when he slapped her ass, spanking her as he gutted her. "That feels sooooo good!" She was coming and he felt it. But he wasn't done. He turned her over onto her back and threw both of her legs over his shoulder and dug her out deep. Celeste could hardly stand it. She hadn't been fucked this good in years. Bryson squeezed her breasts and pounded her out. When he finally came, she could feel him pulsating inside of her. His orgasm was long and intense and he shuddered as the last of it came forth. Breathlessly he lay beside her.

Celeste could hardly look at him. He had fucked her so well that she wanted to get away from him, but at the same time she wished she never had to leave. She reached for her clothes and he pulled her back in bed. "Don't get dressed. Don't fix your hair or nothing. I'm only gonna fuck it up again." He smiled at her and she smiled back. For the rest of the night, he sexed her as if she were the last woman alive. She slept like a newborn child that night, with not a care in the world. Bryson lay beside her fast asleep. And in the morning he greeted her with round two.

Ishmael could tell she was coming. His face was buried in her moistness, and her juices dripped down his chin as he feasted on her expertly. He sucked on her softly and glided his fingers in and out of her wetness. Her knees began to quiver and her voice rose several octaves. He knew he had her now.

"Oh . . . my . . . God!!!!!!!!" Robin screamed as she came in Ishmael's mouth, her body convulsing involuntarily. She grabbed his head and pulled him deeper into her, and he loved every moment of it. He lapped up her creamy center eagerly. For two nights straight she had been Ishmael's dessert after she was done with work and he was done with his hustle. Robin's sister had been kind enough to look after Hezekiah while Robin snuck over to Ishmael's secret apartment both nights. Her sister had been more than happy to watch her nephew, since she could tell by Robin's cheery demeanor that she was finally getting some. To her sister, it was about time! Robin needed to start living before life passed her by.

Right now she had never felt more alive. Ishmael finally came up for air and he kissed her inner thighs, which were still shaking from the explosive orgasm he'd just given her. She breathed heavily as he maneuvered himself sensuously up the length of her body, stopping at her breasts and sucking on them separately. Slowly, he dipped the head of his dick inside her wetness, feeling her legs still trembling.

"I got you, baby girl," he whispered, still teasing her with the tip of his manhood. "Let me in."

Robin did. Slowly he stroked her, the rhythm making her feel weak with ecstasy. He was hard as a rock and she was loving every second of it. She clung to him, pulling him deeper inside of her, and he smiled.

"You want all of it?" he asked.

"Yes!" she answered breathlessly.

Ishmael slid his hands beneath her, palming her ass with

both hands. He plunged deep within her sugar walls and Robin let out a deep moan. Damn, she had some good pussy! She was tight and wet and so warm inside. He couldn't get enough of her.

Robin had let go of all of her inhibitions. This man was the king of lovemaking! She wrapped her legs around his waist and ground herself back at him, matching his strokes with equal intensity. Ishmael tried to hold back his ejaculation. He wasn't ready to come yet. This was getting too good.

He put both of her legs up on his shoulders and stroked her deeply. "Damn!" she exclaimed, and Ishmael knew just how she felt. He had been with many women in his lifetime but could not ever recall a woman who made him feel like this. Suddenly, she pushed him off of her, catching him completely off guard. Before he could protest, Robin pushed him onto his back and straddled him, plunging his ten inches deep inside her as she rode him. Her hips swiveling like a belly dancer, she worked him into a frenzy until he couldn't take it anymore. He grabbed her by her hips to get her to slow her pace before he came too soon. Robin looked into his eyes and smiled.

Ishmael smiled back, pulled her close, and kissed her passionately. He was beginning to wonder if he had met his match. Robin smiled once more. "Can't take it?" she asked with a smirk, still grinding her hips but slower this time.

Ishmael liked a challenge. "I can take it," he assured her.

Robin wanted him to prove it. She began to ride him once again with the same intensity as she had moments prior, and Ishmael did all he could to hold back. He didn't want to give her the benefit of knowing how she had him. He bit his lower lip, willing himself to hold back his orgasm. Noticing this, Robin began to bounce up and down on his dick, her breasts jiggling enticingly. Ishmael reached for them and stroked her nipples and then he felt it. He couldn't hold it any longer.

"I'm gonna come!" he roared, wrapping his arms around her waist and thrusting himself deeper inside of her. She could feel him exploding within her and she clung to him breathlessly. The two of them lay together afterward, breathing heavily and reveling in the feeling. Silently Robin leaned over and kissed Ishmael's luscious lips. Then she sat up and slowly walked to the bathroom, her legs feeling like spaghetti.

Ishmael heard Robin turn the shower on and he lay there, dazed. She had been blowing his mind for two straight nights, and each time was better than the last. He felt weak and had never felt that way after sex before. Usually he felt energized and ready for more. But not with Robin. She took all that he had and then some!

When she came out of the bathroom, she strolled over to the bed naked and he watched her. She bent over and picked up her clothes and began to get dressed. Ishmael immediately protested.

"You don't have to leave so soon," he said. "It's not like I got shit to do, and your son is with your sister, so—" He caught himself sounding like a bitch and cleared his throat. "I'm just saying if you don't want to go I'm not forcing you to."

Robin nodded. "I wish I could stay," she said. "But I have a paper to hand in tomorrow and I have to finish it." She pulled her T-shirt over her head and leaned over to kiss Ishmael on his soft lips. "I'll call you when I get off work tomorrow."

Ishmael nodded, wanting her to stay but not wanting to beg. He watched her slip her feet into her Coach sneakers and waved at her as she walked out the door. When she was gone, he asked himself what had come over him. Robin was making him weak.

Ishmael sat up in bed and looked around the room. They had made love with such intensity that the room was a mess, the lamp was knocked over, and the condom had broken. He smiled at the memory. Robin was one hell of a woman.

He stood up and stretched and then walked over to his computer. He needed to stop thinking about her, since she seemed to invade his thoughts more and more each day. He hadn't been back to the home he shared with Nina since their fight at Charly's shop. Nina had shown him such an ugly side of herself that he no longer looked at her the same way. When he had first gotten with her, what he'd loved about her was her softness, her disdain for drama, and her independence. Those things were gone now, and he was turned off. He logged onto the Internet and checked out his e-mail messages—nothing important besides a few e-mails from former coworkers and some party invitations. He thought about Robin once again, wondering when was the last time she'd been out to a party, and then he chastised himself for even caring. His relationship with her was physical, nothing more. After all, she had a child and Ishmael wasn't eager to get involved with someone who had a kid. What he needed was some time to be a single man again—no commitments, no responsibilities to anyone but himself. He went to his MySpace page and immediately smiled. He read Celeste's message, reached for his cell phone, and dialed her number.

Celeste was just getting into work two hours late after her overnight date with Bryson. Her cell phone rang as she slipped into her office and shut the door. She kicked off her Jessica Simpson heels, trotted over to her desk, and picked up the call. "Hello?" she answered.

"If you miss me, then why did you leave without saying good-bye?" Ishmael asked, a smile still plastered on his face.

Celeste stopped dead in her tracks and felt her heartbeat quicken. She had wondered if he would actually call her, but she certainly hadn't expected it to happen so soon. "Ishmael?" she asked, although she knew that it was him.

"Yeah, it's me. What's good, Celeste? Damn, it's been a long time since I heard your voice."

She sat down at her desk and crossed her legs. "I know,"

she said. "What made you look for me on the Internet? I figured you forgot about me a long time ago with all those women in New York to keep you company." She wasn't joking. She knew that Ishmael was a notorious ladies' man. Although they'd shared an unquestionable chemistry, she figured that in the years since she'd left both Ishmael and Rah-lo had surely moved on.

Ishmael let her know that she was mistaken about both of them. "Nah, I could never forget about you," he said. "Neither could Rah-lo, apparently. I hear he's on his way to find you."

Celeste gripped the phone tighter. "Find *me*? What are you talking about?"

Ishmael walked away from his computer and went and stretched out across his bed. "He left Asia and I haven't heard from him in days. Asia's been calling me off the hook trying to get me to tell her where he went, but Rah-lo hasn't told me shit. I keep ignoring her phone calls and she keeps leaving me these long messages telling me that he left her to run off and find you and that she ain't giving him up without a fight, yada yada."

Celeste couldn't believe her ears. "You've gotta be kidding. Why would he think he could just come and find me after all these years? I moved on with my life. I'm not going backward."

"Not even for me?" Ishmael said it without thinking about it.

Celeste didn't answer right away. She frowned slightly. "What do you mean?"

Ishmael wasn't sure what he meant. But he knew that Celeste held a very special place in his heart. "I mean you don't have room in your new life for an old friend like me?"

She smiled. "Well, obviously I do. I gave you my phone number after all." She knew that Keisha had actually sent him her phone number, but Ishmael didn't need to know that. "But getting back to your boy," she said. "Where is he supposedly looking for me? He didn't come down here to Atlanta, did he? He must be crazy to think he can find me that easily. This isn't such a small town." Celeste searched her memory for ways that Rah-lo could find her. She had been careful not to reveal her whereabouts before she left town. And she hadn't been in touch with any of their old crew since she left.

Ishmael shook his head. "I don't know. All I know is what Asia said. And I haven't heard from him in days, so he's definitely up to something." Ishmael didn't want to talk about Rah-lo anymore. His loyalty to his childhood friend had begun to wane. Now that Rah-lo had all but disappeared, leaving Ishmael to pick up the pieces and carry on their business, he knew that it was time for him to branch out for good. While Rah-lo was out chasing Celeste, Ishmael got busy chasing paper. And to add insult to injury, he had gotten to Celeste first. In Ishmael's mind, Rah-lo had blown his chance with her. Now there was nothing standing in the way of Ishmael connecting with Celeste on a more intimate level—or so he hoped.

"You got a man?" he asked.

Celeste logged onto her computer and thought about Bryson and the wonderful time she had with him last night. "Nope," she said. "But I'm not looking for one, either."

Ishmael laughed. "I hear that."

For close to half an hour they talked like old friends and caught up on each other's lives. Celeste was shocked to learn that Ishmael had been with Nina since the last time they'd spoken years prior.

"Nina? What made you get with her? She never really seemed like your type." Celeste wondered why she was so bothered by this revelation.

"So what's my type?" he asked.

"I don't know. But not Nina. I would've expected you to be bored with her by now."

Ishmael laughed, wondering if Celeste knew how right she was. "Well, it's about to be over between me and her. She's been bugging out lately." He recounted Nina's encounter with Charly and subsequent confrontation with Robin.

Celeste sighed. She didn't miss that type of drama at all. When Celeste had first met Charly—in a hair supply store in Staten Island—the two of them had become friends. Celeste thought Charly was fun and witty. When Rah-lo gave Celeste Dime Piece, she had brought Charly on board as one of

the stylists. It was then, working with her closely every day
of the week, that Celeste began to see how much trouble
Charly really was. When Nina applied for a job as a stylist,
she and Charly had clashed almost instantly. Robin had been
a good addition to the team because she was always desperate to avoid beef and bullshit. That is, until Ishmael came in
the shop and set all three of them at one another's throats.

"See?" Celeste said. "That's the shit I had to get away
from. All three of them are nothing but trouble."

"Robin's not so bad," Ishmael said, defending her. "But
those other two are a handful."

Celeste thought she detected affection in Ishmael's voice
when he mentioned Robin. "Are you still screwing all of
them?" Celeste asked.

Ishmael laughed. "Nah," he said. After all, he hadn't slept
with Charly in years. Two out of three was better than *all* of
them. "I'm a changed man."

Now it was Celeste's turn to laugh. "Yeah, right!"

Before she knew it, an hour had passed and Celeste was
terribly backed up with work. Then she saw her second line
ringing and she recognized Bryson's number. She smiled.
"Ish, I have to go," she said. "I'm late for a meeting. Can I
call you another time?"

Ishmael sucked his teeth. "What kind of meeting do you
have on a Friday afternoon?" He shook his head. "Don't
play with me. Your man is there or something? He's on the
phone? I know you got a man." Ishmael was smiling, teasing

her, and he knew she hated that he knew her so well. "What's his name?"

Celeste chuckled. Ishmael had seen right through her white lie. "His name is Bryson and I just had my first date with him last night. I like him, though."

Ishmael smiled. "Bryson? What is he, a politician or something? Does he wear slacks and penny loafers?" he teased.

"Okay, I'm hanging up now," she said.

"All right, all right. I didn't mean to make fun of ole boy. He's probably very nice. But I thought you said you didn't have a man."

"He's not my man. It was just a date."

"So when can I call you back? It's twelve o'clock, so your little lunch date should be over by one—"

"Excuse you! Since when do you decide how long my dates should be?" Celeste couldn't help smiling. Ishmael was still overprotective of her after all this time.

"Don't make me fly down there," he said, hoping she would extend an invitation for him to do just that.

Celeste almost did just that but thought better of it. "Well, if Rah-lo brings his ass down here you may need to come and get him so I don't have to shut him down. Seriously, Ish, tell him that I left that part of my life behind. I don't want to be caught in a love triangle anymore. He's not ready to leave Asia and I've outgrown all that shit, for real."

Ishmael hoped she hadn't outgrown her attraction to

him, too. "I understand." He hesitated, wondering if he should say what was on his mind. Throwing caution to the wind, he went for it. "Yo, I might have to come down there next week to do some business and shit," he said. "Why don't you let me stay at your house so I don't have to pay for a hotel?"

Celeste held the phone, speechless. Was he serious?

"You can say no," he told her. "Your silence is making me feel bad."

Celeste laughed. "I'm sorry. You just caught me off guard with that one. I mean . . . yeah, I guess so. I don't see why that would be a problem." She frowned, suddenly wondering if this was all a setup. "Ish, did Rah-lo put you up to this? 'Cuz if you're trying to find out where I live so that you can tell him—"

"Nah!" Ishmael asserted, slightly offended. "I see you still think I'm one of Rah-lo's soldiers."

"I'm not saying that, Ishmael."

"It's all right. I guess the last time we saw each other that's exactly what I was. But a lot has changed since then. I'm doing my own thing now," he said. "Rah-lo will always be my boy, but I get money by myself. And I don't do his dirty work anymore. He handles his business and I handle mine." Ishmael knew even as he said it that he wasn't telling the whole truth. Rah-lo had no clue that Ishmael had gone into business for himself, and Ishmael preferred it that way for the time being. He and Rah-lo had established a very successful hustle together. Ishmael didn't want to fuck that up. Instead, he would get money on the side to supplement his income until his own client base grew larger. The last thing he wanted was to piss Rah-lo off.

Celeste bit her lip, wondering what she should do. "All right then. Yeah, you can stay with me if you want to." She wondered why her heart was racing at the mere thought of it. "Just make sure your boy don't find out. I don't want to see him, Ish." It might be hard for her to resist the urge to do all the things she had fantasized about doing to Ishmael once upon a time. But she thought she was up to the challenge. Rah-lo, on the other hand, was not so easy. Celeste feared that if she saw him again she would fall back in love, and that was the last thing she wanted.

Ishmael smiled, happy that she had said yes. Seeing Celeste again was exactly the change of pace he needed in his life. "I got you," he said. "I'll call you tomorrow so you can give me all the info so I can come down there."

They ended their conversation, promising to talk again tomorrow. When she hung up the phone, Celeste thought about all that he had said. Was Rah-lo really looking for her? Had he really left Asia? As Celeste got to work, she wondered why part of her—deep down inside—felt hopeful that Rah-lo would indeed come looking for her. She wanted to believe that she was over him, but deep down she knew that wasn't the case. And what about Ishmael coming to visit?

She wondered what his true intentions were. She reasoned that it would be nice for the two of them to catch up as old friends. After all, all they had ever been was friends. So she questioned herself as to why her heart was galloping in her chest at the mere thought of seeing him again.

CHAPTER TEN

Friend or Foe?

Ishmael's cell phone was ringing, and PRIVATE CALL was displayed on the caller ID. He hesitated to answer it, but since he hadn't heard from Rah-lo, Ishmael picked up the call, hoping it would be him calling. "Yeah," Ishmael answered, entering the house, thrilled that Nina wasn't home, and kicking off his Timbs. He was only there to gather up some of his things so that he could head back over to his sanctuary.

"What up?" Rah-lo said. "I been laying low for a few days. You hear from Asia?"

Ishmael switched on the lamp in his empty living room. "Hell, yeah, I heard from her! How the hell you gonna leave town without telling me, son?"

"Son?" Rah-lo knew it was just a figure of speech, but he didn't appreciate Ishmael's tone. Who did he think he was talking to? "First of all, who the hell said anything about leaving town? I'm over here at my spot on Howard."

"You're still on Staten Island? I was just over there the other day—every day! Nobody's been answering your door."

"I wasn't here. I was over at this shorty's crib for a little while, but I never left the Island."

"So, why does your wife think you went to Atlanta to find Celeste?"

Rah-lo frowned. "Is that what she told you?"

Ishmael was confused. "Hell, yeah, that's what she told me! She said you told her that you were going to find Celeste. That day when I helped you move your stuff when the shit jumped off with Neo. She said you told her that. Then I didn't hear from you for all these days, so I thought that's what you did."

"I went somewhere to get my mind right. I deaded Asia, but it had nothing to do with Celeste. Asia's crazy. She got it stuck in her head that I left her so I could find Celeste, but I never told her that shit." Rah-lo shook his head in frustration. Asia drove him insane sometimes.

Ishmael was relieved that Rah-lo wasn't chasing after Celeste after all this time. "Still. You haven't checked in for days. There's still business we gotta handle out here. And you couldn't even call to tell me what was going on?"

Rah-lo calmed down a little. "I didn't have time to stop

and think about who I should call. I had to get away for a minute."

"Well, your wife has been calling me for days, yo."

Rah-lo thought about it. He hadn't considered the position he was leaving Ishmael in. Not only did he have to keep business running smoothly in Rah-lo's absence, but Ishmael had to deal with Asia's bullshit also. "You're right. I ain't mean to leave you stuck like that. I just started thinking about how much I gave up, trying to be a good father to my kids. And I love my kids, Ish, but I don't love Asia no more. I had to go. Then to find out she was fucking with Neo . . . finding him in my house. I needed a minute to myself."

"I can understand that. But why does Asia think you were going to find Celeste? She left years ago, so it's not like you could just go find her and pick up where you left off. Celeste won't want to hear that shit after all this time." Ish's tone was slightly hostile, and he didn't realize how obvious it was.

For a moment Rah-lo thought he heard a twinge of jealousy. "What's the matter, Ish? You mad you didn't think of it first?" Rah-lo smirked, knowing that Ishmael had a crush on Celeste. He had no concrete proof, but he could tell there was something more than feelings of friendship there.

"What did you say?" Ishmael wanted to make sure he wasn't misunderstanding his friend.

"Why you so concerned about whether or not I went to find Celeste? You sound like you really felt a kinda way about me supposedly going after her. What's that about?"

"Rah-lo, I don't know what you're getting at right now, but let me make this clear. I don't want Celeste. Never have, never will." It was a lie, but it was a necessary one at the moment. "If you decided to leave Asia 'cuz you weren't happy, I understand that, too. It's your life, son. My only concern is that business could've suffered while you were out of the loop for three days. That's all I care about. We already had a bad week. Isn't that what you said?"

Rah-lo didn't answer. But he heard Ishmael loud and clear. As Ishmael told Rah-lo half-truths, Nina came home and was visibly thrilled to see that Ishmael was there. He hadn't been home since she'd caused a scene at Charly's. Nina wanted to set things right. She smiled eagerly and waited for him to get off the phone.

Ishmael concluded his telephone conversation, agreeing to meet with Rah-lo to go over business later that day. When Ishmael hung up the phone, Nina walked over and hugged him tightly. He halfheartedly returned the gesture.

Sensing his reluctance to be nice to her, Nina took matters into her own hands. She stroked his dick inside of his jeans and kept going as he rose to the occasion. When he was fully hard and throbbing, she stepped out of her dress and stood before him in a black bra and a matching thong. He watched her lustfully as she unzipped his jeans. Ishmael was surprised by her silent aggression but didn't resist as she kissed him. He was still pissed off at her for causing a scene at Charly's salon and for confronting Robin. Ishmael enjoyed the feeling as Nina worked hard to make it up to him. Before long he was leading her to the sofa, where she stepped out of her panties as he unhooked her bra.

As she stood before him completely nude, Ishmael thought Nina was such a beautiful woman. She had so much potential, but she was so fucking insecure. If she wasn't so needy and so desperate for commitment, he could see himself loving her for a long time. But lately she had turned into someone he no longer recognized. He didn't want to be with a woman who demanded more of him than he was willing to give. "You're gonna make me leave you," he said.

Nina frowned. That wasn't the reaction she had expected. Ishmael stood in front of her with his dick standing at attention, while she was naked and ready to get it poppin', and here he was threatening to leave her. She was speechless.

Ishmael pulled her close to him and kissed her roughly. She matched his intensity as she kissed him back. He sucked her lower lip, while he slipped his middle finger inside of her. Nina moaned deeply and dug her nails into his back. He slipped another finger inside of her and grabbed her ass roughly with his other hand. "Stop your bullshit," he warned her. "I'm serious."

With Ish's rock-hard dick pressed against her bare belly, his two fingers deep within the wetness of her pussy, and his big, strong hand palming her ass, Nina was in heaven. "Okay," she whispered. She took the lead once more and shoved him down, straddling him. She plunged his stiffness deep within her pulsating walls and rode him in a perfect rhythm. Ishmael rubbed his hands across her body, squeezing her and kissing her all over. It wasn't long before she climaxed, throbbing on his rigid dick and sending him into spasms of ecstasy. Nina kissed Ishmael as he came. She loved him, and hoped that his breathless recovery signaled that he had forgiven her.

She stood and looked at him. "You still mad at me?" she asked.

Ishmael smiled. "Yup."

Nina mushed him playfully and went to the bathroom to clean herself off. Ishmael sat there on the couch and laid his head back against the cushions. Within minutes, he was asleep. Nina returned to the living room and found her man fast asleep. She smiled, grateful that he was home again. Now all she had to do was make sure that he stayed there.

She spotted his phone sitting on a bedside table. She glanced at him once more, making sure that he was really asleep. She heard him snoring softly and she walked over to his phone, picked it up, and headed into the bathroom. Locking the door behind her, she scrolled through his phone and checked to see whom he had been calling. Her heart skipped a beat as she spotted a number she didn't recognize. The area code made her blood pressure rise instantly. She had traveled enough in her days as a stripper to recognize the Atlanta exchange. She hit the "send" button and waited for confirmation of her worst fears.

"Hi, you've reached Celeste Styles. Leave me a message

and I'll return your call." Nina heard the voice message and she felt like the roof of her head was about to blow off. She hung up without leaving a message, and tears began to stream down her face. Checking his call history, she saw that he had also called another number numerous times. She dialed that number and was stunned to hear Robin's voice answer, "Hello?" When Nina said nothing, Robin continued saying, "Ish, stop playing. What's wrong? You miss me?"

Nina slammed the phone shut and charged out of the bathroom. She felt like a damned fool. Storming into the living room, she threw Ishmael's phone at him, hitting him in the chest. He woke up and looked at her as if she'd lost her mind.

"You're fucking around on me, Ish!" she yelled. "I saw Celeste's number in your phone and Robin's, too. You cheating bastard!"

Ishmael knew he was caught. Nina had gone through his phone—a cardinal sin in his book. "Fuck you going through my phone for?" he demanded, standing up and towering over her.

"Don't turn this shit around! You fucking lied to me." Nina began to cry. "You been cheating on me and all this time you've been saying you're not ready for marriage or kids. . . . How could you do this to me?"

Ishmael shook his head in frustration. "I told you I wasn't ready to settle down," he said simply. "You walk around here nagging me about it day in and day out. You forced me to cheat on you!"

"Shut the fuck up, Ish! That's bullshit and you know it!"
Nina was enraged. "Fuck you!" she spat.

Ishmael walked toward the door and Nina threw one of
her shoes at him, hitting him in the head. He turned, ready to
charge at her, but caught himself. Instead, he laughed at her
and shook his head. "Fuck you, too! I'm outta here." He
slammed the door behind him and left her crying in his wake.

Ishmael drove to his secret lair and called Robin on his
way over there. She answered the phone, sounding confused.
"Ish, why'd you hang up on me before?"

He adjusted his earpiece and gripped the steering wheel.
"I didn't call you," he said. "Nina did. She got ahold of my
cell phone and went through all my numbers."

Robin frowned. "I thought it was over between you two.
How did she get your phone?"

Ishmael had to think quickly. "I went over there to get
some of my stuff. While I was there I fell asleep on the couch
and she came in while I was asleep."

Robin didn't buy it. But she wasn't in the mood to play
the role of the interrogator. "Okay," she said. "Thanks for
the heads-up. I guess I should expect some bullshit with her
as a result of all this."

He sighed. "I'm on my way to my spot. Why don't you
come and keep me company?"

Robin rolled her eyes. Ishmael was back on his player
shit again. She was no dummy. She figured that his relationship with Nina wasn't completely over yet. And since she

was acting up tonight he wanted to replace her with Robin. "I can't," she said. "I've already been over there three times this week and I have to study. Finals are coming up."

"Come on," Ishmael coaxed. "Just for a little while. I don't feel like being alone tonight."

Robin shook her head. "I'm sorry, Ish. Maybe some other time." The truth was Robin needed to put the brakes on. She was completely vulnerable as a result of the intoxicating sex they'd been having. She needed space to get her heart in check.

Ishmael hated being told no, but he relented. "Aiight. Just call me when you have some free time." He ended the call and pulled up at a red light. Ishmael leaned back against the headrest and let out a heavy sigh. He had a long and lonely night ahead of him.

"Hello, Rah-lo?"

"Yeah," he answered. Looking at the clock, he realized how early it was. It was just after eight o'clock in the morning. "Who's this?"

She tried to steady her voice, which was laced with raw emotions. "It's Nina," she managed. "I need to talk to you about Ishmael."

Rah-lo was all ears. He had gotten a call from Ishmael late the night before. Ish had told Rah-lo that he was going out of town for a couple of days after having a big fight with

Nina. Rah-lo hadn't questioned it, since he knew firsthand what it was like to feel the need to escape the drama at home. He figured Ishmael would explain what happened once he got back. "Okay," Rah-lo said.

Nina took a deep breath. "Ishmael's a fucking liar. You can't trust him. None of us can." Her voice shook as she spoke.

Rah-lo frowned, wondering what the fuck was going on. "What are you talking about?" he asked. "Calm down and tell me what happened."

"Ishmael told me that you left Asia and that you went to find Celeste."

Rah-lo sighed. "I did leave Asia, but I never said I was going to find Celeste. It was a misunderstanding. Asia got that shit in her head all by herself. Nobody told her that." He wondered if that was what had Nina so upset. He rolled his eyes, hating how women often overreacted. He had no time for Nina's drama right now. He was tired. "Ishmael didn't do nothing wrong. Asia's bugging out. Relax."

Nina couldn't stop her tears from falling. She felt a toxic mixture of hurt, rage, and vengeance. Ishmael was going to pay for breaking her heart. "It was no fucking misunderstanding. He told me that so that I would think he was talking to Robin to try to help you find Celeste. But he was really fucking Robin. And Celeste, too."

Rah-lo's jaw clenched immediately. "What are you talking about?"

"Ishmael is a liar! I found Celeste's number in his phone

and he's been talking to her all this time. All this time he was pretending to be your friend and pretending to be my man and he was playing both of us."

Rah-lo seethed but said nothing.

Nina continued, "I went through his phone and found her number. And when I checked the call history, he had talked to her on the phone the other night for over an hour. Did you know that?"

Rah-lo thought back on his earlier conversation with Ishmael. Not once had he mentioned speaking to Celeste. "Nah," Rah-lo said calmly. "I didn't know that at all."

Nina was satisfied. Misery loves company. "I figured you should know what kind of friend he really is."

Rah-lo's mind was reeling. He couldn't believe that Ishmael would betray him like that. "How long has he been in touch with Celeste?" Rah-lo asked.

"I don't know. For all I know he could've been in touch with her all along, since the day she left."

Nina sounded terribly hurt and Rah-lo wanted to believe that that was why she had made this all up. "Let me get the number he dialed. How do you know it was Celeste?" Rah-lo asked, still giving Ish the benefit of the doubt.

"Call for yourself. If she doesn't pick up, you'll hear her say her whole name on the voice mail. Four-oh-four . . ." Nina recited the number, which she'd memorized.

Rah-lo didn't need to write it down. He committed it to

memory easily and said, "Aiight, Nina. Try to calm down and I'll call you back."

When he hung up the phone, he dialed the number and waited for the answering machine to come on. Instead, a sultry female voice answered, "Hello?"

Rah-lo's voice got caught in his throat. He would recognize that melodic voice anywhere.

"Hello?" Celeste repeated.

"Celeste," he said, his worst fears confirmed. "It's Rah-lo."

Celeste felt her knees go weak and wondered what the hell was going on. Had Ishmael given Rah-lo her number? Damn! "Rah-lo? How did you get my number?"

Rah-lo felt his heart racing in his chest. "Did you ask Ishmael the same question when he called you?"

Celeste didn't know what to say. She held the phone in silence.

Rah-lo didn't know where to begin, so he struggled to find the words. "I'm not with Asia anymore, Celeste. I left her." He hoped that would be music to Celeste's ears.

"Ishmael already told me that. Congratulations," Celeste said flatly. She figured her conversation with Ishmael had been nothing more than a cleverly disguised precursor to this conversation. "What? Are you on your way down here with Ishmael? Y'all planned this whole thing?"

Rah-lo gripped the phone so tightly that he thought it might snap in half. "He's on his way down there?"

Celeste was confused. She had assumed when he called

that he had gotten her number from Ishmael, that Rah-lo and Ishmael had planned the whole thing. "How did *you* get my number if you didn't get it from Ishmael?" she asked.

"Nina gave it to me. She found it in his phone. So I'm curious about how he got your number. How long have you been talking to him? You're telling me he's on his way down there to see you?"

Celeste could hear the irritation in Rah-lo's voice and she knew him well enough to know that he was heated. She still couldn't believe that she was speaking to him after four long years. "I just spoke to him for the first time the other day," she said. Celeste could sense drama on the horizon.

Rah-lo said, "I don't understand. All of a sudden I got my boy's wifey calling me accusing him of betraying me . . . and betraying her, too. And now you're telling me that he just called you out of the blue and now he's coming all the way to Atlanta to see you? What's up with that?"

Celeste was confused herself. She wondered what the hell had happened between Rah-lo and Ishmael to cause them to keep such secrets from each other. And how the hell had Nina gotten involved? "Rah-lo, I don't know what's going on," Celeste said. "All I know is that it's early in the morning on my day off and I'm sleepy. I'm not a morning person."

He smiled. She never had been a morning person. He couldn't believe that she was right there on the other end of the phone. He sighed and closed his eyes. "Damn, baby girl," he said. "It's good to hear your voice." Celeste said nothing in response. Rah-lo forged ahead. "I miss you. I never stopped missing you since the day you left."

Celeste hated herself for being so glad to hear those words. She shook her head as if to shake the feeling off. "I–I can't talk right now," she stammered, and hung up the phone abruptly. "Shit!" she hissed to herself. She couldn't believe he had her number! Rah-lo's voice echoed in her ear, causing her to feel elated and mortified at the same time. She missed him, too— in her heart she did. Her mind was telling her to change her number and forget all about him. It was too late and she had come too far. She grabbed her iPod and her car keys and decided to head to the gym to blow off some steam. She needed to clear her head. Too much was happening all at once.

Meanwhile, Rah-lo headed out to find the man whom he had once considered his friend. Ishmael was a dead man. Rah-lo got behind the wheel of his car and dialed Ishmael's number. He had to find out where Ishmael was.

"Whattup, son?" Ishmael answered.

Rah-lo's face was twisted into a menacing grimace. "What's with this 'son' shit all of a sudden, Ish? You been sounding kinda sure of yourself lately."

Ishmael frowned. "What are you talking about?" He sensed hostility coming from his friend and wondered if he had found out about the side deal Ishmael had cut with Cito. "What's the problem?"

"Where you at, Ish? I need to meet with you *right now*."

Ishmael was in his secret apartment, but he wasn't about

to divulge his whereabouts to Rah-lo until he could figure out why he sounded so upset. "I'll come meet you on Staten Island," Ishmael said. "Where you at?"

Rah-lo was furious. "Meet me at my house on Howard Avenue. Don't keep me waiting, *son.*" Ishmael could hear the sarcasm in Rah-lo's voice. The next thing Ishmael heard was a dial tone, signaling that Rah-lo had hung up on him.

Ishmael threw some clothes on and headed out to Staten Island. The twenty-minute drive felt like it took days, as Ish wondered what the hell Rah-lo's problem was. Ishmael finally arrived at Rah-lo's sprawling second home and parked his car. He pulled his gun out of the glove compartment and put it in his waistband, just in case Rah-lo got crazy. Ishmael had to admit to himself that he felt nervous as he approached the doorway. He rang the bell and waited.

Rah-lo answered within moments. He opened the door and ushered Ishmael inside without a word. He stood in Rah-lo's foyer waiting for him to tell him what this was all about. Rah-lo got right to the point as he stood and faced Ishmael with only feet separating the two friends.

"You betrayed me, Ishmael. After all these years of me thinking that you were like a brother to me, you fucking played me."

Ishmael frowned, confused. Rah-lo obviously knew something and Ishmael decided to address the issue head-on. "What, nigga, you mad about Cito?"

Now Rah-lo was the one who frowned. "Cito? What the fuck happened with Cito?"

Ishmael cursed himself for making an incorrect assumption. Thinking Rah-lo had found him out, Ishmael had spoken too soon. But it was too late to turn back now. "Aiight, listen," he said. "The last time you picked up the money from the workers, it was short. And you know it was short. I don't know if *you* shorted me or if the workers shorted both of us. And, honestly, with all the bullshit you're dealing with from Asia right now, I didn't feel like bothering you with my problems. But I got bills to pay, son. I got moves I gotta make and I can't afford to have a slow week. So I went to Cito and got some work of my own."

Rah-lo stared at his friend for a long time. "You cutting me out of some money now?" Rah-lo demanded, becoming angrier by the minute.

"Nah." Ishmael didn't want to dig himself deeper into the hole that he was already in. "The shit I got going with Cito has nothing to do with you. Me and you still get our money the same. Nothing changed. I just got a lil something going on the side, Rah-lo. It's as simple as that. Like I just explained, I can't afford to have a bad week. This way I got my shit covered and I still got your back with the shit we got going on."

"I can't believe this shit." Rah-lo looked at the ceiling in anguish and let out a deep sigh. "First I find out that you're talking to Celeste behind my back. And now I find out that you got a secret deal with the supplier. You're a fucking snake."

"What?" Ishmael was stunned. "Celeste?" He wondered how the fuck Rah-lo had found out about that.

"Yeah, muthafucka! Celeste. Nina called me and let me know that you've been talking to her. I didn't believe her, so I called the number she gave me and I spoke to Celeste myself. She told me that you're planning a trip down there." Rah-lo stepped closer to Ishmael. "So when the fuck was you gonna tell me that you've been talking to Celeste?"

Ish took a step back. Not that he was scared of Rah-lo. Ishmael just needed a second to get his story straight before this confrontation turned physical. "I only called her because I thought you went down there to look for her. Your wife was calling me every five fucking minutes demanding to know where you were. She kept telling me that you went looking for Celeste. So I called her looking for you."

"How the fuck did you get her number, Ish?"

"I found her on MySpace! I sent her a message and she sent back her number. Rah-lo, Asia said that you went after Celeste. That's the only reason I contacted her. I was only trying to find you so I could tell you that your wife was bugging the fuck out."

"Why didn't you tell me that you spoke to her when I called you earlier? Huh? If all this shit is on the up-and-up why the fuck didn't you mention that you spoke to my shorty?"

Ishmael had to stifle a laugh. Celeste hadn't been Rah-lo's "shorty" in years. But rather than point that out, Ishmael sighed. "I don't know why. Nina came home and I got distracted. It slipped my mind."

"Slipped your fuckin' mind, huh? Word? What about you going down there to visit her? Did that shit slip your mind, too?"

"I was just talking shit when I said that!"

"And what about Cito, Ish? What the fuck is going on with you? All this time I thought you was my man and I could trust you. Now you calling Celeste behind my back, keeping secrets with Cito . . . Tell me something, nigga!"

Ishmael held his hands up in exasperation. "You're taking this shit too far, Rah-lo. Seriously."

"I gotta hear from your girl that you're having late-night conversations with Celeste? I gotta wonder if the niggas I'm doing business with got larceny in their hearts? Nah! Fuck that." Rah-lo punched Ishmael in his face, knocking him off balance. Before Ishmael could regain his composure, Rah-lo was on him again, pummeling him in a barrage of punches.

Ishmael charged Rah-lo, knocking him off his feet. Now that he had gotten Rah-lo off of him, Ishmael tried desperately to get the upper hand. But he was no match for Rah-lo, who was still throwing powerful punches at his former friend. They tussled on the floor for several minutes until finally Ishmael scrambled to his feet and threw his hands up to continue the fight. His gun fell from his waistband onto Rah-lo's hardwood floor, landing with a loud boom.

Rah-lo stood and faced his friend, the gun lying precariously on the floor between them. "You gonna shoot me, Ish?" Rah-lo demanded, his chest heaving.

Ishmael stared Rah-lo down. He didn't want to fight his friend, much less shoot him. "Rah-lo, you got this shit all twisted," Ishmael said.

Rah-lo shook his head and bent down and picked up Ishmael's gun. He handed it to Ishmael and, cautiously, he took it from Rah-lo. He looked Ishmael dead in his eyes. "Get out of my fucking house. Take your deal with Cito and run with it. I'm not fucking with you no more. I can't trust you."

Ishmael felt terrible because he knew how bad this all looked. "Rah-lo—"

Rah-lo shook his head and looked at Ishmael seriously to demonstrate that their conversation was over. He gestured toward the door and hoped for Ishmael's sake that he followed his orders and left Rah-lo alone. "You can't say shit to me. You betrayed me. Leave, Ish."

Ishmael wanted to defend himself but thought better of it. Instead, he headed out the door and shut the door on a lifelong friendship as he made his exit.

"Jackie, can you wash Sabrina's hair for me, please? I need to take the next customer. It's getting too crowded in here."

"No problem." Jackie escorted the client to the sink while Nina called the next lady to her chair. Nappy Nina's was packed for a Thursday afternoon. Nine women sat patiently waiting their turns as Nina, Jackie, and Alesia (the salon's braider) worked busily through the steady stream of clients. KISS FM was playing an old Stephanie Mills joint, and several of the patrons and stylists sang along.

Nina took one look at a client's weave and shook her head. "Uh-uh!" she said emphatically. "You gotta go across the street to the Dominicans and let *them* wash your hair." Nina continued to shake her head as she looked at all the woman's nappy new growth while cutting the weave tracks out of her hair. There was no way Nina was going to dig her well-manicured hands into this woman's matted mane. Nina cut out the last track and repeated herself, shaking her head. "Mmmmm. Go across the street, let them wash you, and come back." The client looked slightly offended, but she grabbed her bag and strolled right across the packed Brooklyn street, looking like Buckwheat's mama.

"No shame!" another client called out. Everyone started laughing.

Nina began applying a relaxer to Ms. Turner's hair, while noticing Ishmael pulling up outside in his truck. She frowned and kept working, wondering what the fuck he wanted.

As he entered the shop, she saw a heated expression on his face. When he approached her, she avoided his gaze and said, "I can't talk right now, Ishmael. You see how packed it is in here."

Ishmael ignored her statement and said, "I need to talk to you outside for a minute."

Nina frowned slightly. She motioned to Ms. Turner and shrugged. The woman had Creme of Nature slathered throughout her head. She wasn't going anywhere. "I can't leave a perm on her, Ishmael. Let me rinse it out and I'll—"

"It can't wait, Nina." Ishmael was dead serious. He hadn't stopped scowling at her since he got there.

"Ish, I can't leave a relaxer in her hair. There's lye in it. It'll burn her hair out. What's the matter with you?"

He stared at her blankly.

"What?" she demanded.

"Get your shit out of my house," he said matter-of-factly. "I'll give you one week and then I want you and all your shit gone! You betrayed me, you little bitch! I know what you told Rah-lo and I swear I want to fuck you up right now. So before I hurt you, get your shit and get the fuck out of my house." He stood with his chest heaving and his hands balled into fists in his pockets. The customers in the shop ceased all conversation and began to pay close attention to Ishmael and Nina's conversation.

"Aww shit," one client said under her breath.

Ms. Turner was all ears. She was glad to have a front-row seat—Nina's chair—for the drama unfolding before her.

Nina was astounded. "Get out of *your* house?" She put her hands on her hips and shook her head. "Your fucking house? I don't think so. My name is on the lease and—"

"Your name ain't on shit," he said. "Don't make this hard on yourself, Nina. If you don't have your shit the fuck out of there in one week, I'll throw all your shit out. Word. Don't test me." He turned to leave, but Nina was hot on his trail.

"Ishmael, it's like that now? Why? 'Cuz I went through your fucking phone?" she demanded.

"What the hell did you tell Rah-lo for?" Ishmael barked, turning to face Nina. He knew that he had beef now.

Nina stood speechless. Ishmael looked at her in disgust. "Get the fuck outta my face." He turned to leave and Nina grabbed his arm.

"Wait a minute!" she cried out desperately.

"Nina, my scalp is tingling!" Ms. Turner called out to her.

Nina ignored Ms. Turner. "Ishmael, how the hell was I supposed to feel, knowing that you been creeping on me? Huh? What about Robin? That shit don't count? I was mad. You gotta take it this far?"

Ishmael shook his head as he looked at her. "You can't be that dumb. Really. You knew when you told him that bullshit that I would never fuck with you after that. Don't act surprised now. Just stay away from me."

"I'm not going nowhere!" Nina stepped back and put her hands on her hips.

Ishmael chuckled right to her face. "You're a crazy bitch!"

Nina hauled off and slapped Ishmael so hard that clients ran for cover, assuming that Ishmael was going to beat the hell out of her in response. He pushed her hard enough to make her stumble backward slightly. She charged at him again, and he pushed her back again, this time causing her to stumble backward into one of the chairs. He didn't want to hurt her, but if she slapped him like that again he knew he might do just that.

Frustrated, Nina began to cry. "Fuck you, Ishmael!" She was embarrassed in front of her clients and her employees and she was losing the man she had wanted to spend her life with. Nina struggled to her feet.

"Nina!" Ms. Turner was not playing anymore. "My fuckin' scalp is on fire. I need to rinse this shit out of my hair now!"

Other clients began to grumble about the scene playing out before them. "This shit is so unprofessional!" one client exclaimed. "If that was me and my hair fell out, I would kick somebody's *ass* up in here!"

Ishmael rubbed his face, which was still burning from the impact of Nina's hellified slap. He wanted to slap her back to show her how that shit felt, but instead he shook his head at her in disgust, turned around, and walked out.

Nina was left standing there with all eyes on her. Jackie mercifully stepped in and ushered Ms. Turner to the sink to rinse out her relaxer. Nina watched Ishmael drive away and she walked out of the shop and stood there, thinking about what had just happened. Behind her she could hear the whole shop buzzing about the scene Ishmael had caused.

"That muthafucka is *fine*! How did she fuck that up?"

"I hate guys like that. He cheated on her and then he turns it around to make it seem like it's all her fault. He did that shit just to embarrass her. He knew what he was doing. Coming in here to tell her to get out of *his* house. He wanted to make her look like a fool."

"She should learn to keep her mouth shut. When I used to get my hair done at Dime Piece, she was always in there telling Charly that she talks too much. Looks like she talks too much, too."

"You know what they say about people in glass houses," another lady observed.

"Did y'all see how hard she slapped him, though?"

"Yeah, but then he pushed her like he wanted to choke the shit out of her instead."

"She's lucky it was him. 'Cause if it had been my man, he would've knocked her straight out!"

"That shit was hilarious. He kept pushing her and she was so mad!"

"I got it on my camera phone!" one girl exclaimed. Everyone in the shop crowded around her to see the instant replay.

Nina had never been so embarrassed in her life. She walked off toward her car, climbed inside, and sped off toward home.

Charly's shop was so packed that there were no more chairs available for the clients to sit in. Every dryer, sink, and stylist's chair was occupied. The seats set up around the perimeter of the salon for customers to sit in while they waited were all taken. There were women lined up against the walls and some sitting outside of the salon, waiting their turns.

Charly had never seen this before. Especially not on a Thursday! She walked over to the sink where Robin and Lauren were washing hair and shook her head. "I wonder where all these people came from. I need y'all to speed it up a little so no one gets impatient and leaves before we get a chance to get that money."

Lauren nodded. "The girl in the red shirt said that there was a fight at Nina's salon and they closed early. So her and her friend came here to get their hair done."

Both Robin's and Charly's ears perked up. "A fight?" Charly asked. "Who was fighting in there today?"

Robin kept washing her client's hair but was focused on the dirt Lauren was dishing. Lauren shrugged her shoulders. "I don't know. I'll ask her when I'm finished with this shampoo."

Charly had no patience. She rolled up her sleeves and stepped in. "I'll finish her shampoo. Just go and find out what happened. The suspense is killing me!"

Lauren laughed and stepped away from the sink. She took a towel to dry her hands and headed over to the girl in the red shirt. Robin and Charly were too far away from the conversation to hear what was being said. So they both watched the body language of the client and Lauren's reaction to what she was telling her. Lauren held her hand over her mouth in shock. The client was animatedly describing the scene in Nina's salon, sitting on the edge of her seat and motioning with her hands as if hitting someone. Robin could hardly stand the wait as Lauren continued to talk to the girl in the red shirt. Finally, Robin saw Lauren making her way back to where the sinks were. When she got there, Charly and Robin were putting conditioner in each of their clients' hair and eagerly waiting to hear the juicy details.

Lauren wasted no time. "She said that Nina's man came in the shop and broke up with her in front of everybody."

"Well, we know he doesn't mean it, because he told her that the other day and he's still dealing with her." Charly was unimpressed with the way this gossip was shaping up. Plus she wanted to rub salt in Robin's wounds. Charly suspected that Robin was still feeling Ishmael.

Lauren continued, "This time the shit sounds serious. She said that Nina punched him in the face and he hit her back and knocked her out."

"What?" Robin was floored. "That doesn't even sound like Ishmael."

Charly cut a look at Robin and wondered how the hell she could possibly know what Ishmael would or wouldn't do. All Robin had ever been to him was a one-night stand. "So what happened after that?" Charly asked.

"Then he left. But some lady got all her hair burned out with a relaxer that Nina left on during the fight. So all their clients came here." Lauren winked at Charly and she smiled. Nina's loss was certainly their gain.

Charly headed back to the front of the salon while Lauren escorted the client to the dryer. As Charly called the next customer, Robin was on her cell phone, calling Ishmael.

CHAPTER ELEVEN

The Second Time Around

It was close to noon when Ishmael got a call from Robin. She was whispering so that nosy Charly wouldn't hear her. "What happened at Nina's shop, Ish? A whole bunch of new clients have been coming in here and saying that you and Nina had a fight."

Ishmael sighed as he leaned his head back against the pillows on the bed in his secret apartment. He figured he'd lay low for a few days to let the drama die down with Rah-lo. "We did have a fight. She told Rah-lo that I had a conversation with Celeste. Now I got this dude looking at me like I can't be trusted or like I double-crossed him or some shit."

Robin listened to Ishmael admit to fighting with Nina

and was surprised at him. "You knocked her out, Ishmael? I heard she punched you in your face, and that's fucked up. But you didn't have to hit her back like that."

Ishmael frowned and cursed the ghetto grapevine for the umpteenth time. "I didn't knock nobody out," he said. "And she didn't punch me in my face, either. We had an argument. She slapped me. Then she kept trying to hit me and I pushed her off me. That was it. Then I left." He sighed. "You see how people lie?"

Robin was relieved to hear that Ishmael hadn't hit Nina. She would have looked at him much differently if he had. "I thought you said that you were helping Rah-lo try to find Celeste. Why would he be mad at you for talking to her?" she asked.

"Yeah, I was helping him find her and I found her before he did. I sent her a message on MySpace and she sent me her number. Our whole conversation was about five minutes long," Ishmael said. Another lie, but he didn't want Robin to suspect that he felt more for Celeste than he should.

Robin wasn't sure she believed him, but she shrugged it off. Celeste was miles away. "You sound tired. Where are you now?"

"At my apartment. Why? You want to come over?"

Robin sighed. "No. I have about three more clients to do and then I have to get home to Hezekiah. My sister won't watch him tonight. She's going out."

Ishmael couldn't help feeling disappointed. "I'm starving right now. I was hoping you could come over here and feed me." His tone was suggestive and Robin smiled, remembering.

"Let me see if I can make that happen. I'll call you when I leave here."

Ishmael agreed and Robin hung up and got back to work.

Two hours later, she called Ishmael on his cell phone. When he answered she was parking her car outside of his house. "Are you still up for company?" she asked.

Ishmael had just woken up from a catnap. "Yeah. You coming over?"

"I'm outside. Come open the door."

Ishmael hung up the phone and trotted downstairs to let her in. He couldn't wait to get her in his bed once again. When he opened the door, he was surprised to see Robin standing with Hezekiah beside her. Ishmael's expression changed visibly and Robin noticed.

"I know this wasn't part of the plan," she said, nodding discreetly toward her son. "But my sister wasn't trying to hear me and I had no choice. You sounded like you needed a friend today, so I came over with food." She held a casserole dish in her hand. Looking at the disappointed expression on Ishmael's face, she wasn't sure that this had been a good idea after all. "If you want, you can take the food and

I'll come back for my dish tomorrow. I understand if you have other plans."

Ishmael wasn't thrilled about kids. He rarely dated women who had them and had only made an exception with Robin because she was so sexy. He looked down at young Hezekiah and the little boy peered back at him through wide eyes. He was a cute kid, Ishmael had to admit. And Hezekiah seemed calm enough not to fuck up Ishmael's high. "Nah," he said. "I don't have any other plans. Come on in."

Ishmael ushered them inside and up the stairs to his apartment. When they got inside, he heard his cell phone ringing and knew without looking that Nina was calling for the millionth time. He picked up his phone and turned it off. While Ishmael and Hezekiah sat awkwardly beside each other on the couch, Robin went to the kitchen and began heating up the chicken, macaroni and cheese, and cabbage she'd made.

Ishmael looked at the little boy and smiled. Hezekiah smiled back and looked around the room, taking it all in. Silence filled the space as Robin got Ishmael's food together. Hezekiah wondered why they were there. He wondered who Ishmael was and why his mom had gone through so much trouble to make sure that dinner was perfect tonight. Ishmael caught Hezekiah staring and he looked away quickly. His gaze fell on a video game system and he shifted excitedly in his seat.

"Is that Xbox 360?" he asked, his voice revealing the enthusiasm bubbling just below the surface.

Ishmael nodded and smiled. "Wanna play?"

Hezekiah nodded quickly and Ishmael passed him the wireless control. Picking up the second control, he challenged the little boy to a game of Madden. "You don't mind if I beat you, do you?" Ishmael asked jokingly.

Hezekiah laughed. "You can't beat me! I'm nice at this game!" Hezekiah sat Indian-style on the floor and prepared for war. They started the game and chose their teams, both of them talking trash. Robin watched them from the kitchen and smiled. They laughed and yelled at the TV when their plays didn't go as planned. It felt good to her to see Hezekiah finally have the chance to interact with a man other than his grandfather. Ishmael connected with the little boy easily and found himself enjoying the game so much that he didn't pause to eat when Robin brought his plate of hot food to him. Instead he gulped down the delicious meal in between plays, genuinely enjoying the battle with the six-year-old. Hezekiah beat him fair and square and Ishmael demanded a rematch. As they played a second game, Robin washed the dishes and imagined that every day could be like this—her, Hezekiah, and Ishmael, one big happy family.

It was close to eleven o'clock when Ishmael and Hezekiah prepared to play for a third time. "I hate to interrupt this little male-bonding session, but Hezzy's bedtime passed a long time ago. I need to get him home."

"Awww, Mommy! I was gonna beat him again!" Hezekiah protested.

Ishmael laughed. "I let you beat me once; you can't do it again."

"Yes, I can! Don't be embarrassed to tell your friends you got beat by a little kid."

Ishmael liked Hezekiah a lot. "Okay. I see you got a lot of confidence, kid. Tell you what. Next time Mommy brings you over to visit me, we'll play our tiebreaker. Whoever wins is the ultimate Madden champion. Deal?"

Hezekiah liked the sound of that. "Deal!" He put the control down and followed his mother to the door.

Ishmael stood tall over Robin and smiled at her. "Thanks for dinner. It was really good. I don't believe you cooked all that all by yourself. I didn't know you could cook like that."

Hezekiah chuckled. "She said it had to be perfect for you—"

"Stay out of grown folks' conversations, Hezzy!" Robin chastised him, embarrassed. She looked at Ishmael and said, "I'm glad you liked it. Next time it's your turn to cook."

Ishmael laughed at that and gave Hezekiah five. "We'll see. See you next time, little man."

"Okay," Hezekiah said, wondering why his mother seemed so shy around Ishmael.

Ishmael smiled at her. "I had fun. I'm glad you brought him over." Ishmael didn't kiss Robin good-bye out of respect for her son. Instead he pulled her into a firm hug and whispered in her ear, "Good night."

She melted. "Good night," she said, and then she and her son went home. On the way, Hezzy couldn't stop talking about Ishmael. Hezzy really liked him. Robin did, too. And she spent the whole drive home reminding herself that Ishmael wasn't the kind of man whom it was safe to give your heart to. Trouble was, it was already too late.

"You dirty, nasty, rotten pussy bitch!"

Robin sat up in bed and held the phone steady, hoping that her ears were deceiving her. "What?" she managed, her voice thick with sleep. It was one o'clock in the morning.

"You wait till I see you, Robin. Just wait. I know where you live, where you work, where your son goes to school," Nina said. "I will catch you. And when I do I'm gonna kick your filthy ass!"

Robin couldn't believe her ears. "Nina, you can't be serious. I know you're not threatening my son, you stupid bitch!"

"I'm not making threats, Robin. I'm dead serious. You'll see." Nina hung up the phone and Robin sat in the dark in disbelief. She dialed Ishmael's number and he answered on the fourth ring.

"Yo, Ish, your girl is really bugging out. She just called me and threatened me *and* Hezekiah."

"What?" Ishmael rubbed his hand across his face in exasperation. "What did she say?"

Robin recounted her conversation with Nina, and Ishmael listened closely. He knew that the shit was out of control now. "I'm sorry, ma. But she ain't really gonna do shit. She's just talking."

Robin shook her head. "I'm not taking no chances, Ishmael. I can't fuck with you no more. If she comes near me or Hezekiah I will kill that bitch. Seriously. And I can't deal with you anymore. This is too much."

Ishmael sighed. "Come on, ma—"

"Nah," she said. "It's over. Deal with your bitch and keep her away from me." She hung up the phone and Ishmael was left sitting in his apartment alone in silence. He lay back on his bed and looked at the ceiling feeling drained. He wished this was all a bad dream. In one day he had lost his childhood friend and Robin as well. As much as Ishmael hated to admit it, he was beginning to develop strong feelings for Robin—and her son. And now, thanks to Nina, Ishmael's relationship with Robin was over.

His phone ringing snapped him out of his trance. He saw Cito's number and quickly answered. "Whattup?"

Cito sighed. "Ish," he said in his heavy Spanish accent. "I cannot do business with you anymore, my friend."

Ishmael frowned. "What? What are you talking about?"

"Rah-lo gave me a call," Cito said. "He said you told him about our deal and he was very unhappy. Basically, what he told me is that if I keep dealing with you, he will find a new supplier. I can't afford that, Ish. Rah-lo brings me a lot of business—more than you will right now. And I assured him that I would not fuck with you anymore." Cito spoke very matter-of-factly and Ishmael was livid.

"Come on, Cito! You can't do this shit to me. I've been working with you just as long as Rah-lo has. How you gonna choose his side in this shit?"

Cito wouldn't budge. "You have both been dealing with me. This is true. But now Rah-lo has the bigger clientele, the bigger empire. He told me that you walked away from your partnership with nothing. That you will be building from the ground up. All the soldiers will remain with him. That means he will be doing bigger business with me than you will right now. You can't give them what he's giving them and therefore you won't bring in the money that he does. It's simple arithmetic, my friend. Rah-lo is a bigger player in this game. So I have to do what's best for my business."

Ishmael couldn't believe his ears. "So now I gotta find someone else to get my shit from. I got money, Cito. I got clientele. You gonna cut me off just like that?"

"I'm afraid so. It's nothing personal. I like you, Ish—"

"Fuck you, Cito!" Ishmael hung up and paced the floor in a rage. Rah-lo was playing hardball.

Ishmael picked up his cell phone and scrolled through

the numbers until he found Celeste's name. He dialed the number.

"Hello?" she answered.

"Hey," Ish said. "Change of plans. I think I'm gonna come down there sooner than I thought."

CHAPTER TWELVE

Georgia on My Mind

Hours later, Celeste's phone rang again. She knew that Ishmael was on his way. He had told her that he would be on the first flight out in the morning. But it was still dark outside. Surely he hadn't arrived so soon. She answered the phone, cursing under her breath, eager for a few hours of uninterrupted sleep.

A familiar voice came through the receiver. "Don't hang up."

Celeste looked at her bedside clock and saw that it was 4:40 A.M. "Rah-lo?" she asked, holding the phone close to her ear. "Do you know how late it is?"

Rah-lo was aware of the late hour but didn't care. He

had to talk to her. "I'm sorry I woke you up. I just had to say this to you and I couldn't wait."

Celeste clicked on her Tiffany bedside lamp and propped herself up on her elbow, sighing. "What?"

"I still love you."

The words hung in the distance between them as Celeste closed her eyes and pictured his face. She thought about all the times he'd said that he loved her over the years, how good it used to feel to hear him say it. But those days were gone. It was too late for that now. "Raheem, I have to work in the morning. . . ."

"I know." He thought about it. "What kind of work do you do?"

Celeste stifled a yawn. "I work in marketing. Advertising, promotion, things like that."

"Wow," Rah-lo said. "That sounds official. You like it?"

"Yeah," Celeste said, rolling her eyes. "But I won't like it tomorrow if you keep me up all night talking."

"I know it's late," he said. "And I don't mean to be inconsiderate. But I need you to know how I feel about you. I never stopped loving you, baby girl."

Celeste shook her head. "I can't do this."

"Just listen. I should have been with you all along. I was just trying to do right by my kids."

"So then what gave you the guts to leave now?" Celeste frowned.

"I asked you to just listen."

She fought the urge to smile. Who did he think he was?

"I got with Asia for all the wrong reasons. By the time I realized how miserable I was, I had three little girls and a wife who was teaching them wrong. So I thought the right thing to do was stay there and be a father to my kids. Asia just came along with the deal. I never loved her like I love you."

"Listen—"

"Nah. *You* listen. Why can't you just understand that I was stupid to let you leave here? I wish I would've come down there to get you when you left. I didn't see how I could have you and my daughters at the same time. Asia wouldn't have let me see them if I left her back then. Now they're older. They understand more, and they can get to me on their own. I just wanted to tell you that I'm serious about seeing you again. I need to look you in your eyes and tell you some things. That's why I contacted you."

Celeste couldn't believe her ears. "Are you done?"

"Yeah."

"First of all you contacted me because Nina gave you the number. Ishmael is the one who found me. So who really wants to see me again, Rah-lo? You or your boy?" Celeste knew she was hitting a nerve and she loved the feeling. "Second of all, you're crazy for even calling me at this time of night. You don't know if I got a man or what."

"Do you?"

"That's none of your business," she spat. "Stop calling

me. I'm not interested in your sob story. You had a wife. You had no time for me. I walked away and you let me."

"Is that how you see it?"

"That's how it is. Good night." Celeste hung up the phone and then turned the ringer off. She threw herself back on the pillows and covered her face with the sheet, hoping to run from Rah-lo's voice in her ears.

In the morning, Rah-lo thought about his conversation with Celeste. She sounded so mad at him, and he hated that. She wasn't giving him a chance to explain. In his mind it wasn't that he had chosen Asia over Celeste. Instead, he believed that he had never had much of a choice to start with. It really was all about his little girls. He reasoned that all he needed was to see Celeste face-to-face to convince her that he loved her. He made up his mind that he was going to Atlanta to get her.

He packed his bags and called the airport to book a flight. Ishmael crossed his mind and Rah-lo shook his head. Yesterday he had paid a visit to Cito. He hadn't confirmed that Ishmael was indeed doing business for himself on the side. Cito refused to go so far as to snitch on the guy. But Cito did acknowledge that Ishmael—and a lot of dudes who played the sidekick role—would eventually get hungry. Cito told Rah-lo to keep in mind that Ish wasn't working a day job anymore. Chances were that Ishmael would want to make more money, and Cito told Rah-lo that he had to expect that. While it wasn't the admission of guilt that Rah-lo had hoped for, his discussion with Cito had been all that Rah-lo needed to hear. He was finished with Ishmael both as a friend and as a business partner. Rah-lo called one of his workers and left him in charge. Then he loaded up his car and headed for the airport.

On the way, Rah-lo scrolled through his Blackberry. Dialing a number, he weaved across the nearly empty expressway. "What up, Uncle James?" Rah-lo spoke into his cell phone. "Yeah, I'm on my way down there and I want to crash at your crib for a while."

Rah-lo's uncle James was older than Rah-lo's mother by seven years, which meant that he was about sixty-seven years old. He had been a very protective older brother to Rah-lo's mom. When she died at the age of fifty, James had taken it the hardest. He left New York City, moved to Atlanta, and had a modest home there, which he shared with his much younger wife and her two young sons. It was the family joke. Clearly, Uncle James was the twentysomething woman's sugar daddy, but he didn't give a damn. Rah-lo had only met his uncle's wife once, and she and her kids had left a lasting impression. Her boys were rude and they asked questions and said things that they had no business asking or saying to grown folks. Rah-lo wasn't really looking forward to spending time with his uncle and his newfound family. But Rah-lo didn't know how long he would be in Atlanta before he found Celeste.

And in the event that he did find her, he might need some place to stay for a while. Staying in a hotel long-term could end up being costly. That's where Uncle James came in.

"Yeah, come on down here, boy. You can stay for as long as you want." Uncle James was thrilled to have Raheem coming to stay with him for a while. Ever since his sister Vivian had died years prior, James had wanted to connect with her son and make sure that the young man was living right. James knew enough about Rah-lo to know that he sold drugs, that he was fresh out of jail, and that he had a wife, with a girlfriend on the side. But James didn't know much more than that. This trip, his nephew coming to stay with him, would be a great opportunity for James to get to know the young man better.

Rah-lo was grateful to have his uncle's house to crash at. James made his living as a loan shark and dabbled in illegal numbers. His house was comfortable and he drove the flyest cars. Rah-lo laughed to himself as he hung up the phone, thinking that his uncle's gold-digging wife was probably driving all the fly cars now. He parked his car in the long-term parking section in the Continental Airlines terminal and dialed Asia's number.

She answered almost immediately. "You can call and talk to the girls and not me?" she asked, not even hesitating to start her usual bullshit.

"Up until now I had nothing to say to you," he told her. "I'm leaving town for a couple of weeks."

"Rah-lo, don't play with me. Ishmael said you been left town." Asia frowned.

"Ishmael don't know what the fuck he's talking about. Either that or he just threw some shit in the game. I never left town. But I'm leaving today. I parked my car at the airport and there's money in the glove compartment. Come get my car and hold it till I get back." Rah-lo knew that he'd never see the money again. And there was a chance that he might not see his car again, knowing Asia. She was likely to do anything. But he knew that she would ensure that his daughters were taken care of as long as he gave her the money to do so. Rasheeda had already told him that they'd been staying at their grandmother's house, with Asia dropping off money every couple of days. Now she could give her mother a lump sum, which would keep Mrs. Hudson's mouth shut. At least then he would know that his girls were safe. Asia's mom may be a bitch, but she took good care of her grandchildren.

Asia couldn't believe her ears. She was excited at the prospect of a lump sum of cash but concerned about where Rah-lo was running off to. "Where the fuck are you going, Raheem? We still never got the chance to talk about what happened."

Rah-lo shook his head. "There ain't shit to talk about, Asia. Just come get my car and get the money. When I get back I'll give you some more dough. Where's the girls?"

"They're at my mother's house," Asia answered flatly.

"They were at your mother's house on Wednesday when I called. What's up with that?"

"Don't worry about it. We ain't together no more, right?" Asia's attempt to make Rah-lo jealous fell flat.

"Right. I'll call you when I get back." Rah-lo hung up the phone and made his way to his departure gate.

Flight 1121 for Atlanta, Georgia, is now boarding at Gate 8A.

Rah-lo walked over to the desk and gave his ticket and ID to the airline employee. She smiled at him, in a manner that was clearly forced, and he walked past her without returning the gesture. Once aboard the plane, he took out a folded-up piece of paper he had been carrying in his pocket. He opened it up and read the note Celeste had scrawled for him when she'd left.

"Life is short and I don't want to look back on mine with any regrets." Rah-lo folded the note and stuck it back inside his pocket. He had read it a million times over the past few years, and he still couldn't believe that Celeste had walked away from him. He thought about all the memories they'd made over the years. The trips, the dinner dates, the rainy nights they spent making love to the rhythm of the drops on the windowpane. He thought about how she looked in the morning when the sunlight caressed her face, and how she looked at him with her eyes so full of love. These were all things he missed about her, things he hadn't found in his wife. Celeste's words rang in his head. *Life* is *short,* he thought, and he was tired of living a life full of regret. He regretted letting her walk out of his life, regretted sacrificing his own happiness for the sake of everyone else's. But he didn't regret leaving Asia. Not for one second.

He glanced out the window on the plane and looked into the clouds that surrounded him. In about forty minutes, his flight would be landing in Atlanta. He intended to find Celeste and to win her back. This time, he was playing for keeps.

Nina walked into Charly's and headed straight for Robin. Robin looked up just in time to see Nina swinging at her, fists balled up and ready for war.

"You thought I was playing, bitch? You wanna fuck my man?" Nina was out of control. Robin ducked and dodged Nina's blows and then jumped on her, knocking her to the floor. Nina kept swinging, catching Robin a few times. But Robin was surprisingly strong and she was soon straddling Nina, punching her again and again. The two women fought like cats as the patrons in Charly's shop looked on in amazement.

The man whose hair Robin had been braiding tried to intervene and separate the women. But he was afraid that he would be hit by one of the many blows thrown between them. Finally, he managed to pry Robin away from Nina and Charly stepped in and held Nina back.

"Calm the fuck down!" Charly yelled at Nina as she tried to get free. "Coming in here with this bullshit. You two should be embarrassed, fighting over Ishmael like this!"

Robin shot Charly an incredulous glance since she herself had fought over Ishmael at one time. As Robin turned her attention back to Nina, Robin's chest heaved with anger. "You're crazy!" she yelled. "He don't want you, bitch. Leave it alone."

"Fuck you!" Nina said. "He definitely doesn't want you! He's only fucking your dumb ass!" Nina tried to charge at Robin again, but Charly held her tightly. "Stay away from him, Robin!"

Robin smirked. "He told me it's over with you and him, Nina. He told you, too. So as far as I'm concerned, he's a single man. I'm gonna keep fucking him for as long as I want. And I'm gonna keep letting him eat my pussy, too, you stupid bitch!"

Robin knew that she was stooping to Nina's level by antagonizing her with the details of her and Ishmael's sex life. But she was heated. This bitch had charged into Robin's place of work and tried to kick her ass. At that moment, rationality went out the window.

Hearing Robin describe Ishmael going down on her was enough to make Charly want to cry. Damn, she missed Ishmael's oral expertise! She was so jealous that she was tempted to let Nina go and let the two women fight all over again. But Nina would probably kill Robin if Charly let her go. And then who would Charly get to braid hair as well as Robin did?

"Nina, get out of my shop," Charly said as calmly as she could. "I don't come in your shop starting shit, so don't come in mine with that bullshit, either." Charly half-dragged Nina to the door. Nina was far from done.

"This ain't over, bitch! I swear to God I will kill you if you ever go near him again!"

Charly ushered Nina outside and she stormed off toward her car. Nina could not stop crying. To her, all of this was Robin's fault. If she hadn't been fucking with Ishmael, he might still be in Nina's life. As of now, Nina hadn't heard a word from him since he stormed out of her shop. She feared that this time he meant business and that it really was over for good. She got into her car and called Ishmael once more. Again, she got his voice mail and she hung up fuming with anger. She dialed Asia's number and was relieved when she answered. Nina needed desperately to commiserate.

"Have you found Rah-lo yet?" Nina asked.

Asia told Nina about her conversation with Rah-lo when he was at the airport. "I'm gonna go down there," she said. "I'm not gonna just let another bitch have my husband."

Nina knew exactly what Asia meant. She wasn't about to let Robin have Ishmael, either. Nina filled Asia in on her fight with Robin and what Robin had said about Ishmael going down on her.

Asia was flabbergasted. "See?" she said, amping it up. "I would have to kill that bitch for saying some shit like that to me."

What Asia didn't know was that Nina had threatened Robin's child as well. Nina had conveniently left that part out. "Have you heard from Ishmael?" Asia asked.

Nina closed her eyes and shook her head. "No," she said. "He won't answer any of my calls."

"Mine, either," Asia said. "Him and Rah-lo are both ignoring my calls and messages."

Nina tried not to cry. "But that's okay," she said. "Ishmael can't ignore me forever." Even as she said it, Nina wasn't so sure. She felt that this was really the end as far as Ishmael was concerned. And it tore her heart into a thousand pieces.

"I'm not letting another bitch just take my husband without a fight," Asia said.

Nina nodded. "I know exactly what you mean," she said. She would do whatever it took to get Ishmael back.

Asia called her mother and explained the situation to her. "I know you've had the kids all week, but I need you to keep them just a little while longer." Asia asked her mother to watch the kids for her while she went and tried to salvage her marriage. "Ma, I know how you feel about him," Asia said.

"Like hell you know. You don't have a clue how much I can't stand that miserable bastard. What do you need him for, Asia? He's not making money the way he used to make it. He's no longer an asset. Now he's a liability. He got arrested with his mistress in a house you didn't even know he owned. What more do you need to see before you make up your mind and walk away from this bullshit? What you need to do is divorce his broke ass and take him to child support court for all them kids you done laid there and had with him. Make that muthafucka pay for leaving you by yourself. And then you go and find you a man who can *really* provide."

Asia rolled her eyes. She hadn't expected her mother to understand that it wasn't so simple for her. Asia didn't really love Rah-lo anymore. She cared about him. But love had gone away a long time ago. Still, she would be damned if another bitch would have him. All the years Asia had put in with Rah-lo were not going to be wasted. She would not allow Celeste to win, to take the man she had invested so many years in and make him her own. No. Asia was going to fight tooth and nail to ensure that her husband came back home to her and their children, no matter how unhappy that home was. "I'm going after him, Ma. Now if you don't want to watch the girls, it's all right. I will ask somebody else. But I don't need the lecture right now. I'm going to Atlanta in the morning."

Mrs. Hudson shook her head. "You don't even know if

he went to Atlanta. What if he went to Chicago or Char-
lotte? For all you know, he could have a chick in every
state."

"I know he went to Atlanta because I checked his checking account statement and he put a one-way ticket on his
debit card. So I'm not just running around the country
looking for him."

"And you just gon' go on down there and chase after
that fucker like he has a golden dick swinging between his
legs—"

"Ma!"

"Ma, my ass, Asia! I raised you better than that. If a man
don't want you, he don't want you. I told you that when you
came crying to me about him having that chick on the side.
I told you that when you kept getting pregnant trying to
hold on to him."

"I wasn't trying to hold on to Rah-lo by getting pregnant," Asia protested, wiping tears out of the corners of her
eyes.

"Yes, you were, and you know it. Every time shit got bad
between you two and Raheem started spending more time
away from home, miraculously you got pregnant. Like
clockwork. You don't fool me."

Asia sat silent, knowing her mother spoke the truth.

Mrs. Hudson knew that her daughter was still on the line
because she could hear her breathing. She decided to ease up
just a little. "You can leave my granddaughters over here so I

can make sure they're okay while you're gone. I'll take them to school every day and to dance class and all that shit you got them signed up for. Bring some money by here before you leave, too! But let me tell you one thing. You have to let him go if he don't want to be with you, Asia. If a man don't love you, there's nothing you can do but let him go. It hurts like hell. I know it does. But you gotta bow out gracefully and let him go so that you can move on with your life and he can move on with his. All this foolishness is affecting your kids. You can go and try and save your marriage if you want to. But you and I both know it's been over for a very long time. If this doesn't work and Rah-lo doesn't come back to you, I want you to pick yourself up and start over again on your own. There's a man out there who will love you for you. Trust me."

Asia felt the tears rolling down her cheeks because what her mother was telling her was truer than she probably knew. But Asia was stubborn. She was hurt that Rah-lo wanted to end their marriage, hurt that he had walked out on her. But what hurt more was the thought that another woman might actually love him the way that Asia knew he really deserved. She also couldn't bear the thought of having to support herself and having to give up the lavish, lackadaisical lifestyle she had grown accustomed to. There was no way Asia was giving all that up without a fight.

She dried her eyes, said, "Thanks, Ma," and hung up the

phone. Asia took a deep breath and began to pack her clothes.

Ishmael stepped off the plane and walked into the airport terminal. Almost immediately he spotted Celeste waiting for him at the gate. Beside her stood another lovely young lady whom Ishmael didn't recognize. He smiled, seeing Celeste for the first time in so long. Despite the fact that they had never even shared a kiss, he felt a strong emotional and physical connection to her. The chemistry between them had been undeniable once. He wondered if that had changed.

Celeste couldn't stop staring at him. He was still so damn fine! Keisha all but jumped out of her panties at the sight of him.

"Hello, stranger." Ishmael dropped his bags and grabbed Celeste in a big bear hug, scooping her off her feet. She squealed in delight and hugged him back tightly. When he finally put her down she was smiling so hard that she was blushing.

"Aren't you gonna introduce us?" Keisha asked, looking Ishmael up and down. She liked what she saw.

Celeste shook her head in amazement. "This is my friend Ishmael," she said, unable to stop smiling. "Ishmael, this is my friend Keisha."

Keisha smiled. "Is he a *single* friend?" Ishmael was a beautiful man! He looked even better in person than he did on his MySpace page. He was tall, had a nice build and a smile that made her want to slip into something more comfortable.

Celeste shrugged her shoulders. "I don't know," she said, looking at Ishmael. "Are you?"

Ishmael smiled and nodded. "Yeah, absolutely." He wondered why seeing Celeste smiling at him was such a thrill. She looked better than she had the last time he'd seen her. Which was saying a lot, because to Ishmael Celeste always looked flawless. "I like your haircut," he told her.

She smiled. "Thanks."

An awkward silence enveloped them and Keisha filled it. "So, are we gonna stand here all day smiling and staring or should we go get something to eat? I'm starving." She had come along with Celeste because Celeste was nervous about seeing Ishmael again after so long. Now that Keisha saw the two of them together she could understand why. Their connection was unmistakable.

Celeste nodded. "Come on," she said, taking Ishmael by the arm. "Let's go feed you some real southern cooking."

They headed to Keisha's favorite soul food restaurant and got comfortable at a corner table.

"So, Ishmael," Keisha said, batting her eyelashes. "What brings you to Atlanta?"

He looked at Celeste and was tempted to tell Keisha that her friend had brought him there. That was the truth. That and the fact that Nina and Rah-lo's bullshit had gotten to be too much for him. But he didn't need to divulge all of that right now. "I had some business to handle down here and I was gonna come in another week or so," he said instead. "But after I talked to Celeste the other day, I felt like I should come down here a little early and get reacquainted with an old friend." He sipped his drink.

Celeste said nothing. She couldn't help noticing that the years hadn't changed him much. He looked good, smelled good, and Celeste was momentarily distracted. She snapped out of it when the waitress came to take their orders. They made small talk until their food arrived. Biting into her salmon, Celeste looked across the table at Ishmael. "I'm glad to see you again, Ish. It's been a long time."

Keisha wasn't letting them off the hook with pleasantries. She wanted to know the real deal. "So, Ishmael, tell the truth. Are you here doing Rah-lo's dirty work or what? Did he send you down here to find Celeste and get her to take him back?" To Keisha, this was better than *All My Children*.

Ishmael shook his head. "Rah-lo don't even know that I'm here."

Celeste was relieved to hear that. Seeing Ishmael again was enough of a distraction from her new life. She didn't need to see Rah-lo and lose her focus completely. "Good," she said. "I came down here to get away from all that bullshit. I got tired of being Rah-lo's secret. And I got sick of all the fighting between me, Charly, Nina, and Robin and Asia. I needed to get away from that."

Ishmael laughed. "I know exactly what you mean." Ishmael explained about Nina and their breakup, Robin and his unexpected feelings for her and how she broke up with him, and Charly and her thirst for drama. He recounted the fight at Rah-lo's house and how their friendship had ended. Celeste listened attentively and so did Keisha. For Keisha, all of this was extremely exhilarating, and she hoped that sexy Ishmael liked Atlanta enough to stay for a long time. She hadn't had this much excitement in years.

They finished their meal and headed out to Celeste's car. Along the way, Keisha and Celeste pointed out Atlanta's hot spots. Ishmael soaked it all up. Celeste drove Keisha home and dropped her off. She felt comfortable enough with Ishmael now and she no longer needed the third party.

Keisha bid them both good-bye and climbed out of the car. "See you soon, Ishmael," she said, winking at him. "Celeste, I'll call you later." Keisha sashayed inside of her house as Celeste drove away.

Now that they were alone, Ishmael couldn't keep his eyes off of Celeste. He remembered when he would've given everything to be with her. But her love for Rah-lo had always prevented that. "Celeste, do you still love him?"

She was caught off guard by Ishmael's question. "Who? Rah-lo?" She took her eyes off the road and looked at him briefly before refocusing on her driving. She sighed, shook her head. But she couldn't deny the truth. "I do love him, Ishmael. I do. I'm just at a different point in my life now. I don't want to deal with all that drama anymore, Asia and all that. I don't want to be involved with a drug dealer, worrying that he's not coming home at night because he could be dead or locked up. Who still hustles at our age?" When she had met Rah-lo, Celeste was infatuated by the lifestyle he lived. The money, the power and respect, the drama, the intrigue, and even the violence were exciting to Celeste in the beginning. She had never been with a guy like Rah-lo. But as she got older and matured, she began to realize what an ignorant mentality she had adopted as a result of the life she was living. The money was intoxicating and the lifestyle was one that most women would envy. But she began to feel empty despite all of that. She began to question whether it was wise for her to be involved in such a serious relationship with a man who was not only married but also deeply rooted in the drug game. Celeste wanted more. She wanted her own success, her own money, and her own man.

Ishmael looked at her blankly. He wondered what she thought of him, since he also hustled. "Well, you know that's what we do, Celeste. So what? That's not good enough for you now that you came to Atlanta?"

Celeste hadn't meant to offend Ishmael. Even though he had worked with Rah-lo, she had never seen Ishmael as just a drug dealer. He had a day job—or at least he did at one time—so she thought of him as a workingman who hustled a little here and there. "It's not that I'm too good for anything. I'm just tired of all of that shit, Ishmael."

He understood. "Well, I can't speak about baggage because my baggage just fucked up my friendship and my sex life."

Celeste laughed. "Well, at least you were smart enough not to get married or have a whole bunch of kids. I dealt with more than some jealous ex-girlfriends. I had a wife, kids, a whole other life that he was living apart from me to contend with."

Ishmael watched her smile fade. He thought Rah-lo was a fool. Having had a few drinks during lunch, Ishmael was feeling loose and began to speak from his heart. "I used to have the biggest crush on you, Celeste."

She smiled, wondering what she should say. She didn't want to act as if she had no idea that Ishmael had feelings for her. She had known that for years. And she'd had feelings for him, too, at one time. But that had been years ago. "I had a crush on you, too. But Rah-lo would've killed both of us if we had ever acted on those feelings."

Ishmael nodded. "I know. But that didn't stop me from feeling what I felt. If you would've told me that you felt the same way that I felt, I would've taken a chance with Rah-lo. By the time he found out about us we could've been long gone."

Celeste smiled but didn't know how to respond. Ishmael could tell she felt uneasy about what he had just said and he decided to correct himself. "I know that sounds foul. Rah-lo is my friend. At least he was. I wouldn't want to hurt my friend. But you can't help who you love. And I think that when you left town I was starting to fall in love with you."

"Really?" Celeste asked, flattered.

"Yeah, really. I thought Rah-lo was a fool for having you wait for him. We meet a lot of women in this line of work. Most of them just want to see what you can do for them. They don't want to do shit for themselves. But you were different. You had goals and you didn't sit around waiting for shit to happen. You made shit happen. I admired that. When Rah-lo was locked up, you were faithful to him. Even though the dude was married to somebody else, you took your role as his shorty seriously and you didn't cheat on him—at least not while I was around. And you know Charly would've ratted you out if she caught you creeping, so I had no reason to believe that you were being anything but a good woman for Rah-lo. It just seemed like every time you needed him, he was nowhere in sight. When Dre did that to you, and then when your shop burned down, Rah-lo was with his wife and his kids. I felt like a good woman like you deserved a man who would be there for her all the time. Not just some of the time. I wanted you real bad back then. And I knew it would cost me my friendship. But at that point I didn't even care about that. I just knew that I wanted you." Ishmael looked at her and waited for her response.

Celeste felt conflicted. Even though she was no longer with Rah-lo, something seemed wrong about having this conversation with his former best friend. "What about Nina? I mean I know she fucked up now. But you did love her before all of this started, right?"

Ishmael shrugged. "Yeah, I guess so. I cared about her. But she wanted too much too fast and I wasn't for that. I was just happy taking it one day at a time and seeing where it leads us. But she wanted it all—the marriage, the kids, the house, the picket fence—right now! She didn't want to wait. And I got sick of hearing her nag me about it all the time. I started flirting with Robin because I was sick of Nina's bullshit. And then me flirting with Robin led to something else. I'm feeling Robin, Celeste. When I'm around her I get like . . . nervous."

Celeste laughed. "Nervous, huh? You?"

Ishmael laughed, too. "Word. Me! I get like butterflies in my stomach. Not just 'cause she looks good, either. She's mad smart, and she wants to do something productive with her life. Nina can draw. The girl has a real talent for art. But she doesn't want to pursue it. She's content doing hair for the rest of her life." He glanced out the window. "Not that there's anything wrong with doing hair," he clarified. "But she can do more than just do hair. She can draw; she can cook. She's like a black Martha Stewart. She's just settling for what she already knows instead of trying to do what she loves. For some people, that's enough. But I just feel like if you got a talent you should use it. Why waste it?"

Celeste pulled up in the parking lot of her condo and parked her car. "Well, this is it," she said, popping the trunk so that he could retrieve his bags. Ishmael climbed out of the car and gathered his things. Then he followed Celeste up to her place. He was impressed. The place was beautiful. Celeste opened her door and heard the telephone ringing. She scurried for the phone and answered just in time.

"Do you know Oslo?" her grandmother screamed into the phone. Nana was eighty-four years old and almost completely deaf. She heard what she wanted to hear, though. Celeste's mother, Zara, called it convenient deafness. But Nana did have a hearing problem, which caused her to scream her words at people as if *they* couldn't hear *her*. Right now, Celeste was wondering if *she* had heard correctly.

Celeste froze. "What did you say, Nana?"

"Who is Rah-lo? Or Oslo or something like that."

Celeste knew who it was. The name alone gave her chills. "Why?" she asked. "Where did you get that name from?"

"Huh?" Nana yelled.

"Why?" Celeste said much louder. "Where did you get that name from?"

"Oh. Somebody called here and said they found our number listed in the phone book. Said his name was Rah-lo or Oslo or—"

"Okay, Nana, what else did he say?" Celeste was eager for details.

"He asked for you. Asked if he had the right number for Celeste Styles, Zara's daughter. I told him that you don't live here, but I am your grandmother. He was very nice. He asked about my arthritis like he knew me or something. I don't know how he knew I had it, but it was sure nice of him to ask."

Celeste rolled her eyes. Rah-lo sure knew how to lay on the charm when he needed to. "Well, Nana, I used to be in a relationship with him back when I was living in New York," she explained. Ishmael sat on the couch, frowning as he listened to Celeste's side of the conversation. She was obviously referring to Rah-lo.

"I see," Nana said, sucking in a deep breath as if she had just been told some deep, dark secret. "Well, he seems like quite a nice young man. He told me that he is in town and he wants to meet with you to talk about some kind of business."

"Business?" Celeste was confused.

"Mmm-hmmm."

Celeste frowned, completely confused. What could he possibly want after all these years? She had already told him to forget about it. She wasn't about to go back to being his mistress, so whatever he had to say would be a waste of her time. She quickly brushed her thoughts of Rah-lo aside and turned her attention back to her grandmother. "Nana, did you talk to him for a long time?"

"Yup," Nana said, as if proud of herself. "Told him that you're still single and I gave him your address."

"What?" Celeste dropped the earrings she had just taken off. "Why, Nana? Why did you do that?"

" 'Cuz he was such a nice young man and you need to meet a nice young man. You don't want to grow old and be all lonely like your mama," Nana said.

Celeste suppressed a laugh. If Zara had heard her mother

say that, there would've been a huge argument. "Nana, please don't give my personal information out to people over the phone. What if I don't want to see this man? Now he knows where I live and he can pop up whenever he wants."

Hearing this, Ishmael shifted in his seat. If Rah-lo knew where Celeste lived he could be on his way there at that very moment. Ishmael couldn't wait for Celeste to get off the phone so that he could find out what was going on. If Rah-lo was on his way over, Ishmael wanted to be ready for him.

"Don't worry about that, baby. I could tell he's a good man."

"Just by talking to him over the phone?" Celeste asked.

"Mmm-hmmm. You don't get to be my age without learning a few tricks." Nana laughed at her own wit. "I just called to tell you that you should be expecting his call. Now I gotta go. *Wheel of Fortune* is coming on."

"Good-bye, Nana." Celeste was pissed.

"Bye." Nana hung up and ran to get her daily glimpse of that cutie Pat Sajak.

Celeste hung up and turned to face Ishmael. "Rah-lo's in town," she said. "And my grandmother gave him my address."

She plopped down on the sofa beside Ishmael. She looked at him to see and gauge his reaction. Ishmael sat expressionless. But in his mind he knew that if Rah-lo came by and caught him there, one of them would be carried out in a body bag. But Ishmael didn't give a fuck. Rah-lo had cut Ishmael off from his money. Any loyalty he had once felt for Rah-lo was gone.

Celeste couldn't imagine why he had come to town or how long he planned to stay. It had been four years since she'd last seen or heard from him. Four years since she had walked out of his life and started over. And now here he was bringing back all the old emotions she had just begun to bury and dredging up emotions she no longer wanted to feel. She wondered if he looked the same, if he was different in any way. And then she was angry with herself for even caring what he looked like or what had changed about him. She didn't want to care about him anymore. She wanted to forget about him and move on with her life at last.

She gave Ishmael a quick tour of her home and then invited him to get comfortable in her spare bedroom. Ishmael brought his bags into the room and Celeste turned to leave. "I'm going out with Bryson again tonight," she told Ishmael. He frowned and then caught himself and brightened up. "Make yourself at home and let me know if you need anything before I leave."

Ishmael nodded. "I'll chill here till you get back," he said. "Tomorrow I need to rent a car so I can do what I came down here to do." He smiled. "I'll let Bryson have you tonight. But tomorrow night don't make any plans. I want you all to myself."

Celeste smiled and felt herself blushing again. She went to her bathroom and took a shower and dressed for her date.

By the time she applied her makeup and went to check on Ishmael, she found him sprawled out fast asleep across the bed, fully clothed. Celeste smiled and shook her head. She headed to the living room and grabbed her car keys off the coffee table. The phone rang once again. She glanced at it on the way out the door and decided not to answer it. For all she knew, it could have been Rah-lo calling. Celeste felt like the walls were closing in on her. She had left New York and here New York was chasing her once more. Ishmael was in her spare bedroom and Rah-lo was hot on her trail. The only thing that could have made it worse was if the Dime Piece stylists suddenly converged on her new town. She got in her car and sped off toward the restaurant to meet Bryson.

"Fuck Rah-lo," she told herself. "He blew his chance." She repeated the phrase over and over in her head, unsure why she was trying so hard to convince herself that she no longer loved him.

"Hello, may I speak to Rah-lo, please?"

Uncle James balanced the phone on his shoulder while he washed the dishes. Wanda's kids loved to eat, but they never took the time to wash out their dirty dishes. The sink was piled high, the kids were running around outside making all kinds of noise, and Wanda was nowhere to be found. James was frustrated, to say the least. "Rah-lo ain't here right now. He should be back later on tonight. Who's calling?" he asked. But the caller had hung up already. James shrugged his shoulders and went back to the chore at hand, grumbling under his breath about his girlfriend's lazy, bad-ass kids. If she didn't make him holler in the bedroom, she would've been history long ago. Her and her damn kids.

Meanwhile, Asia hung up the phone and shook her head. Rah-lo had taken her and the kids down to Atlanta close to six years ago. They had spent a couple of weeks there that summer, getting all of his mother's affairs settled. He had brought his uncle the things that his mom had left for him. A family Bible, photo albums filled with pictures of long-dead relatives, and several other family mementos. It had been a great summer that year, with Rah-lo and Asia reconnecting emotionally and the kids running around in the hot Atlanta sun. When Nina told Asia that Rah-lo had gone looking for Celeste in Atlanta, she wondered if he would pay for a hotel or stay with family. As a shot in the dark, she called Uncle James's house and asked for Rah-lo. James had played right into her hands. Now she knew exactly where her husband was. And she was damn sure going to get him and bring him back to his senses.

Celeste lay beside Bryson and stared at the ceiling. She had slept with him again, and this time was just as good as the first time. She was feeling Bryson. His conversation was great, his sex was even better, and best of all, he was successful and handsome. He had no kids, no wife, no drama. Bryson was a perfect match for her. As she tossed and turned, trying desperately not to awaken him, she wondered why she couldn't get Rah-lo off her mind. She wondered why she even cared that he was in Atlanta. She second-guessed letting Ishmael stay at her place. Somehow her past had come crashing through the door of her new life.

Bryson woke up and caught Celeste lying awake. "What's the matter?" he asked, his voice sexy and heavy with sleep.

"Nothing," she said. "Go back to sleep. I just woke up and couldn't fall back asleep."

"You need some help?" he asked, moving closer to her.

She smiled. She really liked this guy. "No. You're just trying to make me scream again." She snuggled close to him and he wrapped his legs around her. She felt so at peace in his arms, and his heartbeat lulled her to sleep as she vowed that tomorrow she wouldn't give Rah-lo a moment's thought.

The next morning, Ishmael awoke to the sound of his cell phone ringing. He glanced at the bedside clock and saw that it was 11:27 A.M. Celeste must be at work. He stretched his long body and reached over to the nightstand to answer his phone. "Yeah," he said.

"Ishmael, how come you don't answer my calls all of a sudden? I know you got my messages." It was Asia, and Ishmael regretted answering the private number. "I have to block my number in order to talk to you?" she asked.

"It's not like that, Asia. Rah-lo's on some bullshit right now. I don't know what to tell you about your boy."

Asia was all ears. "What do you mean? What kind of bullshit?"

Ishmael replayed his conversation with Rah-lo over in his head and lied. "He won't talk to me anymore. We had a fight and that's that." Ishmael lay back in his bed.

Asia held the phone silently. She thought that Ishmael was lying through his teeth. "Rah-lo is in Atlanta at his uncle James's house. He went down there to find Celeste."

"For real?" Ishmael asked, wondering how the hell Asia knew that.

Asia was enraged, but she kept her cool. "Ishmael, you knew all along where he was. That's why you didn't answer my phone calls."

Ishmael rolled his eyes. He didn't need this drama first thing in the morning. "Nah, Asia. I didn't know that."

Now Asia was incensed. Ishmael was insulting her intelligence. "Nina's the one who told me where my husband is."

Ishmael laughed. "Keep listening to Nina if you want to."

"Ish, please! Don't play games. It's funny how your girlfriend could tell me so much and yet you supposedly don't know shit. After all the years we've known each other, Ishmael.

You had all that loyalty to Celeste, but you treat me like a stranger. All those years you and her got so close. I bet you didn't keep no secrets from that bitch! I know all about how you used to drive her upstate to visit Rah-lo and hang around her hair salon every day. No wonder Nina thinks you wanted to fuck Celeste, too."

"Asia, listen—"

"No, Ish, *you* listen. I'm on my way down to Atlanta now. So, tell Rah-lo that if he's with that bitch Celeste I'm gonna cut his fuckin' dick off!" Asia hung up the phone and Ishmael put his phone back on the nightstand and shook his head. Celeste had no idea that the very drama she had run away from was headed her way.

CHAPTER THIRTEEN

Showtime

Celeste yawned so hard a tear fell from her eye. She was tired. Working late came with the territory, but that was the part of the job she hated most. She had beautiful things and little time to stop and enjoy them. Her night with Bryson hadn't helped matters. He had kept her up all night with his wonderful lovemaking. After a full day at work and a full night sexing Bryson, Celeste was drained. When she pulled into her parking spot, she opened her purse and pulled out her house keys. She turned the car off and got out, feeling drained both emotionally and physically. Ishmael was upstairs in her home and Rah-lo was somewhere in town. Both of them had come back to disrupt the peace she had finally found in her life.

As she made her way through the parking lot, she heard footsteps behind her. She panicked, still fearful of being raped after her close call so many years ago. This wasn't New York City, but the city girl in her always expected the worst. She quickened her pace, only to hear the person behind her speed up as well. She started to run, and tripped on her pant leg. She stumbled and fell on her knees.

"Celeste!" a familiar voice called out.

Celeste looked up and saw Rah-lo standing there. Every thought in her head prior to seeing his face was washed away instantly. She wanted to cry tears of joy and run away at the same time. "What are you doing here?" she asked, stunned.

Rah-lo looked at his baby girl. She was as beautiful as the last time he'd seen her, and hearing her voice, seeing her face, made him want to hold her close to him. She had cut her hair shorter than it was the last time he'd seen her. She looked thinner, too. But she was as lovely as ever. Damn, how he had missed her. Without thinking about it, he walked up to her and held out his hand. Celeste stubbornly refused to take it. She got to her feet on her own.

"I don't need your help," she said flatly. "What did you come here for?"

"I didn't mean to scare you." He couldn't take his eyes off of her. "I had to see you—"

"For what?" Celeste interrupted him.

"I know you don't want to see me. But I think you need

to hear what I have to say." Rah-lo reached to touch her face, but Celeste pulled away.

"Why? You ain't saying nothing new."

"That's not true." Rah-lo was hurt that she was reacting this way. He wanted her to be happy to see him.

"Don't act like that," he said. He shook his head for emphasis. "I missed you."

"What about your wife?" Celeste demanded.

"I left her." Rah-lo looked for Celeste's reaction but got none. "It's over. I know I don't have a right to come back into your life after all these years. You probably think I'm crazy coming down here like this, but I need you."

"You need me for what? I left New York *four years ago*, Rah-lo. I changed my whole life around. Why did you come here *now*?"

"So you changed your life and now there's no room for me?" Rah-lo frowned.

"Get the fuck outta here with that, Raheem! I don't want to hear that shit. You married Asia and let her have your children. Then when I left, all these years you've stayed with her. Don't think you can come back here and pick up where you left off. Nobody sat around waiting for you. I wasn't fucking knitting in the corner waiting for you to finish being married! Rah-lo, fuck you! Get the fuck away from me!"

Celeste hated his guts at that very moment. She wished

she could hurt him the way she had been hurt after years of playing the background. She was done. He could kiss her ass.

"I'm not saying I was right—"

"You *can't* say you were right, muthafucka!"

Rah-lo breathed deeply. "I'm just sayin'."

"What the fuck are you just saying? As a matter of fact, what the fuck are you doing here? What do you want from me? Why can't you leave me alone?"

Rah-lo looked at her and took another deep breath. "I can answer all your questions if you stop interrupting me."

"I don't need your answers, Raheem."

"Okay, I see you're real mad right now." Rah-lo tried not to react to Celeste's bitterness, but she was making it hard for him.

"I'm not mad, Rah-lo," she said evenly. "Never that! In fact, I'm quite happy. So go back where you came from. Back to your fucked-up wife and your kids and leave me alone. She can have you."

Celeste walked away, telling her heart that it better not break. She meant every word she said to Rah-lo. She hated him. But damn if she didn't love him, too. Celeste's heels clicked on the pavement as she stormed toward the exit.

Rah-lo was right behind her. He grabbed her by the wrist and she swung at him with her other arm, hitting him square in the jaw, which made him bite his tongue literally. The pain was evident on his face the moment it happened, and Celeste knew she had gone too far. Thinking she had knocked his tooth out, she reached toward him apologetically.

"Oh, shit. I'm sorry."

Seizing the moment, Rah-lo kissed her softly. Celeste pulled away, but the feeling of his lips against hers lingered still.

She turned to leave and he stopped her, holding her by the arm until she met his gaze.

"I'm sorry," he said.

Celeste shook her head. "I know you didn't think I was gonna just sit around forever and wait for you to get sick of being married," she said.

"I knew you wouldn't." He thought about it and was scared to ask his next question. "You got somebody else?"

Celeste glared at him. She almost wanted to tell him that Ishmael was right upstairs in her house. But she knew that would end badly. She felt the urge to tell Rah-lo that Bryson had been fucking her better than he ever had. But she simply said, "Yeah." She wanted to hurt him and she could tell by the look on his face that she had succeeded.

Rah-lo said nothing at first. He was crushed, although he knew it was selfish for him to feel the way that he did. He had a wife and during the past four years he hadn't been alone. It was wrong for him to expect Celeste to be alone after all that time. "So, I guess I wasted my time coming down here, then."

Celeste didn't understand why she felt sorry for him. And she didn't understand why she was secretly thrilled that he had finally come for her, that he had left his wife, and that he still loved her.

Rah-lo rubbed his hands together. "You want me to leave?"

Celeste couldn't tell him to go, because she wanted him to stay. She realized then how much she still loved Rah-lo. Her gaze fell downward. She couldn't believe that this was happening. Where had he come from? She had convinced herself that Bryson was the type of man she needed in her life. He had stability, intelligence, romance, a legitimate job, no wife or kids, and she felt comfortable with him. Still, he was not Rah-lo. He didn't excite her the way Rah-lo did. And as Rah-lo stood before her she wanted nothing more than to fall into his arms and tell him how much she loved him.

Instead, she took her hand away and shook her head. "Yeah, you can leave. You can't come in and out of my life whenever you see fit."

Rah-lo took her hand back and held it tighter. "I'm here to stay this time. I swear, baby girl."

As much as she loved it when he called her baby girl, Celeste pulled her hand away again and walked inside her condo. Rah-lo stood in her wake, speechless.

Asia stepped onto the elevator at the Embassy Suites Hotel in Buckhead. She had checked in late the night before when her evening flight had landed. The hotel was beautiful and conveniently located, and she felt right at home in her spacious suite. She figured she may as well enjoy cozy surroundings while she was here in Atlanta to fight for her husband. She waited patiently for the elevator to descend and looked around at all the activity in the lobby through the lift's glass walls. The fountain in the lobby bubbled with large tropical fish swimming inside. People milled about on their way to and from their destinations. As the elevator doors opened to the exquisite lobby, she stepped out and strutted out to the parking garage to get started on her way. She looked amazing that day. Wanting Rah-lo to see her in the way he once had, she had gotten her hair done and her nails, too, before she had left New York. She wore skintight capris and a very low-cut top. She wore her GUESS sandals and carried the Dooney & Bourke bag Rah-lo had given her for Valentine's Day. She hoped it was enough to change her husband's mind.

She had rented a car at the airport and was now ready for the drive to Uncle James's house. As she strolled along, her heels clicking on the pavement, she turned several heads and was pleased by that. Since she seemed to be having no problem attracting male attention from passersby on the street, maybe she would have equal success with the man whose attention she was determined to keep. Today was the day she would confront her husband and, she hoped, bring him back home where he belonged.

When she arrived at Uncle James's house, Asia parked the rental car and got out, eager to get inside and surprise her husband. She all but ran up the steps leading to the front door of Uncle James's house and eagerly rang the bell when she got there.

"Hold on; hold on a minute!" Uncle James called out. Somebody was ringing his doorbell like a madman. He was sitting on the toilet in the downstairs half bathroom, and he wasn't done letting his load out.

"I'll get it!" Wanda's son Brian yelled as he ran downstairs. "Damn, you stink in there, James!" Brian fanned the fumes away from his nose as he caught a whiff of what was going on in the bathroom.

"Shut the fuck up and answer the door!" James barked. He shook his head, for the hundredth time wishing Wanda had no kids.

Brian opened the door and smiled when he saw Rah-lo's wife standing there. He remembered Asia from the last time she came to visit. He had a crush on her then, and here she was again. "Hey!" he exclaimed, pulling her into a hug.

Asia felt caught off guard and it showed. "Hi," she said with a fake smile. "What's your name again?"

"Brian." He sized her up. "I haven't seen you in a long time! Why didn't you come down when Rah-lo came the other day?"

Asia smiled. This kid was feeding right out of the palm of her hand. "I wanted to surprise him," she said. "Where is he?" She looked around Uncle James's living room for signs of her man but saw none.

Brian shrugged his shoulders. "He left last night. Right after he had some of my mama's good cookin'." Brian smiled proudly, as if he had cooked the meal personally.

"How is your mama?" Asia asked, not really caring.

"She's fine."

"Good. So did he say where he was going?" Asia asked.

"Right after he ate, he started making phone calls. Said he was trying to find somebody important down here and he wasn't leaving till he did that."

"Find who?" Asia asked.

Brian shrugged. He was smart for thirteen and he didn't want to say too much. Rah-lo had sat up till the wee hours of the morning kicking it with Brian. His little brother, Nigel, had been asleep—just as he was at the moment—and old James had been in his bedroom with Wanda doing only God knew what. Rah-lo had talked to Brian about how it was living in Brooklyn and what it was like being married to one woman and loving another. "Don't get married unless you really love a woman. Don't do it 'cause anybody makes you feel like you have to." That's what Rah-lo had told Brian.

He shrugged his shoulders and ignored the question. "James told him to stay as long as he wants. So he left outta here and he ain't been back since. Did you try to call him yet?"

Asia noticed that Brian had ignored her question, so she in turn ignored his. "He hasn't called since he left?"

"Nope. I guess he'll be back here soon. You can stay here and wait for him if you want." Brian rubbed his hands together. He would love to play peekaboo with Asia.

James came out of the bathroom at last. He wore a pair of red athletic shorts with tube socks pulled all the way up to his knees and a black muscle shirt that showed clearly that he had no muscles. He tried to spray the air freshener discreetly but failed. When he saw Asia, his heart sank. He knew that Rah-lo wouldn't want to see her. But even worse was the fact that *Brian* had been talking to her for several unsupervised minutes. James wondered what his dumb ass had told Asia. James scowled as he entered the room at the kid.

"Hello," James said, pretending to be happy to see Asia.

She smiled. "Hi! Brian was telling me that I missed Raheem. I came to surprise him."

James nodded. "He'll sure be surprised. He didn't seem like he was expecting you."

Asia caught James's meaning. She wondered if she was too late. Had Rah-lo found Celeste already? "He didn't tell you who he was looking for?" Asia asked.

Who had told her that he was looking for someone? James immediately shot a penetrating glance at Brian.

James shook his head. "Nope. He didn't mention any names."

Asia looked at Brian to see if he had anything to add. She wanted to see if he looked like he believed James. Brian shrugged, seeing that she was trying to gauge his reaction. He knew James was lying. But Brian couldn't say so.

James wanted to kick Brian's ass, but the phone rang. "Excuse me," James said, and went into the kitchen to answer it. He hoped it was Rah-lo so that he could warn him of his unexpected visitor. The minute James was out of earshot, Asia turned to little Brian.

"I got twenty dollars if you tell me where Rah-lo went," she said. "I know you know something."

He smirked. He liked her style. She was so "New York"! "You can keep your twenty and let me see your titties," he suggested. She was a dime piece for real!

Asia wanted to slap the shit out of his young ass. "Do you want the twenty or not?" She waved it in his face invitingly. Little bastard!

"Yeah. Rah-lo went to find his old shorty," the kid said matter-of-factly. He snatched the money, smiling. He tucked it discreetly into his sock.

Asia was pissed. "He told you that?"

"Yes, ma'am. He didn't tell me her name, but he said he was here to find her."

James came back into the room and cleared his throat heavily. He shot a look at the kid that made it clear that his input wasn't wanted. The look on James's face said, *Shut the fuck up,* but Brian didn't seem fazed by it. He had a twenty in his sock, and that was all that mattered.

James looked at Asia. "This is Wanda's son Brian," he explained. "She went out shopping again and his nappy-headed ass don't know how to stay out of grown folks' business." James glared at Brian.

Asia suddenly needed to get out of there. She felt like she wanted to burst into tears, but she certainly didn't want to do so in front of Uncle James and his too-mature-for-his-own-age stepkid. "Okay. I'm gonna go. I'm staying at the Embassy Suites in Buckhead."

"You want me to tell Rah-lo you're here?"

Asia was already at the front door. "No," she said over her shoulder as she made a hasty exit. "I'll tell him myself." Asia ran out to her car, got in, and peeled out. She looked in her rearview as she left and saw Uncle James pop little Brian in the head for talking too much. She wiped the tears from her eyes and dialed Rah-lo's cell phone number.

His phone went straight to voice mail and she was furious. When she heard the beep she began her tirade. "You motherfucka! I know you're with that *bitch*! And when I find her I'm gonna kill her, I swear. I went to your uncle James's house, so I know you're not there. And that little bastard he has running around there told me that you went looking for your shorty. Call me back, Rah-lo!"

Asia hung up the phone and immediately redialed. She left five messages and each one was more venomous than the last. As she pulled up at the hotel, she was eager to get to her room so that she could have a good old-fashioned cry.

Rah-lo rang the doorbell and waited. Soon he heard shuffling outside of the door and the locks being undone. A slightly smaller and much older version of Celeste peeked out the cracked door. "Yes?" Nana asked the handsome young man standing before her. Rah-lo was dressed presentably in a pair of jeans and a button-up.

"Hello, Mrs. Styles. My name is Rah-lo. I spoke to you on the phone."

Nana smiled. "Yesssss, Oslo!" she exclaimed, opening the door wider. "Come on in." She held the door ajar as Rah-lo entered. He started to correct her but decided against it. Judging from the volume of her voice, he assumed she was hard of hearing. As he entered the house, a large Rottweiler barreled up to him and Rah-lo was caught off guard. He expected the dog to bark at him and act aggressively. But instead, the dog jumped on Rah-lo and began to lick his face.

"Zeus! Get down!" Nana yelled at him. "He's not usually this affectionate," she said.

Rah-lo smiled. "This is Zeus? I gave him to Celeste as a gift when he was a puppy. God, he got so big!" He petted the monster's large head and smiled.

Nana was amazed. "They say a dog never forgets a scent. I guess it's true." She led Rah-lo into her living room, with Zeus following close behind. "It's too bad you just missed Celeste's mama. My daughter, Zara, just went down to choir rehearsal." Nana gestured toward the sofa, and Rah-lo smiled and took a seat.

"It's all right. I doubt she would want to see me. I actually came to talk to you."

Nana sat down slowly in her rocking chair and kicked her size 6 feet up on the ottoman. "Really?" she asked. "Why me?" She sized Rah-lo up and saw why Celeste was so smitten. Rah-lo was handsome, tall, and strong. He seemed like he'd be a real powerhouse in the sack.

"I came down here to see Celeste," he explained. Rah-lo laid out his entire love life for Nana's inspection. He told her about loving her granddaughter while he was married to another woman. He told Nana about his children, his career choice, his love for Celeste, and his desire to be with her for real this time. Rah-lo spoke about the demise of his marriage and how he'd come to Atlanta to win back Celeste's heart. Nana listened in silence, nodding every now and then, absorbing all that he said.

"So, you say that you love my grandbaby, but you kept her quiet for how many years?" she asked, her brow slightly furrowed.

Rah-lo sighed. "It was a long time, Mrs. Styles—"

"You can call me Nana, handsome."

Rah-lo smiled, caught off guard. "Nana, I really love Celeste. I do. And I did keep our relationship a secret for years. I know I messed up and I never should have let her leave. But I'm here to fix that now. All I need her to do is listen to me. I was hoping you could help me."

Nana nodded. "Let me tell you a story," she said.

Rah-lo sat back and crossed one leg across his lap. He figured that this could be a long one.

"I used to be something in my youth, chile. I had a man I loved back when I was nineteen years old. See, in those days there wasn't no shacking up or sleeping around. You got married or your daddy would whup somebody's ass for messing around with his daughter."

Rah-lo laughed at Nana's narration.

"So when I fell in love with this man—who was twenty-four and married with two kids—I kept it quiet from my family. He kept telling me that he was gonna leave his wife someday soon and he was gonna marry me. I held on and waited and waited. One year turned into the next and before you knew it I was twenty-two and still waiting to be this man's wife. My family couldn't understand why I wouldn't date anybody or try to find a suitable husband. And I couldn't tell them because it was my big secret. I had to keep it to myself. Eventually, I realized that my mister wasn't going to leave his missus. So I finally managed to get over him and I met my husband. We were married, and then two years later Zara was born. A year after that, my husband died from pneumonia. I can't help wondering if all those years I spent waiting for my married man could have been years spent with my husband, enjoying more of his time than what I had with him."

Rah-lo sighed, figuring his attempt to get Nana on his side had been fruitless.

"We women often tell our daughters and our granddaughters to stay away from married men because they never actually leave their wives. Most of the time that's the truth. But you have actually done it. And you seem to be really in love with my Celeste. I think that is beautiful. And I hope it's not too late for you to win her heart. But what's to stop you from cheating on her and leaving her when the going gets tough?"

"Mrs.—Nana. I love Celeste. She's everything I ever wanted in a woman. Smart, funny, motivated, beautiful, supportive. What more could I want? I would never cheat on her. When a man cheats I believe it's because there's something missing at home. I couldn't talk to my ex about what I was missing. She wasn't approachable like that. But I can talk to Celeste about anything. She understands me and I understand her. I can't guarantee that she'll be happy for the rest of her life, but I can guarantee that I'll try to make it that way. For as long she'll let me."

Nana smiled. "Now that was a good answer," she said. She reached for the phone and dialed her granddaughter's phone number. "Hi, Celeste," she said. "Can you come over here as soon as you can? My arthritis is acting up again and your mama is out at the church." Celeste assured Nana that she was on her way and she hung up.

Celeste walked into the house and froze in her tracks. Whirling around, she glared at Nana. "Your arthritis, huh?" She turned back to Rah-lo and shook her head. "You should be embarrassed, using my grandmother to get me to come over here."

Nana intervened. "Hush your mouth!" she scolded. "Ain't no man used me in far too long!"

Rah-lo laughed and Celeste blushed.

"I spent the better part of this afternoon talking to Raheem about how he feels about you. Now this man has come a long way to talk to you I think it's only right that you hear what he has to say." Nana peeked out the curtains. "But your mama will be back here shortly. And you know she ain't gonna like this one bit. Take Raheem on down to the diner and have some coffee with the man. Listen to him. And if you still don't want to be bothered, he said he'll leave you alone for good. Ain't that right, Rah-lo?"

Rah-lo was caught off guard once again. He had never agreed to that and Nana's words visibly shocked him. But he rolled with it and nodded. "I just want to talk to you, that's all."

Celeste looked at Nana and shook her head. She reluctantly threw her hands up in surrender. Then she kissed

Nana on the cheek and said, "I'll call you tomorrow." Celeste led Rah-lo out and turned to face him. "I guess you can follow me," she said, storming off to her car. Rah-lo happily followed after, hugging Nana good-bye. This was his big chance.

Celeste sat across from Rah-lo in the Waffle House and sipped her coffee. Rah-lo had just spent more than an hour explaining his actions and professing his love for her. She tried not to be swayed by his sweet words and sincere confessions. He had told her that he loved her, that he had always wanted her and not Asia. He apologized, made promises, and told Celeste that he missed her. And she was moved by it. She set her cup down and looked into his eyes.

"One thing I always wanted was to be your friend," she began. "I guess when I left and you went on with your marriage I stopped being your friend. But I loved you."

"You don't love me anymore?" Rah-lo asked, searching her eyes for the truth.

"I wasn't finished," Celeste said, dodging the question. "I moved on with my life, Raheem. I don't want to go backward. I have a man in my life who I care about," she lied. Bryson had potential, but she certainly hadn't developed any strong feelings for him yet. And her relationship with Damon was over. Still, she needed Rah-lo to understand that there was no room for him in her new life. "And I just want to move on. But I do want to be your friend. Nothing more than that." Even as she said it, Celeste knew that she didn't mean it. But she was afraid to let Rah-lo back into her life.

Rah-lo sat back and nodded his head. "Okay," he said. "I guess I have to accept that." Several awkward and silent moments passed between them before he said, "Well, since we're friends now we can hang out and shit like that, right? Can I take you out tonight? Just as friends."

She looked away and thought about it. She knew that if she went out with him he would wind up in her bed. Then she thought about Ishmael back at her house and she shook her head. "No. I have a date tonight. But I can call you and maybe we can get together some other time."

Rah-lo felt dejected. He stared at Celeste, wishing he could say the words to change her mind. "Okay," he said. "How about I come to pick you up for lunch tomorrow? You can eat with me and go back to work and that will be that."

Celeste smiled. He was so persistent. "Okay," she said. She handed him her business card and told him to meet her at her job the next day at one o'clock. Rah-lo summoned the waitress and paid the check.

When Rah-lo and Celeste left the diner, she turned to face him. "I guess I'll see you tomorrow," she said. "It's good to talk to you again." She turned to walk to her car, but Rah-lo stopped her.

"Listen," he said. "I asked you a question before and you never answered it." He stepped in close.

Celeste felt her heart racing in her chest. "What question?" He was standing so close that she could feel his breath on her face.

"You don't love me anymore?"

Celeste looked into his eyes in silence, refusing to answer the question. But when he leaned in to kiss her, she didn't resist. And it felt just like old times. He held her close to him as if she might get away again. But Celeste wasn't going anywhere. She clung to him just as tightly and she was so happy that she wanted to cry. Pulling away reluctantly, she said, "I gotta go." Celeste walked quickly to her car, hoping to get away from him before she fell back in love with him all over again.

When she got home she found Ishmael in her kitchen cooking. She smiled, wondering what had prompted this. Ishmael smiled back. "Getting my Rachael Ray on," he said. "I'm making shrimp jambalaya. Hope you like it."

Celeste shook her head. "You are too much, Ishmael. When did you learn to cook?"

He rolled his eyes. "Nina taught me how to make a few things. At least she was good for something."

Celeste sat down at her kitchen table and rested her head on her chin. "Have you heard from her?"

He nodded, stirring the contents of the pot on Celeste's stove. "Yeah, she keeps calling. I keep ignoring her. Eventually, she'll get the point."

"What about Robin?" Celeste asked. "Do you miss her?"

Ishmael shrugged. "Not really. She said it's over and I'm not gonna keep stressing her. It's like R. Kelly said. When a woman's fed up there ain't nothing you can do about it." Ishmael really did miss Robin. He thought about her more often than he was willing to admit. He thought about Hezekiah, too, and wondered what it was about Robin that made him change his mind about dating women with kids. He wished that he had the heart to call her and ask her to change her mind about dealing with him. But he felt that he was too much of a player to beg her.

Celeste sighed. "Well, I wish your boy would give up that easily," she said. "Rah-lo just ambushed me at my grandmother's house."

Ishmael stopped stirring immediately. "What?" Ishmael set the spoon down and leaned against the counter. "What was he doing at your grandmother's house?" Ishmael couldn't believe that Rah-lo was going this far to win Celeste's heart once more.

"When I got there Nana told me that he came to talk to her about me. She heard him out and then tricked me into going over there so that I would talk to him. So I had lunch with him today."

Ishmael felt a twinge of jealousy. He shook his head

disapprovingly. "You're letting him break you down," he said. "What about ole boy? What's his name?"

"Bryson," Celeste answered. "What about him? Nothing has changed. And Rah-lo is *not* breaking me down, Ish. I'm just trying to see if we can salvage a friendship now that our relationship is over."

Ishmael scrunched up his lips in disbelief. "Whatever!" He waved her off and went back to fixing dinner. "Before you know it, you'll be back in love again." He turned his back to her and added some spices to the dish.

Celeste looked at him. "You seem upset. What? Are you mad at me for agreeing to have lunch with him?" Celeste was beginning to have second thoughts herself. Seeing Ishmael's reaction only made her question her decision even more.

Ishmael shook his head. "Nah. Why would I be mad? It's your life."

Celeste watched him, knowing that he was lying. She could tell that he was upset. "You don't think it's a good idea, huh?"

Ishmael finally turned to face her. "You want me to answer that as your friend or as Rah-lo's friend?"

"Well, Rah-lo's not your friend anymore, for one thing. And second of all, when he *was* your friend you never had a problem telling me what you really thought. So don't sugarcoat anything now."

Ishmael nodded. She was right. He pulled up a chair across from her and sat down, leaving the pot simmering on low. "I like you, Celeste. A whole lot. I like you as a friend—and maybe even as more than a friend." He looked into her eyes so that she could see how serious he was. "I told you that I had a crush on you years ago, but as Rah-lo's friend I couldn't act on it. But now you're not with him anymore. And I'm not with Nina. I know you got Bradford or whatever—"

"Bryson."

"Yeah, him. But I can tell he don't move you like a New York thug would."

Celeste laughed. Ishmael was too much.

"All I'm saying is Rah-lo had his chance. He blew it. You shouldn't let him just pop back into your life and set up shop. That's not fair to the rest of us waiting in line." He looked at her and smiled. He wanted Celeste in the worst way. Even the feelings he was developing for Robin paled in comparison to what he had always felt for Celeste. In his mind, she was available now. He could be with her and Rah-lo would never have to know. At that point, even if Rah-lo did find out, Ishmael wouldn't give a fuck. All bets were off as far as loyalty was concerned. "It's not fair to you, either," he said. "Look at what you've done for yourself, Celeste. This condominium is beautiful. You got a great job, friends, money—you don't need him. You've got a whole new life here. Why let him come back and fuck it up? What is it about him that you can't resist for too long?"

She shook her head, not knowing how to answer. "We have a lot of history, Ishmael. He protected me. He supported me, financially and emotionally. He made me feel safe, and loved, and I never had to worry about anything when I was with him—money, power—he gave it all to me."

"He was like a father to you. That's how you're making it sound."

"It's not just that—"

"No, it's not *just* that. But that's a big part of it. He gave you the world and what woman doesn't want that? What woman doesn't want to feel loved and protected and all that? But he's not the only man willing to give you that, Celeste. Do you understand what I'm trying to say?" Ishmael was laying it all on the line. He didn't want to lose Celeste to Rah-lo again. Not this time.

Celeste melted. Hearing Ishmael pour his heart out to her this way was incredibly touching. She shrugged her shoulders. "You're right. I guess there's a part of me that just has a soft spot for Rah-lo, Ish. I mean . . . he was my man for so many years. He took care of me."

"I'll take care of you." Ishmael's words hung between them for several silent moments. They held each other's gaze and waited to see who would fill the void of silence between them. The smoke detector went off, bringing them back to reality. Celeste scurried over to the pot on the stove, which was bubbling over, and Ishmael walked over to the smoke detector and fanned the smoke away from it. When it stopped beeping, he came back into the kitchen and found Celeste at the stove cleaning up the mess. She turned to face him.

"Listen," she said. "Maybe you're right about Rah-lo. After lunch tomorrow I'll fall back. I don't need him coming back into my life now. Not after all that I've done to get myself to where I am." She looked at Ishmael seriously. "And I don't think we should get involved, either, Ish. It's too complicated. I was your best friend's mistress for years. And even though he's not my man now and he's not your friend, either, it just doesn't seem right." She looked at Ishmael's beautiful face and physique and found it hard to turn him down. But something just felt wrong about the whole situation.

He nodded. "Okay. I respect that." He was disappointed and it showed. "Let's eat."

Celeste pulled out some dinner plates and prepared to have a friendly meal with Ishmael. She suddenly felt like she was in way over her head. Rah-lo wanted her; so did Ishmael. And Bryson was also in the picture. She felt flattered by all the attention but overwhelmed by all the decisions she had to make all of a sudden. As she and Ishmael shared dinner, they changed the subject and discussed the weather, politics, current events—anything that would keep them away from the subject of the passion bubbling just beneath the surface between them. After dinner, Celeste watched a movie with Ishmael until he fell asleep on her couch. As he slept, she looked at him lying there just as sexy as ever. She took a shower, threw on some jeans and a sweater, and headed over to Bryson's place for the night. Seeing Ishmael had her yearning to be touched.

The next day, Rah-lo arrived at Celeste's job and signed in at the security desk, saying to the security guard, "Celeste Styles; Miller, Wilson, and Carter." As the guard checked the directory for Celeste's extension, Rah-lo nervously fidgeted with the flowers in his hand. He was not only concerned about seeing Celeste face-to-face again. He was also bothered by the fact that Asia had come to town. Uncle James had informed Rah-lo of her unexpected visit the day before. He now wanted to win Celeste's heart back before Asia got a chance to throw her usual shit in the game. The security guard dialed Celeste's extension and informed her that she had a guest at the front desk. She slid her feet back into her stilettos and grabbed her Coach purse. She eagerly made her way to the elevator bank, and when the doors opened, Keisha stepped off.

"Hey, girl," Keisha said. "Running out to have lunch with fine-ass Ishmael?"

Celeste smiled at her nosy friend. "No. I'm having lunch with a blast from my past today."

"Who?" Keisha asked, curious.

"Rah-lo."

"That bastard from New York with the wife and three kids?"

"Shhh!" Celeste hissed at her, looking around to see if any of their white-collar coworkers were within earshot.

"Shhh, nothing! Are you fucking crazy? I thought you had more sense than that. What is he doing in Atlanta?" Keisha was disappointed. She had heard all about Rah-lo and his reluctance to leave his wife. Celeste had come to Atlanta brokenhearted, and only recently had she started to let go of that pain.

"*He* found *me*," Celeste clarified. "I'm only going to lunch with him to see if we can still be friends. We have a lot of history together. I guess I just need some kind of closure."

Keisha rolled her eyes. "Oh God! What is this shit, the fucking *Young and the Restless*? You know this ain't smart, Celeste. The man is married. He has three little rug rats running around at home. He ain't got no job, no benefits. What's the matter with you? You're smarter than this!"

Celeste shook her head. Keisha was being very dramatic, as usual. "I would love to hear your wonderful lecture, Keisha. But Rah-lo's waiting for me downstairs so he can take me to lunch." She pressed for the elevator again and Keisha looked surprised.

"That thug is downstairs? Here? Right now?"

Celeste nodded. "Yup."

The elevator doors opened and Celeste stepped on and waved good-bye to her friend. Keisha stepped on as well. "Uh-uh, bitch! You can save all that waving for later. I'm going, too. I wanna see the man that has you throwing away all your common sense." Keisha shook her head and looked at Celeste in amazement. "Yeah," Keisha said. "I gotta see this dude up close."

The elevator doors opened and they stepped out. To Celeste's surprise, Rah-lo stood leaning against the wall wearing a pair of khakis, a button-up, and a pair of crisp Air Force 1s. In his hand he held a beautiful bunch of white calla lilies—Celeste's favorite. She smiled as she walked over to him. "Hi. You look nice," she said to him. "Are these for me?"

Rah-lo smiled modestly. "Thanks. And yes, these are for you. I remember that you like these." He handed her the bouquet wrapped in a pretty red satin ribbon.

Celeste sniffed the flowers and was swept away by their lovely fragrance. She had almost forgotten about Keisha. But she was hard to forget about. She stood peering over Celeste's shoulder, sizing Rah-lo up. Celeste took Keisha by the hand and looked at Rah-lo. "This is my friend Keisha. Keisha, this is Raheem." Rah-lo reached to shake her hand but was interrupted by a disturbance to their right.

"Move the fuck out of my way, bitch!" Asia was storming in their direction, pushing executives and clients alike out of her way. Celeste's jaw dropped.

"Look at this shit!" Asia yelled, looking at her husband. "Why you dressed like that, Rah-lo? Where's the hoodies and Timbs you normally wear? You gotta change who you are to impress this bitch?"

Asia got right in Celeste's face as Keisha looked on. "You like fucking bitches' husbands, Celeste? You like taking food out of my kids' mouths so you can have what you want? You fucking home wrecker!" The people in the lobby were staring and a crowd was forming around them. Keisha stepped back slightly, wanting there to be no question about whether or not she was involved in the dispute. This was her place of work, after all. She stayed close enough to Celeste to help her kick Asia's ass if need be, though. Celeste looked like a deer caught in headlights as Asia cursed and made a scene. "You dirty bitch!"

Rah-lo grabbed Asia roughly by the arm and snatched her away from Celeste. He was furious. "Where the fuck did you come from?" he demanded.

Celeste was stunned and terribly embarrassed. She wanted to disappear, and she was mortified that Keisha and several other people on their way to lunch were around to witness this scene unfolding.

"I followed your stupid ass!" Asia yelled. "Some fucking gangsta you are. You didn't even notice."

Rah-lo wanted to choke the shit out of her. "You're crazy, Asia. Get outta here. I'm not fucking with you anymore. Go home!"

"No! *You* go home, Raheem! Go home to New York, to your kids and your marriage and your regular fucking clothes, you sellout!" Asia was so upset that she was damn near out of breath.

Rah-lo was ready to forget about chivalry and whip Asia's ass. Celeste turned and headed back up to her office with Keisha in tow. She was mortified. Security rushed over and asked Rah-lo and Asia to leave. He stormed outside with Asia hot on his heels.

Once they got outside, Rah-lo turned on Asia with fire in his eyes. "Get the fuck away from me before I hurt you!"

"Fuck that! I came all the way down here so we can work this out. You're gonna listen to what I have to say, Rah-lo!" Asia jogged to keep up with his long strides as he angrily walked to the parking garage nearby.

"Fuck you," he spat.

Asia ran ahead of him and blocked his exit. "You're coming up here, dressing all different and trying to impress this chick. Rah-lo, you *can't* leave me." She looked serious. "I'm serious. I'm not having that. We've been together too long, and we got too many kids." Asia saw a glimmer of hope in his eyes when she mentioned his kids. She thought they might serve as collateral. "If you walk away from me, Raheem, you will never see your kids again. This is a package deal. You can't have just *them*. I'm your muthafuckin' wife!"

Rah-lo flashed a sinister grin. "I was wondering when you would use the kids for leverage. You can't stop me from seeing my kids, bitch. I'm their father. Wherever you take them, I will find you. If you take me to court, I'll tell the judge the type of mother you really are. The girls are old enough to tell him themselves. Don't play this game with me." He started to walk away and then turned and walked back to where she stood. "And you're not my wife anymore. I'm divorcing your ghetto ass as soon as I get the chance."

"Ghetto?" Asia asked. "Now I'm ghetto? Why? 'Cause your little girlfriend works and I don't? 'Cause she got a smile on her face when she sees you? That shit is fake. She don't really love you. And you know I do. You can be yourself with me, Rah-lo. I know you grew up in the projects and you sell drugs. No matter how many button-up shirts and khakis you put on, you're still that ghetto bastard you've always been."

Rah-lo shook his head at her. "I'm not trying to be somebody else. Some people can change, Asia. I know who I am. And I know what I want. And I don't want you. Accept that shit. You don't love me, ma. You love what I am and what I represent in your life. It's all about you. Even the way you're talking to me now. I *can't* leave you. *You're* not having it. You'll take the kids. What type of shit is that to say to somebody you love? You're not even trying to change."

"Why do I have to change?" Asia demanded. "I was good enough for you before. You knew how I was, and you never complained. Now all of a sudden I'm not good enough for you." Asia's voice cracked with pain. "What the fuck am I supposed to do, Raheem?" She was crying. "I don't know how you expect me to just accept this shit."

Rah-lo shook his head. "I told you what I can't stand

about you. And not once have you said or done anything to correct that. All you talk about is you. Then you use the kids to make me feel guilty. You don't love me. This shit is over. Let it go, Asia!"

He walked away and left her standing there enraged. When he got to his car, Rah-lo took out his cell phone and dialed Asia's mother. Mrs. Hudson answered on the third ring.

"You need to come and get your daughter before I hurt her."

"Rah-lo?"

"Come and get her before I kill her, Angela."

"What happened?" Angela had just gotten out of a long steamy afternoon bath while her granddaughters were in school. It was the only time she had the house all to herself anymore.

Rah-lo recounted Asia's antics to her mother, and Mrs. Hudson listened in complete shock. This wasn't how she'd raised Asia to behave—not over a man. Angela had often had to fight in her lifetime, and she'd raised her children to do the same. If someone tried to take what's yours, you fight for it. If you were in danger, fight to defend yourself. But she had always taught Asia not to fight over a man. Mrs. Hudson had always taught Asia that men are a dime a dozen. She couldn't understand why her child was now acting like a damn fool. She assured Rah-lo that she would talk to Asia and hung up. Immediately, she dialed Asia's cell phone.

Seeing her mother's number, Asia sucked her teeth. She

didn't feel like talking to her mother right now, but since Asia was concerned that her daughters might be hurt or in trouble, she answered. "Hello?"

"What the fuck is wrong with you?" Angela got right to the point.

"Ma, what are you talking about?" Asia pulled into the parking lot of a nearby Walgreens. She parked the car and lowered the power windows. Lighting a cigarette, she exhaled the smoke.

"Raheem just called me and told me what you did. Why did you go to that woman's job and act like that? Didn't I show you how to be a strong woman, Asia? You never lower yourself enough to make a scene over a man. Especially at somebody's job. And he told you he wants out, Asia! You can't make him stay. I don't know why you're doing all this, because you know he'll take care of his kids. I taught you better than this shit! He doesn't want to be with you anymore. It's over! He's down there with the woman he wants to be with. Let this shit go! You gotta let *him* go, Asia."

Asia wasn't concerned about the tears that were falling from her eyes since no one could see her. But she kept her voice steady as she responded to her mother. "He's my husband," Asia said. "I'm not gonna just let her have him. I came down here to fight for him—"

"You're fighting for a man who doesn't want you! What the fuck is going on with you?" Angela lit a cigarette of her own as she listened to her pitiful daughter.

"Ma, stay out of this."

"How can I stay out of it when you got me all in the middle of it? I got your kids here missing both of their parents. I got your man calling me, threatening to hurt you if I don't come and get you. And not a damn word I say is getting through to you. How can I stay out of it?"

"Rah-lo shouldn't have called you. It's none of your business."

"You're my muthafuckin' business, Asia! Your kids are here missing their mother while you're down there in Atlanta acting like a teenager. Grow up! You got three daughters who watch you to see how a woman should behave. What the hell are you teaching your kids?"

Asia hung up and tossed her cell phone into the backseat. She didn't want to hear that shit right now. She was far from done. She put the car in drive and headed to Uncle James's house. It was time to take this shit to the next level.

CHAPTER FOURTEEN

A Rainy Night in Georgia

Celeste and Keisha sat in Celeste's office, downing a bottle of Southern Comfort, waiting for Ishmael to arrive. She had called him and filled him in on what happened and he assured her that he was on his way there to take her home. Celeste was in no condition to drive after all the drinking she and Keisha had been doing for the past hour or so. After the scene Asia had caused in the lobby of Celeste's job, Celeste had returned to work sick with worry. Thankfully, none of their immediate coworkers had witnessed Asia's bullshit. Still Celeste was concerned that the whole thing could jeopardize her job and her reputation. She had busied herself with work all afternoon to try to take her mind off of it. Keisha had given Celeste space enough to digest what had occurred. But all day she had been eager to vent about the drama that had unfolded with Rah-lo and his wife. Now that it was after hours and most of their coworkers were gone for the night, Keisha sat with Celeste as she filled her in on her feelings about Rah-lo.

"I still love him," Celeste admitted, downing her third cup of Southern Comfort and lime juice.

"You're fucking crazy!" Keisha looked at Celeste with complete disappointment. "You must have lost your mind. Seriously. This man has a wife! He has kids; he sells drugs; he's been to jail. Are you out of your motherfucking mind? What's there to love?"

"No. I—"

"No, nothing! I can understand that the two of you have history. I really can. But he is in your past. That part of your life is over. You're better than all this bullshit, Celeste. This bitch came to your *job,* girl. She put *all* your business in the street." Keisha shook her head. If she were Celeste, she would leave town. But Keisha didn't want to tell Celeste that because she liked having her around. "I'm telling you that wife of his is gonna hurt you." She saw the look of helplessness on her friend's face and felt sorry for her. "What the fuck are you gonna do now?" Keisha asked. She knew that Celeste had a problem on her hands. A *big* problem, because Asia seemed like she was a loose cannon. Keisha could understand Asia's reasoning, though. Her husband was, after all, in love with another woman. But still, Asia was bugging out.

Keisha felt powerless to help her friend. "You better be care-ful," Keisha said to Celeste. "Females like her are dangerous. You have to watch your back."

Celeste agreed. "I know—"

"No, *seriously*. You better listen to me. She knows where you work, so she already knows too much." Keisha looked serious. "You're not the first one this has happened to," she said. "When I was with my ex, Anthony, his baby's mama rolled up on me at work. The bitch caught me when I was working at the bank. It was all quiet in there, all the cus-tomers lined up waiting to handle their business. And this fat bitch got in line. It was a looooong line, too."

Celeste couldn't help laughing as Keisha continued dra-matically narrating her tale.

"She stood on line and inched closer to the front. I sat there, assisting the customers in front of her, stalling, taking my time so that she would go to somebody else. I kept telling myself, 'Maybe that's not her. Maybe I'm bugging.' But it was her all right." Keisha shook her head, distressed at the memory. "I stood there, trying to plot my escape. I held this one customer at my window for the longest time. I must've counted his money four times. And he was a regular, so he was looking at me crazy. He was wondering why I was counting so slowly when I was normally very quick. But Anthony's wife was next in line, so I didn't dare let my cus-tomer go until one of the other tellers called her over to their window. I was so glad when another teller called,

'Next.' I thought I was out of the woods. But Anthony's wife was like, 'No, I wanna wait for her!' and she pointed at me. The guy at my window looked at her; then he looked at me. I wanted to disappear, I swear. I just laughed because I didn't know what else to do. The guy left my window and she came right over, yelling the whole way, 'Bitch, you can't find your own man? You gotta fuck my husband?' I just laughed and told her that I didn't know what she was talking about. All my coworkers were looking at me and whispering to each other. The guy that had just been at my window stood there and he was laughing, too. All the customers on line were snickering and all that. I wanted to jump through the window and beat her entire ass. 'Cuz she was a big bitch, make no mistake about it."

Celeste was laughing so hard she thought she might need stitches. "Did that really happen?"

"Hell, yeah!" Keisha shuddered at the memory and sipped her drink.

Celeste composed herself. "So what did you do?"

"Well, like I said, she was a big bitch. So fighting her was not an option. I stayed behind the glass the whole time she was yelling at me. The guy I was helping came back to my window and smiled. He was like, 'You didn't sleep with that woman's husband, did you?' I said, 'Would I do something like that?' and he laughed. I closed my window and walked to the back of the bank. The wife stood there ranting and raving until security escorted her out of there. It was terribly embarrassing." Keisha gulped her drink and shook her head again. "I could have been fired for that. Even though I wasn't, I had sense enough to quit eventually." She looked at poor Celeste. "Don't let it happen to you again. Handle your business. You need to take a few days off and talk to Rah-lo."

"I can't—"

"Yes, the fuck you can, Celeste! You got all them vacation days, all that sick time. Be sick tomorrow. Talk to the man. Maybe you can convince him to leave you alone and go back to his wife. Or maybe y'all can even reunite and fall in love again. Stranger things have happened. You never know." Keisha shrugged. "But settle your situation with him once and for all. At least make him get that bitch off your back. Force him to control his wife. Once you get Asia out of your way, you can work on seeing what's left between you and this . . . Rah-lo."

Celeste loved her friend. She appreciated that Keisha could relate to her situation. But she couldn't let Keisha off that easy. "Why you keep cutting me off midsentence all the time?" Celeste asked.

"Shut up." Keisha guzzled her drink and tossed her cup in the trash. "I gotta go before I can't drive home, either."

Celeste laughed and hugged her friend good-bye. "Ish should be here soon," Celeste said. "I'll see you in the morning."

Keisha headed home and Celeste sat alone in her office

with a million thoughts running through her head. Close to twenty minutes later, the front desk called to tell her that Ishmael had finally arrived. Celeste straightened up her office and turned off the lights. Then she headed downstairs— staggering ever so slightly—to meet Ishmael.

When she got to the lobby she saw him standing near the security desk looking better than ever. Wearing a simple pair of jeans and a Sean John T-shirt, Ishmael looked sexy as hell. Celeste made her way over to him and threw her hand on his shoulder.

"I had a fucking terrible day, Ish," she said, slurring slightly.

Ishmael looked at her, confused. "Are you drunk?" he asked, smelling alcohol on her breath.

Celeste waved her hand as if dismissing his question and he shook his head. "Come on," he said. "Let's get you home."

A soft May rain fell on the dark Atlanta streets as Ishmael held Celeste around the waist to steady her. He led her to his rental car and secured her safely in the passenger seat. He went around to the driver's side and climbed in. Looking over at Celeste, he shook his head. "You should see yourself," he said. "Your boy Rah-lo and his drama with Asia has you acting real out of character right now."

She leaned her head back against the headrest, her head spinning in a drunken haze. "You were right," she slurred. "I never should have agreed to meet him for lunch. I should have stuck to my muthafuckin' guns and told him to leave me the fuck alone!"

Ishmael tried not to laugh at Celeste's inebriated state. He drove toward her house. He looked over at Celeste when they came to a red light. "I don't wanna say I told you so," he said.

Celeste frowned and glared at him. "You just said it, you son of a bitch!"

Ishmael laughed and brushed her bangs out of her face. He still found her to be a beautiful woman, even pissy drunk. He drove to her condo, listening to her recap what had happened although she'd already told him the story earlier. He let her repeat herself, knowing that she was really embarrassed by the scene Asia had caused earlier. When they arrived at Celeste's place, he pulled his car into the adjacent parking garage and found a parking spot. He turned the engine off and looked over at Celeste. Suddenly, she didn't look so good.

"I have to throw up," she said. Her chest heaved as she tried to fight it. She opened the passenger door to lean out of the car and vomit on the ground. But suddenly she fell over, toppling out of the car and onto the ground. Celeste lay sprawled on the pavement, hurling her guts out.

He got out of the car and rushed to her side. "Are you okay, ma?"

Celeste didn't answer as she wiped the remnants of her vomit off of her chin. Getting back on her feet took much effort, so Ishmael picked her up. "I guess not," he answered his own question. He laughed as he carried her inside while Celeste rested her head on his shoulder. She felt like the world was spinning. Once they got to the front of her condo, he set her down gingerly while he fished her keys out of her purse. He opened the door to her home and led her to her bedroom. He helped her sit down on the bed and she fell back as soon as her ass hit the mattress.

Downstairs, Rah-lo sat in his car parked outside of Celeste's condo, loading his gun.

"Get undressed," Ishmael said, walking to the bathroom to turn on the shower.

"I can't," Celeste protested, sprawled out on her back on top of her king-sized bed. "I'm drunk."

He laughed. "You're kidding! Really?" he asked sarcastically. He came back to her once he got the shower going and he helped her get back up on her feet. "Come on, smelly. You need to take a shower and brush your teeth. You smell kinda bad, ma."

Celeste staggered into the bathroom and began to undress right in front of him. As eager as he was to see her naked, he didn't want to take advantage of her drunkenness. So he turned to leave, closing the door behind him. He went to the kitchen and put some water in her teapot so that he could help her sober up. Once the water boiled, he made a hot cup of chamomile tea and set it on the counter. He heard the shower turn off and within minutes Celeste came into the kitchen with her long black silk robe tied tightly around her thin frame, looking terribly embarrassed. It seemed that the shower had sobered her up slightly.

"Thank you, Ishmael," she said. "I can't believe I fell."

He laughed and shook his head. "It's all right. That's what friends are for."

She leaned against the counter and sipped her tea. She shook her head. "I feel like such a fool."

Ishmael sucked his teeth. "Please!" he said. "Everybody gets drunk sometimes. It's no big deal. You're kinda cute when you're drunk," he said, smiling at her.

She shook her head and smiled halfheartedly. "That's not what I mean. I feel stupid for even entertaining the idea of letting him back in my life, even as a friend. Now I look like a fool in front of my coworkers and this crazy bitch knows where I work."

Celeste felt overcome with emotion. She felt silly; she felt confused. All the drama and mayhem she had run away from was now right at her doorstep. She felt stupid for loving Rahlo still. She hated herself for not being able to stop wanting him. She turned her back to Ishmael so that he wouldn't see her cry. "Why the hell did he even come down here?" she asked rhetorically, wiping the tears that fell from her eyes.

Ishmael hated to see her cry. He came up behind her and put his hands on her shoulders. She felt a chill travel up her spine at his touch and turned to face him. Pinning her against the counter, he leaned in close to her, his lips inches from hers. "Don't cry, ma. Fuck Rah-lo," Ishmael said. "He don't deserve you."

Celeste looked into Ishmael's eyes and was mesmerized. His lips brushed hers and she clung to him. He kissed her slowly, deeply, and she felt light-headed. He ran his fingers through her hair as his tongue explored her mouth, and Celeste did not protest. She wanted him in the worst way. She had wanted him this way for a very long time. Maybe he could make her forget about Rah-lo for good. Ishmael untied her bathrobe and was pleased to find her wearing nearly nothing underneath. Her flimsy nightie was short and silky and he caressed her body through the thin material. Celeste purred in response to his touch.

Ishmael continued to kiss her sensually as his hands explored her body. Celeste wasn't sure if she was feeling light-headed because of the alcohol she'd consumed that night or if it was Ishmael's touch. He slipped his hands underneath her baby-doll nightgown and palmed her ass firmly. Her nipples grew hard as he traced kisses from her lips to her chin, her neck, and her collarbone. Slipping her nightgown off, he caressed her breasts, squeezing her nipples gently and causing a moan to escape her lips. He sucked her breasts as her head fell back in sheer ecstasy.

"Ishmael," she whispered, her senses tingling from the pleasure of his touch.

He kissed back up to her chin and looked her in the eye.

"I'll take care of you," he said. "You don't need nobody else." He scooped her up, naked except for her lace boy shorts, and carried her to her bedroom. He laid her down gently on her bed and pulled his shirt over his head. He climbed on top of her and slowly let his hands explore the length of her body. Ishmael was making her weak.

He slid her panties down to her ankles and kissed and licked her legs. When he reached her inner thighs, he nibbled on them ever so gently and Celeste thought she would come from sheer longing. He spread her legs wider and palmed her pussy, stroking her lips so perfectly. Ishmael toyed with her clit and Celeste moaned his name once more. He licked his lips and dove right in, licking and sucking her swollen pearl as she felt herself bubbling toward climax. "Oh, shit!" she whispered breathlessly. He was making her feel so good.

Just as she felt herself getting ready to come, they were interrupted by a heavy and loud pounding on her apartment door. Ishmael paused and Celeste froze, both of them wondering who would be banging on her door at close to four thirty in the morning. The pounding continued and Ishmael rose. Celeste wrapped her silk Victoria's Secret bathrobe around her small frame as she scurried to the living room. Ishmael was right behind her. He was shirtless and he frowned as he followed Celeste.

"You expecting company?" he asked.

Celeste shook her head. "No," she whispered. "I don't know who that could be." She wondered what was going on.

Ishmael inched toward the door. The pounding continued, and he reached for his gun. Celeste couldn't help admir-
ing his exquisite body as he maneuvered toward the door.

"Be careful," she whispered.

He got to the door and looked through the peephole as a
precaution, and he saw Rah-lo's face looking back at him.

"Shit!" he said. He turned to Celeste and whispered, "It's
Rah-lo."

Celeste panicked. What the hell was he doing here and
what would he do when he discovered that Ishmael was
there? Celeste didn't want her home to turn into a murder
scene. Ishmael turned back to the peephole and saw the look
of pure rage on Rah-lo's face.

"I know you're in there, muthafucka!" Rah-lo barked.

Ishmael turned to Celeste and shrugged. "He already
knows," Ishmael said. Celeste stood speechless and afraid,
not knowing what to do. Ishmael unlocked the door and
opened it. He and Rah-lo stood face-to-face and Celeste
cowered behind Ishmael.

Rah-lo charged right in. He saw that Ishmael had his gun
in his hand but didn't give a fuck. Rah-lo had one, too. He
pointed his nine-millimeter in Ishmael's face. Ish stepped back
and pointed his .40-caliber right back at his friend. Now the
two former partners in crime stood with guns in each other's
faces and Celeste stood beside them, shaking like a leaf.

"Put the guns down!" she yelled. "Please!"

"What's this, your way of getting back at me, Ish?" Rah-lo

asked, his trigger finger itching to blast this bastard. Rah-lo was hurt. He had sat outside in his car for a long time, realizing that if he went inside there would be no turning back. Ishmael was there in Atlanta with the woman Rah-lo loved, and as far as he was concerned, there was no acceptable excuse for that. He knew that if he got out of the car and went to Celeste's door, he would kill Ishmael. Rah-lo had every intention of doing just that. But first he had some questions. "How long has this shit been going on?"

Ishmael shook his head. "It's not even what it looks like. Put your gun down so we can explain."

Rah-lo glared at Ishmael. "I can't believe I used to trust your punk ass."

"I'm trying to explain this shit to you, son. Put your fucking gun down, Rah-lo. You got this shit all twisted."

Rah-lo looked at Celeste briefly before turning back to Ishmael. "You been fucking him all along, baby girl?"

Celeste shook her head vehemently. "Rah-lo, it's not like that. Please," she said. "I'm begging you to put the gun down and leave. Go get your wife and get out of my life."

He slowly lowered his gun and turned to Celeste and looked at her like she was crazy. Ishmael lowered his gun as well and stood waiting to see what Rah-lo would do next. "You want me to get out, Celeste? Why? So you can finish fucking this nigga?" He looked at Celeste half-dressed and Ishmael standing bare chested and wanted to kill them both.

"I didn't fuck him!" she yelled.

"I saw him carrying you from the car. I watched you!"

"I was drunk!" she explained to Rah-lo. "After your crazy wife came to my job and caused a scene I sat in my office getting fucked up and I called Ishmael to drive me home. I fell out of the car because I was so drunk, and he carried me inside."

Rah-lo stared at Celeste, wanting desperately to believe her. He couldn't accept the thought of Ishmael having Celeste physically. "Why is he down here in the first place?"

Celeste shrugged her shoulders. "He came to visit, Rah-lo. It was innocent."

"He came here to visit you for *what,* Celeste? What kind of shit is going on here?" Rah-lo's voice bellowed and echoed off the walls in her spacious living room.

"I came down here to see my friend," Ishmael answered for her. "You don't own Celeste. She can have company if she wants to—" Ishmael was interrupted midsentence by Rah-lo's pistol cracking against his skull.

Ishmael fell to the floor, clutching his bleeding head. He gripped his gun tighter in his hand and stood back up. He charged at Rah-lo and grabbed him, pointing the barrel at Rah-lo's temple.

"Ishmael, don't!" Celeste yelled. She was crying now. "Put the gun down, please!"

Rah-lo smirked sinisterly at his friend. "You wanna kill me, Ish? Go 'head."

"Ishmael!" Celeste had tears in her eyes. "Put the damn gun down!"

Ishmael was still bleeding from the wound on his head, the blood dripping into his eye. He didn't budge. Celeste walked over to him and touched him softly on his back. "Please," she begged. "Come on. Put the gun down."

He blinked against the blood in his eye and lowered his gun. Celeste took it from him and then reached out her hand to take Rah-lo's as well. He pulled back from her, scowling at her as if she were the filthiest person alive. "Don't touch me, you fuckin' bitch. Of all the niggas in the world you pick my man?" he spat. "I hate you."

Celeste stood speechless. Rah-lo had never spoken to her like that. She knew that he was hurt and she felt tremendous guilt. Ishmael was Rah-lo's friend. The whole situation had gone too far. "Rah-lo, nothing happened," she said. "I swear."

Ishmael's blood spilled from his head like a geyser, but he didn't care. He wanted to fuck Rah-lo up for hitting him like that.

Rah-lo's jaw clenched and he never wanted to kill a man more than he wanted to kill Ishmael at that moment. He knew that if he stayed a moment longer he would kill Ishmael—and probably Celeste, too. Without another word, Rah-lo turned and walked out. He walked to his car, put the key in the ignition, and sped off toward his uncle's house.

Rah-lo trembled with rage. He knew that he would kill Ishmael at a time when there were no witnesses present. Ish had just sealed his own fate.

Nina was tired of calling Ishmael and sick of waiting around to kick Robin's ass. She wanted a face-off and she wanted that shit now. "Asia," Nina spoke into her cell phone. "I'm calling to find out if you heard anything about Ishmael. Has Rah-lo heard from him since he's been down there?"

"Nina," Asia spoke into her cell phone. "Girl, Rah-lo's little grown-ass cousin has been filling me in on what's happening. I have to pay the little bastard, but he's giving me good information. The little fucker told me that Rah-lo came into his uncle's house this morning furious. Turns out your man is over at Celeste's house as we speak."

Nina gulped hard. "What?"

"Yes, girl! How soon can you get here?"

CHAPTER FIFTEEN

Day of Reckoning

"Grandma, when is Mommy coming back?" nine-year-old Raven asked Mrs. Hudson.

Asia's mother rolled her eyes as she stood loading dishes into the dishwasher. She couldn't wait for her daughter to come back for her kids. Angela Hudson loved her daughter and her grandchildren. She loved her son, Larry, and his two kids by two different women also. But Angela loved them *all* from a distance. Since her husband had died several years ago, Angela was living the single life like the old eighties group Cameo had sung about. She was happy having her house to herself. She had white furniture, which sat atop plush white carpet, and all of it was spotless. It stayed that way because she seldom had children over her house. She had no time for that. Kids made messes and Mrs. Hudson's home was decorated with valuable antiques, expensive artwork, and designer furnishings. She didn't want any messes, any spills or accidents, so her grandchildren didn't visit much. She preferred to visit them in their homes rather than have it the other way around. Having Asia's daughters in her home on a daily basis took some getting used to. In short, she wanted her life back. And she wouldn't get it back until Asia came back and picked up these kids.

Angela turned and looked at sweet-faced Raven and forced a smile. "Your mommy will be back soon. You can call her later on if you want to talk to her." Angela finished loading the dishwasher and then started it.

"'Sheeda said that Daddy ain't coming back. She said Mommy played herself and was cussing at Daddy. Now Mommy's trying to apologize, but Daddy ain't trying to hear it. 'Sheeda said he went to find him a new mommy."

Mrs. Hudson looked at her granddaughter and frowned. "Your little grown ass needs to stay out of people's business." She pulled Raven into the living room by her shirtsleeve and called upstairs to Rasheeda, "Come down here now!"

Rasheeda came downstairs and Raleigh was right behind her. Mrs. Hudson noticed and got upset. "Who called *you*?" she asked Raleigh.

Raleigh shrugged her shoulders and sat in the recliner with her chin in her hands. She looked like she was about to watch a movie when in fact it was some real-life drama she hoped to witness. Mrs. Hudson shook her head in disgust. Asia wasn't doing shit with these kids. They were too grown and too nosy for Mrs. Hudson's liking. She decided to address it then and there.

"Sit down," she told them. Raven and Rasheeda sat down and had innocence plastered across their young faces. Mrs. Hudson knew that they were far from innocent. Raleigh continued to sit with her chin in her hands, waiting to hear what Grandma had to say.

"You all need to listen to me very closely," she said. "Raven came in here today and asked me about your mama." Mrs. Hudson looked at Rasheeda. "She said that you told her some things about your mother and father that she has no business hearing at the young age of nine! Your mother is going through something right now. Your father went down to Atlanta because he has some things he needs to think about. You-all are not dumb. You know what's going on and I understand that. But you have to be careful what you say to your sister. Raven is too young to be hearing all that. And you all are too young to be involved in your parents' business as much as you are."

Rasheeda spoke up. "But, Grandma, they *put* me in the middle of their business. I came home the other day and they were fighting. And Mommy wouldn't let me leave when they started talking about all the stuff I shouldn't hear.

It's not my fault that I heard what I did. Mommy said that I should hear the truth." Rasheeda paused. She knew where her grandmother's loyalties lay—with her daughter. And so Rasheeda was hesitant to be as candid as she wanted to be. But taking a gamble, she forged ahead. "Mommy always talks bad about my dad. She tells me that he cheats on her, that he sells drugs for a living, and that type of stuff. I know that all of that is wrong. But if he's so bad, why does she stay with him? I feel like . . . I feel bad for Daddy."

Raven and Raleigh were all ears. Asia's mother was also listening closely. Mrs. Hudson asked, "Why do you feel bad for your dad?"

Rasheeda shrugged her shoulders. "Because Mommy always pushes him to the limit. She stays out late and hardly ever cooks for us or cleans the house. He has to do everything around the house and make money to pay the bills, too. It's not fair. And she's always nagging him. She picks fights with him and she's always cursing at him, making him mad. She's like a bully around the house. And she drinks all the time and gets high."

"High?" Mrs. Hudson asked, her eyebrows raised. "What do you know about somebody getting high?"

"I know she smokes weed, Grandma," Rasheeda said. The look on her face signaled that she was no longer a naive little kid.

"How do you get high off of weeds?" sweet Raven asked.

Rasheeda shushed her little sister. "*Weed,* Raven. Not weeds. Mommy smokes *weed.*"

Mrs. Hudson was mortified. She felt like she was talking to mini-adults instead of young children.

Rasheeda continued. "Mommy makes me mad," she said. "Daddy takes good care of us. He makes sure we have money every day when we go to school. I have a lot of friends whose parents don't give them nothing. He drives us to school every day and picks us up. He helps us with our homework and makes us dinner. Mommy doesn't do any of that stuff. She only uses him for his money. She shops and she gets her hair done every week. But she won't even take the time out to see if Daddy needs something. She's using him and then she wonders why he cheats on her." Rasheeda sighed, relieved to be finally getting all of this off of her chest. "When he left, he told me that he loved us and that he wasn't leaving *us.* He was leaving *her.* And I can't blame him. I would want to leave somebody like her, too, if I was him. Why would he want to stay with somebody who acts like Mommy? She treats him like dirt and it makes Daddy feel bad. *That's* why he cheats on her."

Angela Hudson took a deep breath. She could see that she wasn't dealing with naive youngsters. These were young girls who had seen and heard far more than they should have. "Okay," she said. "I have a lot to say about that." She sighed. "There's no excuse for any man to cheat on his wife. When you get married, you agree to be with this one person until you die. That's the bottom line." As she said these words, Mrs. Hudson thought about her own marital vows. She had cheated on her husband several times. Though she had never gotten caught, the hypocrisy she was preaching made her suddenly feel guilty. She had to admit that hearing her grandchildren describe their mother had a ring of familiarity to it. When she had been younger and was raising Asia and Larry, Angela had seldom been home. Their father had taken care of them far more than she ever did. And when she *was* home, she hadn't been the Suzy Homemaker type of wife and mother. She had seldom cooked for her family, was constantly hanging out at parties and card games, and had stumbled home drunk on many an occasion. She, too, had spent most of her time shopping or getting her hair and nails done. She had spoken to her husband in derogatory terms quite often over the years, and she realized now that Asia had learned her poor behavior from her mother. Angela heard her grandchildren describing not just their mother; they were describing her, too. She felt her stomach do a flip-flop as the truth hit home. She looked at her granddaughters and sighed. She lit a cigarette and inhaled. "Your mother is wrong."

All three of her granddaughters looked surprised to hear those words come out of her mouth. Over the years they had all heard Mrs. Hudson talk shit about their dad. How he was nothing more than a hoodlum, a fake-ass hustler, a criminal.

To hear her now telling them that their mother was at fault was a surprise.

Mrs. Hudson continued. "Your mother got married for the wrong reasons," she said. "And so did I."

Raleigh frowned. "You wish you didn't marry Granddad?" All three girls missed their grandfather terribly. He had always played with them, given them candy and piggyback rides. He had been fun.

"No, that's not what I'm saying," Mrs. Hudson clarified. "I'm glad I married him. He was a good provider, just like your father. The bills were always paid, and he always gave me money. And when he died, he left me with a big inheritance. This house, the car I drive, and the jewelry I wear are all because of him," she said. "But I wasn't in love with him. I married him for money, and that was wrong."

Raleigh listened closely, then said, "But you didn't make him marry you. He wanted to."

Mrs. Hudson nodded. "That's true. But a real woman makes her *own* money. She doesn't use a man for *his* money." She exhaled her cigarette smoke. "I didn't make my own money. Neither does your mom. That's where we went wrong."

Raven shook her head in disappointment. "Mommy's not a real woman."

Mrs. Hudson laughed. "Yes, she is. Don't get me wrong. A man should provide for his family. That's his job as a man. Don't ever settle for a man who doesn't contribute to your family financially and otherwise. But it's important that you have your own money, too. You have to know that if a man leaves you, you can provide and take care of yourself and your children. Even though your husband may take care of you, you have to always make sure that you take care of yourself. 'Cause if he leaves you, you don't want to be stuck with nowhere to go and no way to take care of yourself."

The girls nodded in agreement as their grandmother continued, "Your mama loves you girls. She wants the best for you. But she's selfish and she got that selfishness from me." Mrs. Hudson was being honest with her grandchildren as well as with herself. For the first time, she was seeing her own actions clearly and seeing how those actions had impacted her daughter's life. Mrs. Hudson was also realizing for the first time how what she had taught Asia was affecting her daughters. She knew that the time had come for complete honesty. "I taught your mother to take advantage of men," Mrs. Hudson said. "Most of the time you hear about a man breaking a woman's heart. You hear about men leaving women penniless with a whole bunch of kids and you hear about men cheating and lying to their wives. I tried to show your mother that all of that didn't have to happen to her. I tried to show her that if she followed her head and not her heart, she could make smarter decisions that would make her life more comfortable long after her man was no longer interested in her. But sitting here, listening to you girls talk about Asia, makes me want to cry." She dabbed at her eyes and then continued, "I didn't realize how selfish my daughter is. She sounds just like me when I was younger. Even now. I don't go out with any man who can't pay my bills or finance my lifestyle. That may be wrong, but that's the way I am. The trouble is that when you find a good man, you should be able to turn that coldness off and appreciate the man that you have." She glanced over at her late husband's picture on the mantelpiece. She missed him. And she realized now that she had not appreciated the good man she had. "I know that your mama loves you. She loves your father, too. She just doesn't always show it the best way. You have to excuse her for that."

Raleigh shook her head. "Ain't no excuse for that, Grandma."

Mrs. Hudson smiled. "Yes, there is. She didn't have a good role model to follow. All the things she does to your father are things she watched me do to my husband. So that's her excuse. She's only doing what she was taught. Now with you young ladies there will be no excuse. You can recall this conversation right here when you become grown-ups. Remember what I told you about appreciating a good man."

Raven frowned. "What did you say again?" she asked innocently.

Angela Hudson laughed. Having her granddaughters around had been such an annoyance for her in the beginning. But now she was so happy to have them there. She smiled at little Raven. "Okay," Angela said. "I'll tell you one more time. Don't let a man take advantage of you. A good man will contribute to his family financially and emotionally. Don't settle for less than that. But if you find a man who treats you nice and takes care of you, you have to appreciate that man. Show him and tell him that you appreciate him. And most important of all, don't forget this part of the lesson, ladies. Always be able to take care of yourself. No matter how much money or status your man has. It's important that you have enough to take care of you, no matter what. Got that?"

All three girls nodded. Rasheeda smiled. She had expected her grandmother to defend Asia and to condemn Rah-lo. But Angela Hudson had pleasantly surprised Rasheeda. She walked over to her grandmother and hugged her. Raleigh and Raven followed suit and the three of them embraced her in a big group hug. Mrs. Hudson couldn't help giggling at her silly grandchildren. "All right, all right!" she said. "Enough of this mushy shit. Let's go get some of those Ralph's Italian ices you guys like." They quickly let their grandmother go and ran to get their shoes on. Mrs. Hudson smiled. Asia had no idea what a blessing she had in her children. Angela planned to point that out to her daughter the next time she spoke to Asia.

Asia and Nina sat in the lobby of the Embassy Suites enjoying the free drinks that were served to guests of the hotel each day at six o'clock. Asia had picked Nina up at the airport that afternoon and filled her in on the previous days' events. "We have more in common than I thought," Asia said to Nina. Asia sipped her red wine and nodded her head. "That bitch Celeste has both your man and mine wrapped around her finger. Ishmael played you. Rah-lo played me, too."

Nina agreed. "I knew Ish was a dog when I met him. I just loved him anyway." Nina took a long sip of her Rémy and set her glass down heavily on the table.

Asia watched Nina closely. She was tossing back drinks like they were water and she was clearly feeling the effects. Today she looked lovely in a simple black T-shirt and a pair of jeans. Her hair was pulled back by a black headband, her baby hair slicked down to perfection. Asia looked across the table at Nina. "This shit ain't over," Asia said. "If you love Ish, don't give up on him," she advised. It was like the blind leading the blind, her giving advice to Nina. "I'm damn sure not gonna give up on my husband." Asia was on her third glass of wine, and she was feeling slightly tipsy.

Nina shook her head, reeling from the news that Ishmael had been fucking with his best friend's ex. "I knew he loved her. Ishmael admitted to me that he had feelings for Celeste. It was a long time ago. Back when we first got together and we were trying to see if we could be happy together. I told him about how I used to strip for a living. It was late one night and we were both talking about how we grew up. We were really honest with each other that night and he admitted to me that he used to want to be with Celeste. I told him that I thought he had feelings for her because of how they looked at each other. They used to play around a lot. And I caught them getting ready to kiss one time. I knew there were feelings between them. Ish said that he had a lot of respect for Rah-lo as his friend, so he would never cross the line. But he felt that if she gave him a chance he could be better to her than Rah-lo was since he was married to you." Nina took another sip of her drink before continuing. "But I thought that shit was over after all these years. I thought he got over her."

Asia nodded, paying close attention. Nina was getting drunk and spilling more details than Asia had ever known.

"When Rah-lo was locked up, Ish used to drive Celeste upstate to see him. He used to come to get her and his whole face would light up when he saw her. When he looked at her it was like all the rest of us weren't even there." Nina paused, reflecting on the memory. "All of us hated it, but Charly was the most vocal about it. She let it be known that she saw what was going on. We all saw it. Ish had it bad for her, and she felt the same way. I don't know why I thought I could change his mind."

Nina was a pretty girl, but to Asia it seemed that she was very sad and needy. She seemed so consumed by—even depressed about—the fact that Ishmael was through with her. Asia didn't see that she was behaving the same way. "Damn, I had no idea, Nina. I thought Celeste was only in love with

Rah-lo. Up until yesterday I had no clue that she wanted Ishmael, too. She's a scandalous bitch."

Nina nodded in agreement. "She definitely wanted Ishmael, too. I could tell when I had a fight with Robin. Robin and Charly had ganged up against me. They were hating on me. Mad 'cause Ishmael wanted me and not them. And I had got into a fight with them outside the shop. Celeste called me and Robin into her office. She yelled at both of us for making a scene in front of the shop. Then she told Robin to leave so that she could talk to me alone. When we were alone she asked me why I was dealing with Ishmael knowing that he had been with Robin and with Charly. She said, 'Ishmael doesn't love you.' I took that shit personally 'cause who the fuck is she to tell me who loves me and who don't?"

Asia listened closely. This could be good news for her. Now that Celeste was focused on Ishmael once again, maybe Asia could get Rah-lo to come home. She excused herself briefly and went to replenish their drinks. She came back, sat down, and crossed her legs.

Nina kept talking. "I told her that he didn't love her, either. She didn't like that shit." Nina was letting the liquor talk for her. "I told her, 'Rah-lo loves you. That's all you need to worry about.' She got real defensive then."

Asia was feeling defensive also. She wondered if this drunk bitch knew that she was telling Rah-lo's *wife* that he loved another woman.

Nina kept right on talking, though. "Then she told me don't bite the hand that feeds me. I remember that bitch called me sweetie like she was better than me. I quit right then and there. I should have beat the shit out of her." Nina took a long sip of her fresh drink. "She was right, though. Ishmael never loved me. I can see that now. But why did he waste my time? I could have found a man who would love me for who I am." She took another swig of Rémy.

Asia watched Nina unraveling and felt sorry for her. To Asia it seemed that Nina was drowning in her sorrows. She kept talking about Ishmael as if she would die without him. Asia had gotten what she needed and she was done with the pitiful woman who sat across from her. She had her own problems to focus on. She had to get her own man to come home where he belonged. Nina could go drown on her own now. Asia asked, "What are you gonna do now? You think this stuck-up bitch Celeste will be with Ishmael now?"

Nina shrugged her shoulders. She felt more alone than she ever had before. She had no family, no friends, and she was hurt that the man she loved no longer wanted her. She excused herself and went back to the bartender for a refill.

Asia watched Nina get another drink and couldn't help feeling sorry for her. She was a sad sight as she staggered slightly on her way back to the table.

Asia drank the rest of her glass of wine and folded her

arms across her chest. "I have to go see Rah-lo in a little while, so I guess I'll wait for you to finish your drink."

Nina looked up at her. "Oh. Okay," she said. She swallowed the rest of her drink easily and placed her glass back on the table with a thud. "You can go."

Nina was so accustomed to people walking in and out of her life now. She had been enjoying venting to Asia. But obviously Asia was done listening.

"Are you going over there to confront him?" Asia asked. She had given Nina Celeste's address at both her home and job. Asia figured that with Nina and Ishmael keeping Celeste occupied, she could focus on Rah-lo without any unwelcome distractions.

Nina nodded. "I'm going there right now. I want him to look me in the eye and tell me why he hurt me like this." She shook her head. "Him fucking with Robin was bad enough. But to come all the way to Atlanta to find Celeste . . . he just never should have wasted my time all these years." Nina blinked back tears, unwilling to fall apart publicly. Asia stood to leave and Nina followed. The rain was coming down hard when they parted ways in the parking garage, both of them hell-bent on getting answers.

"I'm gonna go back to New York today," Ishmael said as Celeste sat staring out her bedroom window lost in thought. She turned to him and looked him over. He stood with his bags packed by his side and his hands in his pockets. Ishmael was so damn handsome. After Rah-lo had left last night, the two of them had retreated to separate corners of the house. Celeste had gone into her room and locked the door, feeling like her sexual encounter with Ishmael had been a terrible mistake. She told herself that the alcohol had caused her to spread her legs for him, but in her heart she knew that it was more than that. Seeing Rah-lo so hurt had broken Celeste's heart. She hated that she still loved him so much.

When Rah-lo left, Celeste realized just how much she wanted him to stay. She had a connection with Ishmael that was undeniable. But it was nothing compared to the intense love she still felt for Rah-lo after all this time. She had lain in bed wide awake, thinking about her history with Rah-lo and with Ishmael and about the future she might have with Bryson. She was filled with regret. She regretted allowing Ishmael to come to Atlanta to visit her. It had caused them to take their flirtation to the next level and Celeste realized now that that was not what she wanted. She couldn't be in a relationship—physical or otherwise—with Ishmael when she still loved Rah-lo. Seeing how hurt he was had hurt her as well. *And what about Bryson?* she asked herself. How could she still feel love for a thug like Rah-lo when she had the man of her dreams digging her back out on a regular basis? It wasn't just the sex. Bryson had the total package, and Celeste wondered if she would be foolish enough to risk that for Rah-lo.

She nodded at Ishmael's announcement. "I think that's for the best." She looked back out the window feeling conflicted.

He walked over to her and sat down next to her. "I guess we say good-bye now, huh? You shut yourself in your room last night after he left and I sat there waiting for you to come to me. You never did. So I guess it's safe to say it's a wrap, huh?"

Celeste looked at him. She reached for his hand and held it in hers. "I care about you, Ishmael. I really, really do. You are very special to me. So is Rah-lo, but in a different way. I was so crazy about him once. I think I might still be crazy about him like that. And you . . . you and I . . . I just think I want to leave us at friendship. Anything else would be too complicated for me. Being with you after being with him for so long just seems kind of . . . twisted."

Ishmael understood. He wasn't happy about it, but he understood how she felt. He nodded. "If you ever change your mind, I'll come running back," he said.

Celeste looked at him and had to fight back tears. She threw her arms around his shoulders and hugged him tightly. Then she kissed him softly on his luscious lips. He caressed her cheek affectionately and stood to leave. "Let me treat you to breakfast before I go. I wanna have one more meal at a Waffle House before I go back to New York." He forced a smile. "Afterward I'll come back and then we'll say good-bye." He was dreading that very much.

She smiled at him and nodded. "Let's go."

They walked outside and headed for the parking garage arm in arm. This would be a bittersweet meal for both of them. Celeste knew in her heart that this was good-bye. Seeing Ishmael again after today would be too painful. Ishmael knew it, too. This meal would be an unspoken farewell between them. As they walked to the parking garage, neither of them noticed the gold Ford Taurus parked across the street.

"What are you gonna do now?" Celeste asked. "Go back to Robin?" She forced a laugh.

Ishmael shrugged. "I don't know. I think she might be the best one for me. She makes me feel good. She has a good head on her shoulders; she's smart, motivated, and all that. Plus I like her son a whole lot. I never thought I would be into a kid like that who wasn't mine. But I really like Shorty. Maybe me and her can make it happen. We'll see."

"Take it slow, Ish. You're a good man. Make sure that the next girl you give your heart to deserves it."

Ishmael smiled at her. "Ditto." He put his arm around her shoulder and pulled her close. "Promise me you'll never settle for second place again. Not with anybody."

She nodded and wrapped her arm around Ishmael's waist as they strolled along. "I promise."

Nina sat in her car, furious. She watched Ishmael holding Celeste, walking with her as if he was head over heels in love with her. Nina was so angry—and drunk—that her hands trembled as she gripped the steering wheel. She had expected to come here and have a confrontation with Ishmael and Celeste. But before Nina could even put the car in park, she saw Ishmael and Celeste walk out, saw him hold her close. And now the two of them were walking along, talking and gazing at each other without a care in the world. Nina was blinded by her fury. She hated Ishmael at that moment. Hated Celeste, too. Nina put her foot on the gas just as Ishmael stepped into the street to cross it. She wanted to kill that womanizing bastard—and his little bitch, too!

The Taurus accelerated toward Ishmael and Celeste so quickly that they almost didn't see it. At the last second, Ishmael shoved Celeste out of the way, causing her to fall backward onto the sidewalk. The car hit Ishmael at eighty miles per hour, sending his body flying through the air. He landed several feet away, falling hard with a lifeless thud, and Celeste screamed in horror. Ishmael wasn't moving. Nina had barrelled down on Ishmael with such speed that she lost control of the car. Gripping the wheel tightly, she attempted to make a sharp turn at the corner only to slam head-on into a utility pole. The twisted wreckage smoldered far from where Ishmael's body lay motionless in the street. Celeste got up and ran to where Ishmael lay. She frantically dialed 911 from her cell phone. Several passersby stopped and tried to help resuscitate Ishmael. Others ran over to Nina's car, hoping to pull her to safety. But Nina was dead, her open eyes staring back at her would-be rescuers in wide-eyed shock. Sirens could be heard in the distance and Ishmael's pulse was weak. Celeste could only sob and talk to Ishmael reassuringly as the paramedics swept in to try to revive him.

CHAPTER SIXTEEN

The Prognosis

Rah-lo arrived at the hospital and found Celeste sitting in the waiting room, staring off into space. He rushed toward her, his heart racing. Celeste had ridden to the hospital in the ambulance with Ishmael. He had never regained consciousness and she was distraught. Not knowing who else to call, she had dialed Rah-lo's number and frantically explained what had happened. Nina was dead and Ishmael was near death, from the looks of it. Rah-lo had dressed quickly and sped to the hospital. He was only moderately concerned about Ishmael's well-being after the way he had betrayed him. But Celeste sobbing uncontrollably on the phone had tugged at his heart. He was still hurt that he believed she had crossed the line with his friend. But Rah-lo still loved her tremendously and wanted to calm her down. Celeste sounded like she was on the brink of a nervous breakdown.

Celeste looked up at Rah-lo as he approached her. "They don't think he's gonna make it."

Rah-lo didn't know what to feel. He was heated that Ishmael had been with Celeste. Ishmael had violated the boundaries of their friendship. Maybe this was divine justice. But at the same time, the man had been Rah-lo's friend once. The two of them had grown up together, grown in the game together. Rah-lo couldn't help feeling kinda bad for the guy.

Celeste sat in stunned silence. Ishmael could die. She couldn't believe that only an hour ago she had been talking to him and now he might never talk—or breathe on his own—again.

The doctor came out of Ishmael's room and explained to them all that Ishmael was in grave condition with severe head trauma, several broken limbs, and a collapsed lung. Ishmael was hooked up to a respirator and his vital signs were steady at the moment. The doctor assured them all that he would do everything possible to keep Ishmael alive but warned that if he survived that might be only half the battle. Ishmael could be brain damaged or a paraplegic. The doctor gave Celeste Ishmael's personal effects—his cell phone, wallet, and car keys. She held them in her hands, feeling terrible. She would forever be grateful to Ishmael for saving her life.

"What happened?" Rah-lo asked. "How did Nina know where y'all were?"

Celeste shrugged. "I don't know. We didn't even see her until about a second before she hit him. Ishmael decided that he would leave today and go back to New York. So we were gonna go get something to eat before he headed to the aiport. We were walking to the parking garage and we were talking about last night." She looked up at Rah-lo, her eyes filled to the brim with tears. "We didn't have sex, Rah-lo. You don't have to believe me, but that's the truth." She got lost in thought momentarily, remembering how Ishmael's kiss had made her weak. She continued, "As we were talking about it, we heard a car coming fast toward us. I looked up and saw Nina driving, but it all happened so fast that the next thing I knew Ishmael had pushed me out of the way. He pushed me so hard that I fell backward onto the sidewalk. And then I heard a loud *bang,* and that was when she hit him." Celeste's voice cracked, and she fought back tears, recalling the terrible sound Ishmael's body had made when it hit the ground. "She was driving so fast! He pushed me out of the way at the last possible second."

Rah-lo listened to her and watched her fight the tears that threatened to plunge forth at any moment. One lone tear escaped her eye and slid down her cheek. Rah-lo gently wiped it away and stroked her face softly. She looked up at him and their eyes locked. He was still incredibly hurt, still wondered if she was telling the truth about not sleeping with Ishmael. But Rah-lo loved her and hated to see her so distraught. His cell phone vibrated and he saw Asia's number on the display. He stepped away to answer it in private.

"What?" he answered flatly.

"Don't 'what' me, Rah-lo. Don't tell me you're out chasing Celeste around again. I'm here at Uncle James's house with Wanda and these bad-ass kids and you're not even here. I need to talk to you, Raheem."

He sighed. "Ishmael was in an accident. He's in the intensive care unit. . . ."

"What happened?!?"

"Nina ran him down with her car."

"What?"

"She's dead."

"W-what? I don't understand. . . ."

Rah-lo explained to Asia what had happened and that Celeste had barely survived. He told Asia Ishmael's grim prognosis and she held the phone, stunned.

"Oh my God!" she said at last. "What hospital is he in?"

"Don't worry about that. You don't need to come here. You've done enough." Rah-lo hung up the phone and went back to sit beside Celeste.

Asia rushed upstairs and asked Wanda for names of hospitals in close proximity to where Celeste lived. She called Patient Information at each facility until she found the one to which

Ishmael had been admitted. She raced out the front door. Asia felt terribly guilty. Nina was dead; Ishmael was in the hospital. Was it all her fault? She arrived at Emory Crawford Long Hospital and raced into the emergency room. When she walked in, she saw Rah-lo sitting in the waiting room, comforting Celeste as she wept on his shoulder. For a flashing moment Asia wished Nina had succeeded in killing Celeste. At least then Asia would be rid of this bitch. She looked at Rah-lo and wondered what had happened to the man who hated Celeste's guts just the day before. Little Brian had said that Rah-lo was furious with Celeste. It suddenly appeared that he had forgiven her, and Asia was steamed.

"Rah-lo," she said, approaching the two of them. "How is he?"

"Don't worry about that," Rah-lo hissed. He was sick of Asia's presence. "I told you not to even come here. You and Nina came down here chasing men that don't want you. I told you back in New York that it was over and you came down here anyway—causing scenes, starting trouble, fucking up friendships. Ishmael told Nina that it was over, too, and she couldn't accept it. What's it gonna take, Asia? You wanna kill me since you can't have me, like she did to Ishmael?"

Asia listened to what her husband was saying to her. "You gotta talk to me like that in front of this bitch?"

Celeste glared at Asia, and pressed her lips together in order to keep from going off on Rah-lo's wife. She looked right back at Celeste and tilted her head to the side. "What?

You don't like being called a bitch? That's what the fuck you are."

Celeste had enough. "You know what *you* are, Asia?" She stood nearly eye to eye with Rah-lo's wife, tired of her shit. "You're a miserable bitch, a terrible mother, a sad excuse for a wife, and a fucking stalker who can't accept that your man doesn't want your sorry ass anymore!"

"All right, that's it. This ain't the place for this shit," Rah-lo tried to intervene, but both women ignored him.

Asia stepped closer to Celeste and looked her dead in the eye. "That's supposed to upset me, Celeste? All you ever were was a fuckin' jump-off. A fuckin' ho he could stick his dick in without having to marry you. You's a dumb bitch! Why do you think *you're* not his wife? Huh? If he really loved you he could've divorced me and been with you years ago. Why do you think *you* never had any of his kids? 'Cause he didn't want you for anything more than that beat-up pussy of yours. So now you fucked him *and* Ishmael and you think he wants you now, you filthy whore?"

Celeste smirked. "Well, he damn sure don't want you, Asia. How does it feel to have to beg a man to love you? How does it feel to have to fly around the country chasing your 'husband' when he's professing his love for someone else?"

Asia suddenly charged at Celeste and smacked her hard across the face. She grabbed Celeste by the hair. Holding her hair tightly, Asia swung Celeste around like a pendulum. Asia stopped swinging Celeste long enough to punch her repeatedly as Rah-lo tried in vain to pull Asia off of her. Anarchy erupted in the emergency room waiting area as the two ladies tussled. Rah-lo pried the women apart and he pushed Asia toward the door. "You gotta get the fuck outta here!"

"Tell *her* to leave, Rah-lo. What the fuck do I have to leave for?"

"What the fuck did you come here for in the first place, Asia? It's over with us!" he insisted. "I'm not in love with you anymore. I don't want to be with you anymore. It's a wrap. I don't know how else to say this shit to you! It doesn't matter what you try to do to make me change my mind. Even if Celeste don't want me, I still don't want *you*. I'll be by myself before I go back to being in a marriage feeling unappreciated and disrespected. I'm asking you to leave me alone. Go home to our kids, Asia. Stop calling me. Stop following me. Stop causing scenes. *Get the fuck outta here!*" Rah-lo shoved Asia toward the exit just as security came over to ask them to take their fight outside. Celeste stood behind Rah-lo, angry that Asia had gotten the best of her in their fight. But she was also strangely moved by how Rah-lo had stood by her side and taken a stand against Asia for once and for all. Security ushered Rah-lo and Asia outside as a triage nurse came over to tend to Celeste's bloody lip. Celeste shrugged the woman off and stormed off to the bathroom, where she could be alone. She watched Rah-lo and Asia walk outside, where they continued their argument.

Rah-lo looked into Asia's eyes and saw the emotions

written on her face—hurt mixed with rage. She glared at him. She hated him at that moment but loved him at the same time. "How could you do this to me, Rah-lo?" The pain in Asia's voice was very evident. "All those years you cheated on me with her. And now you come down here and try to get her back? Did you have to talk to me like that in front of her, push me away and all that? How am I supposed to feel?"

"I told you it was over with me and you before I left. So don't act surprised now, Asia."

She shook her head. "You still haven't answered my question. How am I supposed to feel knowing that you came all the way down here just to fuck her again?"

Rah-lo shook his head. "That's not why I came down here."

"So then what was it?"

Rah-lo stared at Asia for a long time, wondering if she could handle what it was that he needed to tell her. "I love Celeste."

Asia laughed. He sounded crazy. "You don't love her. You love the fact that she keeps letting you have your cake and eat it, too. If you loved her, you would've been with her years ago."

"I should've been with her years ago," he said. "But I tried to stay with you for the kids. I thought that was the right thing to do."

"That *is* the right thing to do, Raheem!"

He shook his head. "No, it's not. I'm not gonna be unhappy anymore so that everyone else can be happy. And I
don't think I owe you an apology for wanting to walk away
from a marriage neither one of us is happy in."

"But you do," she clarified. "You owe me an apology for
a lot of things. I'm your wife and you're down here chasing
after another woman."

Rah-lo ignored that comment. He had no intention of
apologizing to Asia for finally finding the courage to leave.
"Why did you come down here?" he asked, shaking his head.
"You don't even want me. You just don't want her to have
me. I told you back in New York that I was done with this
shit. I don't want to be with you anymore. I'm tired of fighting with you."

"Rah-lo, I don't want to hear that shit! We're not just
boyfriend and girlfriend. You can't just break up with me
and then that's the end of the story. I'm your muthafuckin'
wife!"

"Then when were you gonna start acting like it? When?
Now that I walked out you wanna claim your spot as my
wife. Get the fuck outta here with that!"

"What did I do that was so bad, Raheem? What did I
do?" Asia's yelling caused several people to turn and stare at
them. "You want perfection and I'm not fucking perfect.
Nobody's fucking perfect! Not even that bitch you keep running back to. She has flaws, too!"

Rah-lo nodded. "Yup. Everybody has flaws. But not the

kind of flaws that make a man want to hit his wife. You jump all up in my face, constantly bitching and complaining, getting high and drunk, coming in late, neglecting your kids and shit—"

"*I* neglected the kids, Rah-lo? You can't be serious! You walked out on them!"

"No, I didn't. I walked out on *you*. I will always be there for my daughters no matter what. And you should know that by now. I never gave you any reason to doubt me as a father. I'm there cooking, cleaning, and all that shit while you're out in the street acting like a fucking teenager!"

Asia hated what she was hearing, mainly because she knew it was true. She hadn't been the best mother, nor had she been the perfect wife. Far from it. She had been selfish and she knew that. But that didn't mean that she was going to roll over and play dead while Rah-lo rode off into the sunset with his bitch. "You're crazy! I was the one who was there with you when you were nobody."

"Please!" Rah-lo spat at her. "You were only with me because I *am* somebody. Don't act like you just loved me all along and now you're destroyed because I don't wanna be with you anymore. You were caught up in who I was and what I represent and how it could benefit you. It was never about me. Don't insult my fucking intelligence!"

"You know what, Rah-lo? Fuck you!"

It was Rah-lo's turn to laugh. "You only want me to come back so that you don't feel like you lost some stupid game. It's a game for you to be with me and be my wife. You love the privileges. You don't love me. The only reason you want me is to keep somebody else from loving me. You know that another woman will appreciate me."

"You think you're all of that, Raheem. What the hell is there to appreciate about you? You cheat on your wife! You're a liar and a fucking sneak! You act like it's all about you, but it's not."

He nodded. "Exactly. With you, it's not all about me. It's all about you and what you want and how you look and what you can get out of it. I don't want that anymore. I want a divorce. Let me be happy and you can find somebody who can make you happy."

Rah-lo turned to leave, and Asia stood in his way. "Tell me what I have to change and I'll change it," she said, her voice wavering slightly. This was uncomfortable for her—conceding defeat. She choked back a sob as she tried to block his exit. "I'm sorry," she offered. She was desperate to change his mind. "I'm sorry for the way I was acting. Can't we fix it? Please."

It pained Rah-lo to see her this emotional. Asia had never softened this much around him. She was always so tough, so stoic and frigid. Now she stood before him with hurt etched on her face and tears sliding down her cheeks. He wiped them for her and lightly touched her face. "No, Asia. It's over. I just want to move on. Let me do that. Go home and get the kids. When I get back I'll come over and we'll talk to them together. Don't make this harder than it has to be."

Asia's pain turned to sheer rage as she listened to her husband dismissing her like she was nobody. She had let down her guard and shown him what was in her heart and still it wasn't good enough. Asia couldn't stand the idea that even when she cried and pleaded with him it wasn't enough to make him stay. She reached to kiss him and he pulled away. Asia swung at him and Rah-lo deflected the blow and shook his head in disgust.

"See? That's why I don't wanna be with you anymore." He shook his head. "I'm gonna tell you one more time to leave me alone. I'm not gonna say it again. Please don't make me hurt you. Seriously, Asia. Go home." He stepped around her and went back into the waiting room, leaving Asia crying in his wake.

He found Celeste in Ishmael's room. Rah-lo stood beside her and saw his friend lying there with tubes running all over the place, a respirator breathing for him. A monitor beeped softly near his bedside and the IV dripped steadily into his veins. Ishmael's head was wrapped in gauze and visibly swollen. His eyes were puffy and his legs were both encased in casts. Celeste stood with her hand covering her mouth and shook her head in disbelief.

"Oh my God," she sighed.

Rah-lo stood beside her and looked at his friend. Celeste went to his bedside and touched his hand lightly. He was covered almost head to toe in bruises and casts, sutures and gauze. "Ishmael," she said. "Hold on. You're gonna be all right." She began to cry softly. Rah-lo ushered her out of the room and into the waiting room, where he rocked her in his arms to calm her. She took some deep breaths and he handed her a cup of water from the nearby cooler.

"I need to talk to you," Rah-lo told Celeste. She nodded and he led her to the other side of the room. "I want to apologize about what happened with Asia," he began. "I'm sorry."

Celeste shook her head. "You're not the one who should apologize."

Rah-lo looked at the floor and then at Celeste once more. "I love you," he said. "I know I don't always have the best way of showing it. But I never loved any woman the way that I love you. I didn't expect all of this to happen when I came down here. I thought I would come here and find you and then we would see if we could have another chance to be together. But Ishmael came to see you and Asia followed me down here and then . . . this ain't how it was supposed to end up."

"You don't have to apologize for all of this," Celeste said. "I know you didn't mean for this to happen."

Rah-lo shook his head. "My marriage is over, Celeste," he said, looking directly into her eyes. "I swear it is. I don't want to be with Asia or with anybody else. I just want to be with you. Can we have a second chance?"

Celeste looked away and said nothing for a long time. "I

don't want to live like this anymore. Fighting, bitter exes . . . all of that shit surrounds you. Rah-lo, I love you, too. I probably always will. But I came down here to get away from all this. I came to Atlanta to have peace in my life and I didn't ever want to have to deal with this kind of drama again. If you and Asia are finished, I think that's great. But she's always gonna be in your life. You have kids together. And she'll do everything she can to make our lives miserable."

Rah-lo shook his head. It seemed that all he ever heard from Celeste these days was "no." "So you're gonna let her win? You're gonna let her keep us apart?"

"It's not about letting her win. It's about accepting the situation for what it is." Celeste was feeling overwhelmed by everything. In the past few days the man she loved had come back into her life, along with his friend, with whom she'd shared a physical and emotional chemistry; his wife, who was bitter; and the type of drama that Celeste had hoped she'd never see again. It was all too much at once. She wanted nothing more than to go back to her new life with Bryson, spending her Sundays with her mother and Nana and having her after-work drinks with Keisha. All this drama was for the birds.

Rah-lo knew that Celeste meant what she said. He could see the conviction on her face and hear it in her voice. But he couldn't give up that easily. He stood beside her, knowing that he had to do something drastic to get her to see things clearly. He walked over and asked the doctor on call whether

Ishmael could regain consciousness any time soon. The doctor shook his head, explaining that Ishmael was heavily sedated and would be asleep for hours. That was all that Rah-lo needed to hear. He walked back over to Celeste and grabbed her by the hand. She looked at him, confused. "Where are we going?" she asked.

"To your house. I need to talk to you without a million people standing around, without Asia starting her bullshit, without Ishmael—just me and you."

Celeste looked at him but didn't protest. The truth was she needed to get out of there just as badly as Rah-lo did. She felt drained and she desperately wanted to go home. Waiting around for Ishmael to wake up was fruitless. She and Rah-lo headed out to his car and drove the whole way to her house in silence. Both of them were lost in their own thoughts, processing what had happened over the past several days.

When they pulled up in the parking lot of her condo, Rah-lo parked his car and they headed toward the entrance. Just as they reached the lobby door, Rah-lo stopped her. "Listen," he said. "I need to say this to you before we go inside." He stepped in close.

Celeste felt her heart racing in her chest. "What?" He was standing so close that she could feel the breath on her face.

"I'm willing to do whatever it takes to have you back in my life. If I need to move down here to be with you, I'll do it. I'll get out of the game. Shit, I've wanted out for a long time now. Maybe this is the push I need to do that. I'll keep Asia out of our life."

"How? You can't even keep her out of your life *now*."

"I swear she won't bother us again. I promise, Celeste. Just don't say no to me anymore. Please."

Celeste looked into his eyes and saw that he meant what he said. Without second-guessing herself, she took him by the hand and led him into her place. They were silent the whole way. Once inside, Rah-lo looked around and was impressed by all that she had managed to accomplish on her own. Her home was so beautiful and so meticulously decorated. He hadn't noticed that last night when he had been fighting with Ishmael. But despite how proud Rah-lo was, he had more pressing matters to attend to. Celeste was here with him, and there was no one or no thing around to interrupt them. Celeste was feeling the exact same way. It was almost too good to be true. Without a word, Rah-lo walked over to her, led her by the hand to her huge master bedroom, and made love to her until the sun went down.

In the morning, she called in sick to work and watched Rah-lo sleep. She couldn't believe that he was back in her arms, in her bed, after so many years. She wondered if she had made the right decision by sleeping with him. But one flashback to the night before and she no longer second-guessed herself. She recalled the way his luscious lips had felt pressed against hers, the way his big, powerful hands had felt as they explored her body, how he had felt inside of her. She thought about the way they'd moved together with a cadence that was as close to perfect as anything Celeste had ever known. Watching him now, sleeping peacefully naked beneath the sheets beside her, she almost wanted to cry. She had missed him so much, and now here he was.

She reached over and touched his face, just to make sure that she wasn't dreaming. Rah-lo stirred in his sleep and slowly opened his eyes, squinting against the sunlight peeking through her sheer curtains.

Seeing Celeste beside him, he smiled and turned to her, scooping her into his arms in a warm embrace. "Good morning," he said. He hadn't been this happy in years. Waking up beside the woman he loved so much made him feel euphoric.

She smiled as he held her close. "Good morning." She couldn't understand why she suddenly felt shy like a little girl. She had known Rah-lo for over ten years. The two of them had practically lived together when she was in New York, and they had had sex in various degrees of intensity over the years. Rah-lo had fucked her, made love to her, seduced her, ravaged her, and seen her in every position imaginable. He knew all of her dreams, her fears, her triumphs, and her disappointments. He knew what made her happy, what made her cry, and all the things that made her smile. Rah-lo knew Celeste like no other man—or woman for that matter—had ever known her. He had been her best friend. But that was long ago.

Now she felt as if a familiar stranger was lying beside her. She pulled the sheet up closer to her chin and rested on her elbow as she faced him. Rah-lo noticed her covering up but didn't comment on it. He wondered what was on her mind, so he asked her, "What are you thinking about right now?"

She shrugged. "Whether or not this was a good idea," she said honestly.

"Why wouldn't it be a good idea?" he asked, frowning. "Because of your man?" Rah-lo hated the thought of any man kissing her, touching her, or, worse, making love to her. He knew all along that in the four years that had passed she had probably had sex with another man. Still, the very thought of that made Rah-lo sick to his stomach. So he didn't ask her for details or press her on the topic. But he did want to know how serious she was about this dude. Because Rah-lo was there to take his baby back, whatever the cost. "What's his name, anyway?"

"Bryson," she said. "But that's not important. It's this that I'm worried about . . . us. I don't want to get caught up with this," she said, motioning at the bed in which they lay naked together, "and forget the problems that we still have to face." She looked at him seriously. "It felt so good to be with you last night."

"Tell me about it," he said, smiling.

She smiled back but then forced herself to be serious again. "But we still have a lot to talk about."

Rah-lo nodded, agreeing. He linked his fingers together behind his head and lay back. "Where do you want to start?"

Celeste looked at him. Such a beautiful man. She got comfortable and asked, "What do you want from me now?"

Rah-lo sat up and pulled the sheet off of Celeste. "I want to see your body, baby girl. Don't cover yourself up like you don't know me anymore. I thought about you so much all this time, imagining the way you looked when we used to spend the day in bed together. Don't hide from me now."

She sighed, and felt more at ease with him seeing her in her birthday suit. He looked at her from head to toe and smiled. "That's more like it," he said. Rah-lo told Celeste about how his life had changed when she had left town so suddenly. He told her about his attempt to reconnect with his wife, including the family trip to Florida, and the fact that he had been feeling like he desperately needed to leave the drug game alone. He painted a picture for Celeste of a man who loved his children and had grown accustomed to a lavish and privileged lifestyle. But also a man who wanted peace and needed the comfort of not having to watch his back all the time. He was tired of looking over his shoulder 24/7, waiting for some enemy from some past beef to come back seeking revenge. Rah-lo was sick of the empty marriage he had found himself in, and sick without the woman he truly loved—Celeste. They ordered food from a restaurant down the street and ate it in bed, talking and catching up on each other's lives. Celeste listened to him insist on how much he loved her, missed her, and how sure he was that his relationship with Asia was over. And Celeste was encouraged. They laughed together, just like old times. They had a pillow fight when she made fun of his few stray gray hairs. For the first time in a long time, they were enjoying each other's uninterrupted company and reestablishing their beautiful friendship.

She told him about her life since she'd moved to Atlanta. How she'd enrolled in college and lived with her mother until after she graduated. Celeste described for him the rapport she had built with her mother and her grandmother. Nana was so full of wisdom, although she was growing slightly senile as she got older. Celeste told Rah-lo how Nana's anecdotes about love and life had changed her perspective on many things. She also told him how her mom had stayed up late with her while she completed important assignments while she was in college. They had supported Celeste from start to finish. She told him about landing her dream job and purchasing her condominium and how good it felt to buy her *own* car for once and the joy she found in decorating her new home. She had lost weight, cut her hair, and changed her whole life around and it felt so good. She spared him the details of her new romance with Bryson. "But I did miss you," she admitted.

Rah-lo was so happy to hear that. He looked into her eyes seriously. "That night we met on Targee Street, I was there for a reason. I feel like I was there that night waiting for *you*." He kissed her again. "I'm sorry," he said. "I never should have let you walk away from me."

He kissed her, and made love to her once more. Later, Rah-lo relaxed in the huge claw-foot bathtub with Celeste perched comfortably between his legs. She needed to soak after all the sex they'd been having. Her head rested on his chest, his arms held her close to him, and the steamy water engulfed them as they sat together, reconnecting after so many years. They sat in silence this way for a long while. Both of them were relishing the feeling of being back in each other's arms again, the feeling of not having to worry about time or spouses or responsibilities. They were in a world all their own.

"I love you," he said, breaking the long silence.

She smiled. "I love you, too." She scooped up some vanilla and jasmine–scented bubbles in her hand and wiped them on Rah-lo's face. He laughed. So did she. As they sat together in the bathtub, playing and talking and enjoying each other's company, Celeste realized that this was what she had always wanted. She sat with her head on his chest and listened to the sounds of his breathing, the rhythm of his heartbeat, and she fell in love all over again. This just felt so right.

She turned over on her stomach and kissed him. Rah-lo held on to her big booty for dear life and felt so full of love for her at that moment that he would have asked her to marry him if he wasn't already married to Asia. When their kiss finally ended, he looked at Celeste lovingly and he began to wash her body tenderly. He lathered her up and kissed her all over when she was clean. It dawned on Celeste that he was there to stay. There was no more wife to contend with, no more of Rah-lo's hurried exits soon after their lovemaking ended. This was the real thing. When he finished bathing her, she returned the favor. She couldn't stop kissing him. His lips seemed to be calling her name. His hands began to roam across her body and she was ready for another trip to paradise.

That afternoon, the hospital called. Ishmael was showing signs of consciousness. The two of them went back to the hospital and went to Ishmael's bedside. He lay there looking at them, but unable to speak with a tube down his throat.

Celeste squeezed his hand. "Ish, we're here. You're gonna be okay," she reassured him. To her delight, he squeezed her hand back. She smiled at Rah-lo, her eyes full of hope.

Rah-lo smiled weakly. He looked at his former friend and then turned to Celeste. "Let me get a minute with him alone please?" Rah-lo asked. Celeste nodded and exited the room, leaving Rah-lo alone with his friend.

Rah-lo sat in the chair next to Ishmael's bed and looked at his friend. "Ish, listen," Rah-lo said, unsure whether Ishmael was too drugged up to listen. But Rah-lo had some things to get off his chest. "I won't sit here and act like I'm not still mad at you. I am. I know that you have love for Celeste. But you know how I feel about her—how I've always felt about her. And still you kept pursuing her in a sneaky way—calling her without telling me, coming down here when you knew that I still wanted her." Rah-lo shook his head and looked at Ishmael. He was weak and heavily sedated by all the painkillers. Rah-lo almost felt bad for what he was saying, but it was the truth. Ishmael had betrayed Rah-lo in more ways than one. "Then there's the shit with Cito. I thought we were boys." Rah-lo looked at his friend and forced a smile. Ishmael looked like he was slipping away. Rah-lo had to accept that this could be his last conversation with his friend. "I guess we both made some mistakes and shit," he managed. "I just want to say that I forgive you. And I hope that you forgive me too for whatever I did to hurt you." Ishmael stared at Rah-lo, unable to respond. But Ishmael heard what Rah-lo had come to say.

"Remember when we were kids, Ish? Every dime piece in the hood had a crush on you and you used to be a little Casanova." Rah-lo smiled at the memory. "That never changed. But when you walk out of here, you're gonna stop that. These women are losing their minds these days and that shit is out of hand now. Nina's dead. She tried to kill you and she killed herself instead. But that's not your fault. You didn't make her go crazy. Just like I didn't make Asia a fucking madwoman. But still, we gotta be easy from now on. I'm done with that player shit. I think Celeste is gonna give me another chance. This time I'm not gonna fuck that up."

Rah-lo sat with Ishmael for a while longer, offering him reassurance that he would pull through. The doctor interrupted and asked Rah-lo to leave so they could run some tests, and he stepped back into the waiting room. When he came out, Celeste sat alone. She looked up at him and offered a smile. He sat down in a chair beside her and sighed. Within minutes, Rah-lo had dozed off. He was awakened by Celeste's wailing cry. Opening his eyes, Rah-lo looked around and saw the doctors trying to calm her down. Immediately, Rah-lo's heart sank. He looked to one of the nurses for clarification. She shook her head at him somberly.

"Your friend Mr. Wright passed away a few minutes ago. Every effort was made to resuscitate him, but we were unsuccessful. I'm sorry."

Rah-lo pulled Celeste into a tight embrace and held her as she was wracked with sobs. Ishmael was dead.

CHAPTER SEVENTEEN

Clean Slates

Asia dialed her mother's number and dried her tears. Hearing her husband dismiss her for the hundredth time in the past week was more than she could stand. She felt helpless and hopeless and tired of trying to convince him to stay with her. Asia knew that Nina had gone too far. But truthfully, Asia might have done the same thing had she seen Rah-lo with Celeste. Asia had finally admitted to herself that it wasn't about her loving Rah-lo as much as it was about her not wanting to lose him to Celeste. She finally wondered if this whole thing had gone too far. Ishmael lay dying and Nina lay cold in the morgue.

Mrs. Hudson answered and was relieved to hear her daughter's voice. "Chile, you have no idea how worried I've been. I keep dreaming about funerals and I don't know if it's yours, Raheem's, or that mistress of his!"

Asia sighed. "It might be one of Rah-lo's friends. He got run over by a car and he's in critical condition."

Mrs. Hudson gasped. "That's terrible. Are you okay, Asia? When are you coming back home?"

Asia shrugged. "I'll be back soon. Rah-lo won't listen to me and I'm tired of fighting for him. I guess it's over."

Angela Hudson heard the pain and resignation in her daughter's voice. Mrs. Hudson had never been the type of mother to hold or coddle a child. But at that moment, she wanted nothing more than to hold her daughter and tell her that she was going to be all right. "You're strong, Asia," she said. "No man is strong enough to break you. Remember that."

Asia wished she believed that. But she didn't. She felt broken. Rah-lo had tossed her aside like yesterday's newspaper.

"Rasheeda wants to talk to you," Asia's mom said, handing her granddaughter the phone.

"Ma?" Rasheeda said.

"Hi," Asia said, sounding tired and fed up.

"Ma, when are you coming back? I miss you."

Asia felt her heart melt. She and Rasheeda fought all the time. Rasheeda was a daddy's girl and always had been. To hear her express that she missed her mom touched Asia profoundly. "You do?"

"Yeah," Rasheeda said. "It's nice here at Grandma's

house, but we want to go home." Rasheeda thought about her parents' marriage and how she'd overheard her grand- mother on the phone telling someone that Asia just couldn't accept that Rah-lo didn't love her anymore. "Ma, even if Daddy wants to leave, it's okay. You still have us. Raleigh and Raven are being good for Grandma. And I haven't been cut- ting class or none of that. We know you need us to be good right now, so we're not trying to add to your stress. Just come home. We love you."

Asia felt tears cascading down her face as she listened to her daughter pour her heart out. "Thanks, 'Sheeda," she managed. "I love you, too. All of you. Daddy does, too." She sighed. "We're not gonna be together anymore, but he'll still be there for you guys. He promised me that. I'm gonna come home tomorrow morning." She thought for a mo- ment about the things Rah-lo had been saying lately. She took a deep breath and then said, " 'Sheeda, I know I haven't been the best mother in the world. A lot of what your father said about me was true. And I'm not gonna pretend that I'm gonna be perfect when I come home. But I'm gonna work on being a better mother to you all. I really am."

Rasheeda smiled. "Come home, Ma," Rasheeda urged.

Asia concluded her conversation with her daughter and began packing her things. Going home was exactly what she intended to do. She may have lost her husband. But she fi- nally appreciated the blessing she still had in her daughters— and in her mother, too. Asia decided that it was time for her to start fresh, and that's just what she would do when she got back to New York. Asia had finally found the strength to stand on her own two feet and the courage to let Rah-lo go.

The day of Ishmael's funeral in Brooklyn was a solemn one for all who attended. Even members of rival crews came out to show their respect for one of the last Brooklyn dons in the game. Rah-lo paid all of the expenses, and he hosted the funeral repast at Akwaaba Mansion in Stuyvesant Heights. No expense was spared and Ishmael was given a send-off fit for royalty. Despite their differences, Ishmael had been one of Rah-lo's lifelong friends. Instead of focusing on their differences at the end of Ishmael's life, Rah-lo remembered the good times. And there had been a ton of them.

For the first time, Rah-lo, Asia, and Celeste were present at an event simultaneously. But Asia behaved and kept her distance from Celeste. Celeste was respectful and kept her distance from Rah-lo, focusing instead on grieving for Ishmael for herself. Robin sat in pained silence, rocking Hezekiah in her arms for much of the night. Charly came decked out in a curve-hugging black suit with a big dramatic hat atop her head. At first glance, anyone would have assumed that she was Ishmael's widow. She cried and carried on the loudest and sat up front in the family pew as if she belonged there. The shock and sadness among all those present was palpable. Ishmael hadn't deserved what had happened to him, and the tragedy made them all appreciate life a little bit more.

Celeste sat behind Rah-lo during the funeral. At the repast she watched him from across the room. He stood with his daughters and he looked so powerful, so in control. The way he directed the caterers and the staff to keep everything running smoothly, even the way he held his youngest daughter's chin in his hand—he exuded power and strength. Celeste loved him more than ever. Along with Ishmael, she and Rah-lo had buried their past, and now they looked forward to forging ahead once again—together.

She had gone to talk to Bryson soon after Ishmael's death. It was one of the hardest conversations she had ever had. As she walked into Bryson's house and sat down, she wondered if she had completely lost her mind. He was a single heterosexual man with a great job, no kids, and no crazed ex wreaking havoc in his life. He had no felony convictions, no lengthy rap sheets, and no beef in the streets. He was handsome, his sex was utterly amazing, and she still couldn't make herself feel more for him than the love that she felt for Rah-lo. She felt like such a fucking idiot.

Bryson noticed that she seemed upset. She wasn't her usually happy and seductive self. Bryson had really begun to care for Celeste. He liked having her around and was wondering if they could build something together. "What's the matter?" he asked. "Looks like you have something on your mind."

Celeste sat forward in her chair and played with her hands. This wasn't going to be easy. "Bryson, I think we need to fall back," she said.

He frowned. He wanted the opposite. "Why?" he asked. "Did I do something wrong?"

She shook her head. "No. You did everything right." She sighed. "I mean that. You have been perfect!" She shook her head, again wondering what kind of spell Rah-lo had cast on her to make her walk away from this man. "But I have some unfinished business in a past relationship. And I don't want to keep seeing you while I try to sift through whatever's left of my past. I just think you're a great man and I could really be with you . . . but right now I have to fall back and sort things out with my ex before this goes any further."

Bryson nodded. He appreciated her honesty. At least she wasn't the type of woman to carry on two full-fledged relationships simultaneously the way that his ex had. "Okay," he said, the disappointment palpable in his voice. "I respect that."

She hated that he was making it easy. But she also appreciated it. She did love Rah-lo, whether it was smart to do so or not. She couldn't help it. As hard as it was to walk away from a man as good as Bryson, she had to follow her heart. She stood and kissed Bryson good-bye, and he hugged her tightly.

"I can't kiss these lips anymore?" he asked.

Celeste smiled. "Don't tempt me," she said. She picked up her purse and walked to the door. Turning around to look at him one last time, she winked at him and waved. As she walked to her car, she wondered how long she would continue to second-guess the decision she had just made.

EPILOGUE

Life After Death . . .

Rah-lo had been eager to get out of the game for years, and now was the perfect chance for him to do that. All of his crew was gone. Ishmael, Pappy, and J-Shawn were dead and Harry was in jail. It was over. Celeste had been right. Rah-lo was getting too old for that lifestyle now. Plus, Asia would love nothing more than to see him go back to jail. He knew that he couldn't trust her since he'd walked out on her. He was sick of looking over his shoulder, waiting for some past wrong to come back and haunt him. He had to do the right thing in order to maintain both his freedom and his status as a role model for his daughters and as the man in Celeste's life. So Rah-lo took a portion of the money he had managed to save over the years despite all of

Asia's lavish spending and wasting, and he started a moving company with Asia's brother. Rah-lo didn't do any of the day-to-day work for the company. He had no interest in that. Instead he financed the whole thing and left Asia's brother in charge while he moved down to Atlanta to be with Celeste. Asia didn't appreciate it one bit. Not only had Rah-lo gone legit, but he also had given her newly paroled brother a reason to like him. What Asia had wanted was for her family to shun Rah-lo because he had left her. Instead, they seemed to be rallying around him in support. Rah-lo mused that he had gotten the second chance he had been looking for. With Celeste, he had the chance to be happy on his own terms for the first time since before his children were born. And he was going to give it his all.

Asia eventually got her act together. She went back to school (at Rah-lo's expense) and became a nurse's aide, working part-time in an adult-care facility. She felt better with her newfound independence, and her daughters were extremely proud of her. Rah-lo sent for his daughters every summer and school holiday and they spent time with him and Celeste in Atlanta. They loved Celeste. She was so opposite their mother—calm, fun, happy. They all hit it off beautifully. Despite Asia's attempts to poison her daughters' young minds against Rah-lo's new love, the girls were old enough and smart enough to make up their own minds. And they adored her. They simply never mentioned that when their mother was within earshot so as not to hurt her feelings.

Rah-lo flew to New York for every recital, every play, every game, and they loved him for it. Asia was served with the divorce papers six weeks after Ishmael's funeral. To Rah-lo's surprise, she signed them without putting up a fight.

Asia continued her affair with Neo and actually accepted his unexpected marriage proposal. This surprised everyone involved until it was revealed that Neo had taken over the business that Rah-lo and Ishmael had forfeited. Asia had gotten herself another boss, and all of her family and friends were happy for her. But Neo was swooped down on by the Feds and was facing decades of jail time for drug crimes. Asia left him before the ink was dry on his arrest warrant. Soon, Asia was back on the prowl looking for another sucker.

Charly continued her search for her own baller. She sparred with the stylists in her shop daily and continued to create confusion wherever she went. She wondered what might have been had Ishmael never gone down to Atlanta in search of Celeste. And from time to time Charly wondered if her own instigating had inadvertently led Nina to go over the edge. But Charly pushed those thoughts aside when they invaded her mind. After all, Nina was the psycho, not Charly. She went on with her life and didn't change one bit. She was fine just as she was!

Robin graduated from college and quit her job at Charly's. She went to work as a social worker for wayward teens at a local group home. She loved her job and the lifestyle it allowed her to give her son. Hezekiah was growing up to be a wonderful young man. She was extremely proud of that. She often thought about Ishmael, wondering what might have been had he never gone to Atlanta. Unfortunately, she would never have the pleasure of knowing that deep inside he really did care for her.

Celeste accompanied Rah-lo to New York one summer to pick up the girls. When they got to Staten Island and picked up the girls, Celeste convinced Rah-lo to stop at the mall so that she could run a quick errand. The girls were thrilled at the thought of a shopping spree, and Rah-lo was outnumbered. As they drove around Staten Island, Celeste looked around at the borough she had once called home. In the years since she had last been there, things had changed drastically. Town houses now stood in places where once only woods had been. Traffic was bumper-to-bumper, and new stores had opened up all over the borough. The borough that had once been known as a small suburban community now looked like all the others, overcrowded and bustling with activity. So much had changed in so little time. Including her relationship with the man she loved.

Celeste, Rah-lo, and the girls arrived at the mall and headed inside. While Rasheeda dragged her father into Forever 21, Celeste ducked into CVS. She hadn't been feeling well lately and she needed to find out what the problem was. Not wanting to trouble Rah-lo, she didn't tell him what was wrong. She decided to confirm her suspicions first and made her purchase, then headed into the food court bathroom nearby.

Celeste came out of the ladies' room with a huge smile plastered on her face. Rah-lo now sat on a bench, waiting for his daughters to finish shopping for cell phone accessories. Celeste came and sat beside him. "Baby," she said. "I have something to tell you."

Rah-lo looked at her and smiled back. "What's the matter?" he asked.

"Rah, I'm pregnant."

He stopped talking and stood up with his mouth open in shock. "What did you say?" he asked.

Celeste repeated herself. "I'm pregnant. I missed my period. I thought my cycle might just be changing or whatever, but deep inside I knew that I was pregnant. I just took a pregnancy test and it turned blue!" She smiled so hard her jaw began to ache.

Rah-lo smiled as he listened in stunned silence. Celeste misinterpreted his speechlessness for disappointment. Maybe Rah-lo didn't want another child.

"Are you happy?"

Rah-lo laughed. "Of course I'm happy!" he said. He kissed her and hugged her tightly. Then suddenly he jumped up and said, "Wait here. I'll be right back."

Celeste sat there looking confused as Rah-lo ran up the escalator. She had no idea where he was going or if he was really happy about her announcement. When he came back, he had a pair of blue baby Jordans in his hand. Celeste laughed as he approached her with a Kool-Aid smile on his face. "These are for the baby," he said.

She shook her head. "How do you know it's gonna be a boy?" She motioned to his three daughters headed their way. "You don't really do boys."

"I know I made one this time. I can feel it." The girls approached and saw Celeste holding the baby sneakers. They frowned, confused.

"Who are those for?" Raleigh asked.

Rah-lo smiled and rubbed Celeste's flat belly. "Your new little brother," he announced proudly. It took the girls a few moments to catch his meaning. When they finally did, the three of them jumped up and down excitedly, yelling happily. Celeste smiled as they headed out to the parking lot.

On the way to the bridge, Rah-lo told Celeste that he had to make a detour through Park Hill. "I have to run in this store real quick to see my boy. I'll be right back." Before she could protest, Rah-lo sprang out of the car and into the variety store. Celeste sat in the car with the girls parked in front of the pay phone, wondering why he had to stop here of all places. She looked around at all of Park Hill, bustling with activity. She glanced at her watch, growing impatient as she waited for Rah-lo to come out. As she looked up, she spotted him coming across the street in her direction. He glided toward her and it struck her how eerily reminiscent the whole scene was of the day they'd met. Rah-lo walked toward the car smiling. He motioned for her to get out of the car and she did. Celeste couldn't help smile, although she was still confused about what was going on.

Rah-lo reached the spot where she stood and towered over her. "What's going on?" she asked.

Rah-lo smiled. "Don't worry about all these people out here. They're not used to seeing someone as fine as you are standing on the block like this."

Celeste frowned, smiling at the same time. This was like déjà vu. She recalled the night back in 1992 when she had met Rah-lo on this very spot and he had said something to her that was very similar.

"I don't understand," she said.

Rah-lo grinned, the same sexy grin she'd fallen in love with. Then he got down on one knee and pulled a ring box out of his pocket. It was the real reason he had run upstairs in the mall. The baby sneakers had only been a clever distraction from what he had really gone to buy. Celeste gasped and covered her mouth with her hands.

Rah-lo smiled at her. "I love you, Celeste. I wanted you to come back here where we met 'cause I think we've come full circle. It's been a long time since the day I came across the street and fell in love with you, and as I came across the street just now I fell in love with you all over again." He took the ring out of the box and held it up for her to see. The diamond gleamed in the sunlight. "Will you marry me?"

Celeste began to cry, and Rah-lo's daughters jumped around excitedly inside the car. "Say yes!" they yelled.

Rah-lo smiled at Celeste as she managed to say, "Yes," and he hugged her tightly. "I love you," she said.

Rah-lo kissed her softly. "I love you, too." He rubbed her still-flat belly and smiled broadly. "Finally!" he yelled. He picked Celeste up off her feet and swung her around with pure joy. He felt like the luckiest man alive. He had changed his life and gotten the girl and now she was having his baby. He knew that all the trials and tribulations they'd had to endure to get to this point had been worth it. It was the happiest moment of his life.

They welcomed a ten-pound, four-ounce baby eight months later. They named him Raheem after his father. Asia, in turn, took Rah-lo to court for child support. He happily paid it each month, knowing that she was bitter only because Celeste had given him the son that had eluded Asia three times. Rah-lo and Celeste flew to Negril and got married on the beach the following summer in a quiet ceremony attended by only close family and friends. Rah-lo and Celeste beamed with joy the entire time. It was as close as they could come to happily ever after and it was about damned time.